AF599246

HUNTER'S BLOOD

CURSED BY BLOOD: SHIFTERS

MARIANNE MOREA

CURSED BY BLOOD: SHIFTERS

HUNTER'S BLOOD

MARIANNE MOREA

This book is a work of fiction. Names, characters, places, and incidents either are products of the author's imagination or are used fictitiously. Any resemblance to actual events or locales or persons, living or dead, is entirely coincidental and not intended by the author.

HUNTER'S BLOOD
Cursed by Blood: Shifters, Book 1

COVENTRY
An imprint of City Owl Press
www.cityowlpress.com

Cover Design by MiblArt. All stock photos licensed appropriately.

Edited by Ink it Out Editing Services.

For information on subsidiary rights, please contact the publisher at info@cityowlpress.com.

Paperback Edition ISBN: 978-1-964951-12-6

Hardback Edition ISBN: 978-1-964951-00-3

Also by Marianne Morea

The Cursed by Blood: Vampires

Blood Legacy

Collateral Blood

Condemned

Of Blood and Magic

The Cursed by Blood: Shifters

Hunter's Blood

Twice Cursed

The Lion's Den

Power Play

Club Vampire: The Red Veil Diaries

Choose Me

Tempt Me

Tease Me

Taste Me

Bewitch Me

Shifter Romances

Her Captive Dragon

Taming Their Tailfins

The Siren's Mate

The Wolf's Secret Witch

Never Cry Wolf

The Demon Hunter's Wolf

The Wolf and the Rose

Torn Between Two Alphas

Syndicate Clan Series

The Vampire's Daughter

Lady Wolfe

Queen's Gambit*

Rebel Witch*

*Releasing in 2025

Whisper Falls Holiday

A Little Mistletoe and Magic

The Blessed

My Soul to Keep

CIA Rogue Operative

Dangerous Law

CLUB VAMPIRE

Special Edition RED VEIL DIARIES Bundle

PRAISE FOR MARIANNE MOREA

"*Hollow's End* is the perfect read for a misty autumn night! Filled with everything one would want in a ghost story, this one will make your fingers tingle and your heart race! Morea has taken the well-known tale of Ichabod Crane and the Headless Horseman and thrown it's after effects right into the 21st century... This truly is a scrumptiously scary story that incorporates historical fact while spinning reality, leaving the reader biting their nails and turning the pages!" – *InD'tale Magazine*

"If Sherrilyn Kenyon and J.R. Ward's writing had a child, it would be Marianne Morea's writing. She creates a world that comes to life with richness and detail that pulls you straight into the story and keeps you hooked from start to finish... *Condemned* has an abundance of mystery and suspense intertwine with a beautiful and rather sweet romance that bursts with sizzling heat. I don't want to give anything away because all of these discoveries that come to life as you read is a such a wonderful part of the magic in reading this book!" – *The Red Hatter*

"Ryker and Camille and scorching dragon heat! *Dragon My Heart Around* is engaging from start to finish. Of course, there's also the amazing Gerri Wilder in the flesh, cause where would all the unmated shifters be without her incredible gift of sight. Highly recommended read!" – *USA Today Bestselling Author Gina Kincade*

"Morea has a way of captivating a reader with every word, and Lily and Sean make the perfect, heart-throbbing pair. The mysterious premise will excite you, as will Lily's inner fight when she must choose between her role as mate to Sean and her penchant to be a hunter...I thoroughly enjoyed the spicy scenes between Lily and Ryan, the mix of the real world and the supernatural, and the adventures Morea really spun in Twice Cursed." – *Nadège Richards, author of the Bleeding Heart series*

For my Dad

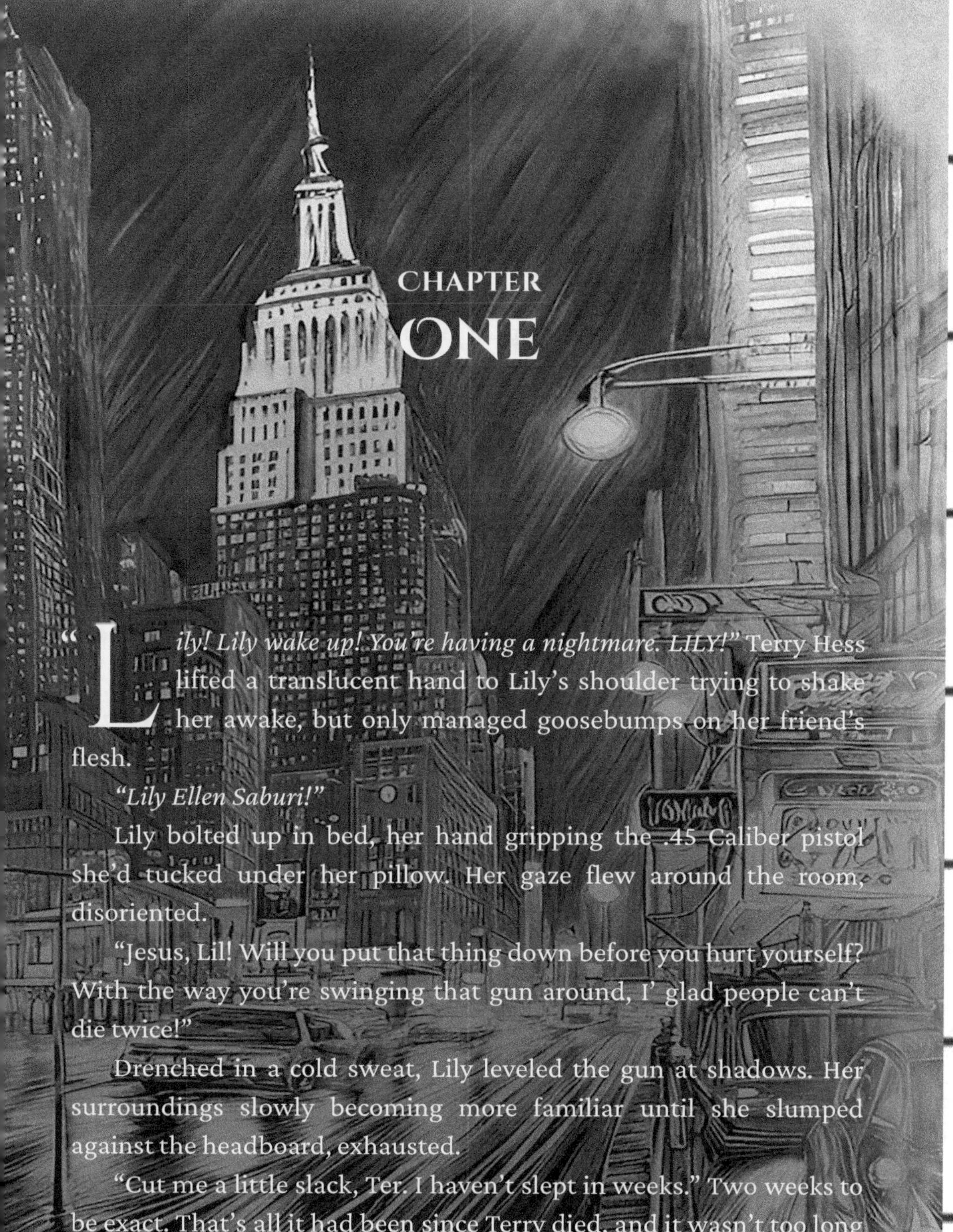

CHAPTER ONE

"Lily! Lily wake up! You're having a nightmare. LILY!"* Terry Hess lifted a translucent hand to Lily's shoulder trying to shake her awake, but only managed goosebumps on her friend's flesh.

"Lily Ellen Saburi!"

Lily bolted up in bed, her hand gripping the .45 Caliber pistol she'd tucked under her pillow. Her gaze flew around the room, disoriented.

"Jesus, Lil! Will you put that thing down before you hurt yourself? With the way you're swinging that gun around, I' glad people can't die twice!"

Drenched in a cold sweat, Lily leveled the gun at shadows. Her surroundings slowly becoming more familiar until she slumped against the headboard, exhausted.

"Cut me a little slack, Ter. I haven't slept in weeks." Two weeks to be exact. That's all it had been since Terry died, and it wasn't too long afterward that her friend appeared in her new ethereal form.

Lily exhaled, placing her gun on the nightstand before taking a cigarette from the pack beside the cheap lamp bolted to the pressed wood. The room was dim. The ambient light from the motel's neon vacancy sign its only illumination.

Sticking the cigarette between her lips, she lit it, and then blew smoke into the already musty air.

"I wish you wouldn't do that," Terry said from across the room.

"Which? Smoke, or wake up screaming from nightmares haunting me since the night you were murdered? Take your pick."

"Neither, but you don't have to be so bitchy about it."

Hmmph. "What time is it?" Lily asked, squinting at the clock radio next to her gun.

"Almost eleven p.m."

Throwing her legs over the side of the bed, Lily stretched. "Time to get moving." With a wink, she took one last drag of her cigarette before stubbing it out in the half-filled ashtray. "Almost witching hour."

She padded barefoot into the bathroom and snapped on the light. Its harsh fluorescent glare made her lack of sleep all the more obvious. She grimaced at her pale reflection and the dark smudges under her eyes.

The water in the tap was ice cold, but she splashed her face anyway. Water droplets dripped from her chin to her chest when she looked up to find Terry's translucent form staring back at her from the mirror.

"Don't do this tonight, Lily. This isn't who you are."

She grabbed a towel from the wire rack above the sink and patted her face dry. "Yeah, well. Maybe that was true two weeks ago, but not anymore."

She dropped the towel onto the edge of the sink and then walked out, leaving the bathroom light on as she headed to the small round table in the corner. On top, sat enough weaponry to outfit a small army.

"Lily, please—"

"Shut up, Terry. This isn't your concern." She didn't bother to look up as she loaded another clip into the magazine of her gun.

"It certainly *is* my concern! *You're* my concern! Lily, for Chrissake! Revenge is not the answer!"

Lily's lip curled. "Yeah, but it feels fucking great," she shot back, but quickly lost her satisfied smile when she saw tears glistening like diamonds on her friend's cheek.

Momentarily stunned, Lily didn't realize ghosts could cry. *Great, one more thing my psychic ability did not pick up on.*

With a sigh, she put the gun down and walked around the bed to where her friend sat— well sort of sat— on the edge of the dresser. "Terry, don't."

Lily reached toward her friend, then shoved her hands into her pockets. She wanted to hug Terry, tell her it would be okay, but couldn't. Her hands would pass through.

At the impotent feeling, her anger bubbled to the surface again. It was fathomless, and every time she thought of that night it crashed through her thin veneer of calm, flooding her with bitterness.

Pressing her lips together, Lily fisted her hands inside her black leather jeans against the onslaught.

"Lil, you've got to stop this. It's not doing either of us any good. What's the purpose? Do you want to get yourself killed so you can join me? I'm a shade because I chose to stay on this plane, even though my time here is done. I've made my peace with what happened. Why can't you? You're the only reason I'm choosing to stay earthbound. You need to get past all this hate and resentment. For both of us."

Lily didn't say a word. Instead, she sat on the edge of the bed and continued to pack her weapons despite Terry's frustrated sigh.

"I've watched your guilt and your anger eat at you, driving you crazy since I died. I even convinced myself that it too would pass.

Never in a million years did I think you were serious about this revenge ride you've been on— that is until you started your little practice runs. *Christ, Lily*! You tracked another vampire last night! What are you looking to do? Become a vigilante against the entire supernatural world?"

Lily shrugged. "Pretty much."

It amazed Lily how easy it was to recognize supernaturals now she was attuned to them. It didn't take much to spot the vampire last night as it tracked potential prey in Grand Central.

As much as she hated to give them credit, the bloodsuckers were patient hunters. Then again, so was she.

She watched the vampire focus on a solitary male heading unsuspectingly out the 42nd Street exit. However, it wasn't until its potential victim crossed 5th Avenue and passed the darkened entrance to Bryant Park that it attacked.

The memory brought a smirk to her face. Stepping out of the shadows, Lily pointed her gun at the vampire's head. "Hungry tonight?" she taunted. The fanged creature jerked its head in her direction and hissed, baring fangs.

What sounded like a half-swallowed whimper sprang from its victim, followed by the pungent smell of urine as the terrified guy stood too scared to move.

"Now would be a good time to run," she said, not taking her eyes off the vampire. Reading the creature's fury and its thirst, Lily knew it was going to strike. With its fangs dripping saliva, the vampire lunged, its clawed hands reaching for her throat. Time seemed to slow as she swung the crossbow from under her duster. The look on the leech's face was priceless. He never saw the point blank arrow coming.

"Well at least that kill didn't make the papers," Terry grumbled, her voice an aggravated sigh.

"Vampires are already dead. They turn to ash when staked, so there wouldn't be anything left for the papers to report." Lily shrugged, tying her boot. "Then again, remember that naked guy they found in Central Park near the fountain? He had been shot in the head, right." She looked up, arching an eyebrow for effect. Tagging the werewolf had been a hard chase, but worth it.

"Lily, please tell me that wasn't you because I'm seriously starting to get scared. I convinced myself this was just one of your knee-jerk reactions, like when you spray painted phallic symbols all over Chris Crowley's car for cheating on you senior year of high school. At least then, no one got hurt. It kills me it doesn't bother you in the slightest you took those lives. That you plan on taking more."

Lily stiffened at Terry's choice of words. "I don't understand why this is so hard for you. The guy in central park was a werewolf! And in case you forgot, it was a *werewolf* that killed you, Terry!"

Squeezing her eyes shut, Lily swallowed against the guilt biting into her gut. She wanted was to scream or cry, anything to drown out the little voice in her head chanting, *your fault... all your fault.*

Tightening her jaw, she forced herself to meet Terry's translucent eyes. "Every one of the supernaturals I hunted was out to take a human life. I was in their psyches, Terry. I saw their intent. Whether you want to admit it or not, my actions saved a few innocent lives."

Except for the one that mattered. Lily ignored the voice in her head.

"But what about innocent supernaturals?"

Lily snorted her reply. "I'll let you know if I come across one."

"Now you've dragged us back to Maine in the hopes of what? Finding this one particular werewolf? And how do you propose to locate this creature? Or are you planning to use yourself as live bait?"

"I've sensed it in this area for a week and managed to narrow its trail to a stretch of woods not far from here."

"That's if it's even still around. It might even be dead." Terry ran her hands through her hair causing it to glitter when it floated back into place.

"It's not dead. I'd sense it. Even *you'd* sense it. I'm tracking this creature, regardless of what you say. All my practice runs, as you call them, have been nothing more than a prequel to this moment. I will kill the beast that took your life or die trying. So will you please stop nagging me?"

"You didn't even take the precaution of telling anyone you were coming here. What if something happens?"

"You'll know."

"Considering the fact you're the only person who can see or hear me, that's not such a great plan." Terry crossed translucent arms at her chest.

Lily shrugged again, shoving wooden stakes into the side of her boot. She was hunting tonight, despite how much Terry disapproved.

Loose bullets suddenly ricocheted past Lily's head making her duck. "What the hell, Terry!"

"I acquired a few abilities in the past couple of weeks, so your portable armory might not be where you last left it."

Bullets rolled on the uneven floor from where they hit the wall, and Lily bent to retrieve them. "You know, if it weren't for the fact my hand would pass right through you, I'd punch you dead in the face right now."

"Dead is the operative word, don'tcha think?"

Lily shot her a look.

"Don't go, Lily. Please. I've got a terrible feeling in the pit of my stomach."

"First off, you haven't got a stomach anymore. Second, forget it. I'm going— and no, you cannot come with me, so stop with the cheap parlor tricks!"

"Oh, I'm coming with you all right, and there's nothing you can do to stop me. I move in a decidedly different way from you these days, and I can sense where you are and what you're doing at any time. So don't piss me off."

She smiled at her friend. Ghost or not, she was still the same old Terry, and Lily's throat tightened even as her heart ached. "If you're that set on coming, then let's go. We're wasting time."

Picking up the last few things from the table, Lily turned, dangling her car from her fingers. "Would you care to drive?"

"Funny. I always said you should have been a comedian." Without a word, Terry blew right through her friend, leaving her shivering in a seventy degree room.

Lily rubbed her arms. "Always has to have the last word," she mumbled, snapping off the lights and closing the door behind her.

CHAPTER TWO

Lily pulled her car to the side of the road and cut the engine. Except for the wind and the distant echo of the waves crashing against the cliffs, it was silent. Mouth tight, she closed her eyes, focusing all of her clairvoyance on the psychic thread she'd been following the last few miles.

Her senses were spread as thin and taut as trip wire in all directions, making the hair on her arms rise. Looking down the deserted stretch of rural highway, she took note of her position, and where she was in conjunction to the thread pulsing in the wind and decided to go on foot.

"Showtime," she muttered, getting out of the car.

"Why are you parking so far from the perimeter?" Terry asked, materializing behind her.

Lily whirled into a defensive stance. "Will you please stop doing that? It's starting to creep me out!" she ground through her teeth.

"Some psychic. Don't you think it would be wiser to park a little closer in case you need a quick getaway? You can't just dematerialize like me, you know."

"I know what I'm doing so just hush up, okay? Don't distract me, anymore. If you're going to be here, then hang around and be quiet. Float to the top of a tree or something. Just stay out of my way."

Terry hmphed but didn't say another word.

Quietly making her way across the road, Lily trekked through the scrub on the shoulder before stopping inside the woods to check her weapons.

With a .45 caliber pistol shoved into the waistband of her leather jeans, and a 9mm semi-automatic at the small of her back, the feel of cold steel sent thrills shooting across her belly. The same eager thrill she always got before a hunt.

A compact crossbow slung low across her back, as well, and a silver-plated knife and sharpened stakes were tucked firmly into her boot. No matter what kind of supernatural crossed her path tonight, she was ready.

Lily glanced at the sky. Its quiet blackness reminded her of the weekend hunting trips she and Terry took as teens with Terry's dad, Carl. He had trained them well, regardless of how many times Terry's mom, Beverly, balked at the idea. She'd mutter how a girl's weapon of choice should be her charm, and not a gun or a bow. Somehow, Lily knew tonight would be an exception to the rule.

It was dark and cold, but the refracted moonlight coming through the clouds gave her enough light. The sky had been ominous all day, but the threat of early snow held off, covering the ground with just half inch of fresh powder. The air carried a lonesome quality, and the forest was still. Almost too still.

Squatting down, she sent her senses out again, tracking the exact direction of the supernatural thread before heading deeper into the woods. She opened herself entirely, not wanting any surprises tonight.

The creature's trace pulsed like a neon sign in her mind, and she smirked. It was almost too easy. She moved quickly, following the thrum through the dense forest, and navigating trees and brush like a familiar obstacle course.

As she rounded a wide thicket, she caught a flicker on the edge of her mind. The feel of the new trace was different, and its pulse loosely cloaked. She needed to investigate, but out here she was too exposed. Ahead, low brambles twisted into a rough, barren hedge, and she crouched beside it for cover.

The trace's cadence was human, but not, and its feel was unquestionably male. He headed southeast toward the cliffs, the same direction as she. Lily exhaled, sending a quiet stream of expletives into the wind. She'd be damned before allowing anyone or anything to get in her way tonight.

With a cleansing breath, she focused her senses and grabbed hold of the new pulse. She needed calm and absolute stealth before merging her mind with this gate crasher. A wave of vertigo hit as she made contact, overwhelming her senses with the sensation of flight.

Lightness enveloped her, yet she remained aware of her body's position in the scrub. Nausea crept up the back of her throat, and she grimaced. The last thing she needed was motion sickness when she was stock still. Perhaps this was some version of astral projection, but whatever the feeling, she needed to be the one in the driver's seat.

Lily scooped up a small handful of fresh snow and wet her tongue. She swallowed her queasiness and adjusted her focus, attuning herself to the peaks and valleys of the man's flight. Whoever this guy was, he was too intent on his target to distinguish her presence. But what was he hunting?

Merged, she soared with him above the tree line and watched as he canvased the ground below. His distraction made it easy for her to advance, and she crept further into his mind, allowing herself to see through his eyes.

The outline of reflected body heat from potential prey radiated in shades of red and blue, but it was clear his interest was elsewhere.

Either he doesn't know I'm here, or he does, but doesn't consider me a threat. Maybe he's just out for a joy ride, and I'm being paranoid. No. Supernaturals are never out for no good reason. He's hunting something...

A disgusted sound left her mouth, and she sat back on her heels. Chewing her lower lip, she weighed the odds. This was too much of a coincidence not to be sure. She dug her fingers into the earth on both sides of her legs to ground herself, before dropping deeper into his psyche.

Her stomach clenched with the effort, her mind spinning from the unaccustomed depth of her probe. Within seconds, a snarl reverberated up her spine and she shook under the weight of its menace. If he didn't sense her presence before, he certainly sensed it now.

Without warning, he reached out with his own mind and seized control of their merge. His mental grip was like iron, but effortless. Panic threatened as she struggled against his hold, gulping down air while trying to stay calm enough to focus. What the hell was he?

His mind probed hers looking for the same answers Lily wanted from him. He stripped away layer after layer of memory and thought, and she screamed at the violated feel.

Self-preservation kicked in, and she slammed doors shut all over her mind. There was no way she'd allow some stranger to mind-rape her, even if she was guilty of trespassing first. She had to keep him out or risk him learning why she was in the woods tonight.

The man exuded raw strength as the sarcastic timbre of the words *nice try* echoed through her mind along with a glimpse of a slow, seductive, and decidedly male grin.

Heat poured through her body, pooling between her legs. Her breath caught in her throat, and she went weak, pitching forward to land on her hands in the cold snow. She sucked in air and tried to sit back, but another wave of desire hit her point blank.

Almost of their own volition, her hands trailed the length of her thighs, grazing her sex through her leather pants. The friction nearly sent her over the edge. As she struggled to maintain control of her body, she heard his deep chuckle. Whatever he was, the son of a bitch was enjoying himself at her expense.

With a snarl of her own, Lily centered her strength and shoved against his hold, managing to slam down a wall and shut him out.

Drained, she slumped forward into the snow. *Stupid.* If she lost the creature's threat because she allowed herself to veer off task, she'd kill the first thing that crossed her path— starting with that fly boy supernatural.

On rubbery legs, she crawled forward and grabbed onto a raised tree root, pushing herself up. She brushed the snow from her pants, careful to keep her mind guarded.

Steeling herself, Lily walled off any errant thoughts or emotions and sent her senses out again, this time focusing solely on the creature. She'd have time later to reconcile herself with what just happened. She had a score to settle, first.

The creature's trace was still there, and she offered a silent thank you to the universe she hadn't lost her chance. She followed its pulse undeterred, even as the scent of salt air and the sound of the ocean grew louder with every step.

She was angry at herself, but that was nothing new. Her anger gave her an edge. Only now she wasn't just angry. Whoever he was, that supernatural had rocked her to her core. He had taken her control, and she hated that. Without a single touch, he made her body come alive. Like some sort of a puppet master. Well, she was nobody's private doll. Not if she had anything to say about it.

Amid her angry reverie, the thread ignited to a pulse stronger than before, closer, yet filled with a snarl of incoherent threads too tangled and enraged to decipher, and too complex to be strictly animal.

This was it, the moment she had been waiting for. All previous thoughts vanished, and her mind focused entirely on her target.

The tangle of threads spread across her mind in the same pattern of frenzied thought that rampaged through her consciousness the night Terry died. The psychic footprint was an exact match, and there was no question this was the same beast that had ripped her friend to shreds.

"I've got you now, you son of a bitch," she muttered through clenched teeth, taking off through the trees,

Her fingers coiled around the grip of her .45 as she pulled it from her waistband and unlocked the safety. The beast's hostility spurred her racing heart, growing louder and more frantic. It was hunting.

Lily ran with desperation, picking up speed while images of Terry's torn and ravaged body ripped through her mind. Heat flamed in her cheeks, twisting her mouth with the angry memories. She'd never forget or forgive those responsible for Terry's death.

Herself included.

The forest thinned the further east she tracked the creature, and now the beast was no more than a bullet away from where she stood. It had dragged a deer onto the bluff. The gentle animal was barely alive, its skittering heart like a stone on Lily's chest.

The wind was wild. The spray from the waves crashed against the rocks, a tempest in the background. The sound was unforgiving, as if heaven itself demanded retribution along with her.

Stepping out from the shelter of the trees, Lily raised her .45. "This is for you, Terry!" she shouted against the wind, pulling the trigger.

The gun exploded in her hand, and the beast's head jerked up from its bloody feast with a shriek. The bullet hit home. The creature staggered backwards, and Lily waited with her gun poised for the death drop.

To her horror, it steadied itself instead, leaping vertically over the deer's carcass. The beast landed a few feet from Lily in an ugly parody of a four-legged stance.

Growling, it moved fast. Too fast. She jammed the pistol into her waistband and then reached for the 9mm from her back holster. A .45 could blow a hole the size of a manhole cover in most anything, but right now she needed speed.

She fired, her arms jerking with each round, but the beast kept coming. Blood poured from its wounds, its mouth foaming and frothing in a rage.

Lily twisted to get away, but the beast closed the distance between them in seconds. In a downward slash, its claws raked her shoulder, neck, and chest, missing her jugular by less than an inch.

She staggered back, but not before it rebounded with a backhand that sent her crashing into a tree. Her body slumped to the ground. Her mind vaguely aware the creature lumbered close, ready for the kill.

"Lily! Shoot it!" Terry screamed, materializing toward the center of the cliff.

Terry's voice was thick and slow in Lily's ears. Her .45 was nowhere to be found, but she managed to lift the 9mm and fire. The bullet missed its mark, and the beast bounded onto her chest. Instinctively, she brought her knees up between them, struggling to keep it at bay.

Using every last ounce of strength, she tried to sweep it off balance by pushing at its hips with her feet, but the beast was too strong. Its sharp teeth cut her hands as they grappled, its fetid drool dripping onto her open wounds.

Snarling, the creature's jaws bit down on Lily's forearm. She screamed in pain and at the sound of her bones breaking. This was it. The creature would rip her apart, same as he did Terry.

"Let her GO!"

The beast released Lily's arm at the sound of Terry's voice. Maybe it recognized another supernatural. Or maybe it thought it was outnumbered. Either way the startle didn't last long, and it lifted Lily by the throat, shaking her like a ragdoll.

Her eyes bulged and her vision dimmed, yet through the haze she saw Terry gathering form behind the creature. But how?

Finding the .45 on the ground, Terry leveled the gun at the beast. “I said... Let. Her. GO!”

Before she could pull the trigger, a man leapt from the trees. He grabbed the creature by its shoulders, yanking it backward. Whoever it was, they were strong enough to break the beast’s hold, and Lily slumped to the ground, again.

Still in a semisolid form, Terry rushed to Lily’s side. She knelt on the blood smeared ground, lifting her friend’s head onto her lap. “I’m so sorry, Lily. I wasn’t fast enough.”

Lily tried to speak, but pain seared her crushed throat. Terry wasn’t to blame. Hunting the creature was her choice, no matter the consequence. She shook her head, but the effort left skirting consciousness. She collapsed back, only this time she sank halfway through Terry’s lap.

The ghost’s corporeal form was temporary and fading fast. Powerless, Lily watched her friend struggle to summon whatever magic had made her substantial, but it was no use. Instead, she lay Lily gently on the ground, and held her hand while she still could.

A loud crack jerked both their heads around. The beast was locked in battle with their nameless champion. Despite her haze of pain, Lily watched him fight the creature barehanded, amazed at his strength and skill. The man fought with stealth and determination and seemed to have no fear.

With a brutal howl, the beast leaped to the trunk of a nearby tree. Its claws pierced the bark like a mutant before propelling itself with a shriek onto the man’s chest. If he died, the creature would finish her off as well.

Adrenaline raced through Lily’s blood giving her borrowed clarity, even as pain screamed through her body. With the last of her strength, she lifted herself and the 9mm that had fallen to her side and aimed for the beast's head.

Squeezing the trigger, she sent one last bullet flying towards its target. This time it hit. The back of the beast's head exploded like an overripe melon. It crumpled to the ground, blood pooling beneath what remained of its matted hair.

"Damn you, Lily!" Terry railed at her friend's motionless form. "You just had to have your way! Don't you dare give up now. You hear me? Don't you dare! I'll get 911 here somehow."

Sensing movement behind her, Terry whirled around. She held her breath half expecting to see the beast, but her shoulders slumped in relief when she saw it was the other man.

He had managed to get himself out from under what was left of the creature and was trying to clean himself off.

"I don't think they've got 911 responders this far out. In all likelihood, they'd probably dispatch the state police, but considering the circumstances, I don't think that would be such a good idea." He looked right at Terry. "Don't you agree?"

The ghost was dumbstruck. Especially since was no longer corporeal. "You can see me?"

"Apparently. And hear you, too." Walking over to where Lily lay, he squatted down beside her body. "Don't look so surprised." He barely spared a glance for her stunned, yet translucent face. "Your friend is in pretty bad shape. We should probably get her to a hospital. Problem is, the closest one that can handle this kind of trauma is hours away. I do have a private facility, though. It's actually not that far."

Terry sputtered a little. "Yeah. I mean, thank you. That would be great."

"You don't look so good yourself. Why are you so washed out?" he asked, finally looking up.

Turning her insubstantial hands over in front of her, she

shrugged. "I'm not really sure. Probably over extended ectoplasm, or backlash from a ghostly adrenaline rush. Take your pick."

Terry's eyes met his, and she exhaled. "Look, I don't know what went on here, and since I feel as if I'm evaporating, I don't have time to play twenty questions. Take care of Lily. Do what you have to, but you keep her alive. Okay?"

Terry's eyes followed his as he looked down at Lily's crumpled form. There was no hiding his reaction when he brushed the hair away from her friend's face. Lily was beautiful. Like a porcelain doll, silent and unmoving.

Clearing his voice, he met Terry's anxious gaze. "Don't worry. I'll see to everything. She'll be fine."

He doubted that as much as she did, but she nodded her thanks, even as she continued to fade.

"Who are you, anyway?" he asked.

Looking over at Lily, a sad smile spread across her almost invisible face. "I'm her best friend," she said, and then vanished altogether.

CHAPTER THREE

Sean Leighton leaned against the polished edge of his desk, his torn and bloodstained jacket tossed diagonally across its expanse. "Is that everything, Jack?"

His lieutenant placed a box of weapons on the conference chair to the front of the shined mahogany. "Yes, sir. It's everything we found on the girl when you brought her in. Marcus is running a search on the information we got from her personal effects. He said he'll be up shortly with a dossier."

"Good. Is she upstairs as I asked?" Without waiting for an answer, Sean picked up the preliminary medical report on the girl's condition and frowned. His own injuries began to heal by the time he carried her in from the cliffs, but it didn't appear as though she would be so lucky.

"We put her on the top floor of the manor for extra security, just in case she decides to bolt. But by the look of things, she's not going anywhere for some time. She's in pretty lousy shape. The doc gave her heavy meds, so it's going to be a while before we can even talk to her."

"Doesn't matter. The last thing we need is panic down in the main clinic. It's better she's out of the way, at least until we know a little more about her."

The lieutenant shifted a bit on his feet. "Is there anything else you need me to do?"

"No, that's all for now. Take everything downstairs and tag it, For Council Eyes Only, Jack...got it?"

"Got it," he replied.

The lieutenant lifted the unwieldy box to his hip, transferring its weight to the edge of the desk, adjusting some of its contents. Picking up the crossbow, he turned it over in his hand before putting it into the box. He reached for the bowie knife next. "*Jesus*. Silver plated. Makes you wonder what the hell she was doing out there."

Sean didn't comment, but his eyes were hard as he watched the implications flicker across his lieutenant's face. Any speculation about what transpired on the cliffs wasn't good. Curiosity led to rumor, and in this case, rumor would lead to panic.

"Just take care of that for me, will you? And tell Mitch to catch up with me at some point today. I need to brief him on what's been happening."

"No problem, boss," the younger man said lifting the box and heading out.

Sean took a deep breath and let it out slowly. It had been a long night. Sitting, he leaned back in his chair and stretched, wincing as fresh pain tore through his arms and chest. He was bloodied and sore from his fight, but there was still too much to think about, regardless of his exhaustion.

A frown formed between his brows as he glanced at the door to his office. Too much to think about indeed. Who was this girl? She was a mystery, and one more complication in an already difficult situation.

So much had happened in such a short amount of time, but the Alpha didn't always have the luxury of time, especially when it involved the safety and security of the Compound. He scrubbed his face with the palm of his hand, the rough stubble under his fingers prickling his skin. He hadn't slept in days. Then again, since this experiment in accord had begun sleep was at a premium.

Alpha Council of the Brethren. He shoved a hand through his hair. His title, like the idea of the Compound, was a relatively new concept.

The Compound of Shifters had been met with strong opposition since its start not long ago. The notion of different species living and working together, rather than struggling separately for limited space and resources, was a concept some had difficulty accepting—and this situation with the girl, was just one more argument the Compound's detractors would use against them.

Sean had been chosen to lead, and in accepting that responsibility, had been given the task of protecting them all. The Hunter's Council had been formed to help him carry out that undertaking, with all shifter groups represented in its membership. As the Alpha Council, Sean alone had been granted the ability to shift into any form. What better way to know and understand each species under his command?

He walked into the bathroom, wincing as he peeled the ruined shirt from his back and tossed it in into the trash. He turned on the shower and stripped off the rest of his clothes. The spray jetted against his skin, and he let the hot water cascade over his sore body. Blood and dirt pooled at his feet, and he watched it swirl toward the drain, his guilt and pain swirling along with it. His brother was dead—or at least whatever was left of him. It was over—until he needed to hunt one of his own...again.

Sean's thoughts drifted to the girl. Verifying her identity was high on his list of priorities, and not just for obvious reasons. Was she the same one he'd caught trespassing in his head right before he got to the cliffs? It was too close to be just coincidence.

No one had ever been strong enough telepathically to shut him down, especially not when he had them in a mindlock. Certainly not a woman. If they were one and the same, then he didn't quite know what to make of it—and the information he gleaned from her mind just added to his reservations. She was a killer.

If the memories he saw were real, then he had more to worry about than just rabid shifters gone rogue. But humans as a species were prone to self-delusion. What intrigued him the most were the contradictions he'd read in her mind. How could a woman so resolute in purpose, carry such guilt and shame? It was clear she killed in cold blood. So why had she left herself prone to his seduction tactics? A hardened killer would have simply ignored the attempt. Either that or tried to turn the tables. She did neither.

Sean turned off the shower and grabbed a towel. After drying off he pulled on a clean pair of jeans and slipped a shirt over his head just as Marcus knocked on the door.

"Sean, I've got as much *intel* on the girl as I could find in a quick and dirty search," he said handing him the file. "She's a pretty well-known psychic investigator. Been successful in solving cold cases for the New York City Police Department."

Sean's fingers closed over the basic beige manila folder. "Find anything that might give you a clue as to what she was up to last night?" he asked, sitting at his desk before opening the file.

"According to my sources she was up this way about two weeks ago working on a routine haunting outside of Ogunquit. There was an accident, and her partner was killed. A woman by the name of Terry Hess. Medical Examiner has the cause of death as animal attack."

Sean's head jerked up, and the two men looked at each other. Glancing at the photo stapled to the inside of the file, Sean just frowned. It all made sense now. The weapons, the shade. He exhaled. It looked as if the girl in his head and the injured girl upstairs were unquestionably one in the same. However, what worried him most was he wasn't the only one hunting last night.

CHAPTER FOUR

Lily opened her eyes. Everything hurt, even her hair. She tried to move but winced as every muscle screamed in protest. She had no idea where she was. The room was dim and unfamiliar, but she was in no condition to complain.

"Terry?" she croaked, surprised at the hoarse sound of her own voice.

"Well, look who's finally awake," a soft, feminine voice said from the door.

Lily squinted in the shadowy light trying to see who had spoken. An older woman walked quietly to the side of the bed and snapped on a soft light. She wore a white nurse's uniform and smiled warmly as she stuck a thermometer into Lily's mouth and lifted her wrist to take her pulse.

The thermometer beeped, and the nurse smiled again as Lily's temperature flashed a normal *98.6* on its LCD display.

"Looks like your fever is finally gone," she said depositing the plastic probe cover into the waste bin next to the bed.

Lily tried to sit up, grimacing in the process.

"Slowly, sweetheart...not so fast. Here, let me help you." She nodded, carefully sliding her arm under Lily's, helping to prop her up with pillows.

"Thanks," Lily croaked again. "Can you tell me which hospital I'm in?"

The nurse just smiled. "Actually, you're not in a hospital. You're a guest at Leighton Manor."

"Where?"

"Leighton Manor. It's a private estate a little north of Ogunquit, Maine. You were mauled pretty badly in the woods not far from here. Mr. Leighton was the one who found and brought you back."

A little stunned, Lily looked at the woman. "How long have I been here?"

"Oh, about a week. You were pretty out of it when they carried you in. I thought for sure they were making a mistake in bringing you here instead of a hospital. You looked as if you needed to be in intensive care, but I have to admit you're healing at an exceptional pace."

"I don't remember. Was I conscious?"

"No, honey, you weren't."

"I see. Is there anyone I can speak with about what happened to me? It's all a big blur."

The nursed nodded brightly, fluffing a third pillow to stick behind Lily's head. "Sure. Mr. Leighton comes in often enough to check on you, so I'm sure he'll introduce himself at some point. In the meantime, you certainly should rest. I'm glad to see you're up and awake. Are you hungry? I can bring you something, but nothing too heavy, no cheeseburgers yet," she teased warmly.

Lily smiled. "Maybe just something hot to drink, my throat is very sore."

"No problem." The nurse nodded and left the room.

Lily lay back on the pillows. She must have drifted off because when she popped awake, a carafe of hot tea and a tiny dish of honey sat on a tray next to the bed.

Struggling to sit up, she noticed the thick bandages covering her chest and shoulder. It was then she remembered the beast's claws and closing her eyes she unconsciously ran her hand across the path they cut, shivering at the thought.

"It's not a very pleasant memory is it?" a deep male voice asked from across the room.

Lily's eyes snapped open tracking the voice to its owner. Shocked at who was standing across the room she gaped, "You!"

"Guilty," he said with a shrug. He was sitting in front of the hearth, a low fire burning in the grate. Closing the book, he'd been reading, he got up and walked toward the bed. Lily's body tensed as he moved toward her, a predator's grace in his gait.

"Sean Leighton," he said with a hint of a bow. "It's nice to finally make your acquaintance."

"Lily. Lily Saburi." Still a bit stunned, a flush of self-conscious heat flooded her pale face. He was the last thing she expected to wake up to. He was gorgeous, and she felt like what the cat dragged in. She swallowed painfully. "Forgive me. I'm still a little bit fuzzy. How did I come to be here?"

Sean gave her a quizzical look. "You *do* remember what happened, right?"

Lily nodded but didn't say anything else, waiting for him to continue.

"You were badly injured, so I brought you here. Considering the circumstances, I thought it better for you to be treated at my private facility rather than at a regular hospital. Still, don't worry, there's a STAT MedEvac helicopter on the premises. If it had become necessary, we could have transported you to the trauma center in Portland at any time."

"Impressive. I'm sure the helicopter must come in handy during rush hour," she answered absently still trying to puzzle it together. Her eyes swept the room. It certainly didn't resemble any hospital room she'd ever seen. The place was posh.

She glanced at the hospital gown synched up around her thighs, and her face grew warm again, embarrassed by the fact she wasn't wearing anything beneath it.

"Where are my things? I know I was wearing a little more than this last night."

"Actually, it's been a week since you were brought in. Your clothes were ruined, and, unfortunately, we couldn't find any other personal effects. I'm sorry. If you'd like, I'm sure we can find something else for you to wear once you're feeling better."

Lily's mind was a jumble. She closed her eyes trying to collect herself as her memory came back in bits and pieces. "Wait a minute...," she paused, frowning in confusion.

"I remember you fought that creature barehanded. You were hurt. I'm sure of it. So how come you're walking around fine and I'm the one looking like I should be having last rites?"

"You actually look much better than you probably are. In fact, I think you look pretty good, considering. Still, if you must know, my injuries were mainly superficial."

Lily watched his face. His eyes were intense despite his relaxed pose. She tried to sit up only to have her shoulder and chest scream in protest. Slumping back, she turned to say something, but when she looked at him her throat went dry, and she couldn't remember a single thing she wanted to say.

Perhaps it was the pain meds being pumped into her I.V., but her limbs were heavy and her muscle like rubber. She couldn't look away, and his gaze made her want to slap on some lip gloss and run a brush through her hair.

Lily's eyes traveled the length of his body, and she couldn't help but stare. It seemed impossible he could look so good after the fight he had. She remembered with distinct clarity his skill as he fought—his power and his strength and how his body moved.

Leaning against the back of a chair, his long legs were crossed nonchalantly in front of him. He wore jeans and a fitted, long sleeved tee, and she couldn't help but notice how the soft denim hugged his sculpted thighs. Though his arms were crossed in front of his chest, there was no denying the six-pack hidden underneath, as well.

She knew he was speaking to her, but for all she heard he might as well have been speaking Greek. Lily blinked.

What's the matter with me? I'm laid up like death warmed over, and all I want to do is lick his thighs! Maybe I hit that tree harder than I thought...

Her cheeks flushed, and she glanced away hoping he hadn't caught her staring.

"Lily, are you all right?"

Self-conscious she cleared her throat, grimacing slightly at the soreness. "I'm fine...you were saying?"

"Still pretty bad, huh?" he said, pouring her a cup of tea with a generous dollop of honey. "This should help ease the rough spots. In the meantime, rest. I'll be back later. There'll be plenty of time for questions when you're better."

"Wait," Lily croaked, but when he turned all she managed was a weak smile. "Thanks."

With a nod, he slipped quietly out of the room and Lily sank deeper into the pillows, exhausted. A hundred questions already whirled in her head, including why she felt like a cat in heat every time he looked at her.

Hands in his pockets, Sean walked quickly down the main staircase, the thick Aubusson runner muffling the sound of his hurried footsteps. His eyes narrowed as he glanced up the stairs, wondering about his unusual guest.

He should be wary of her. Based on what he already knew, it seemed to follow she was some kind of bounty-hunter. The supernatural community had faced their fair share of those over the years, but his gut told him there was more to it—more to her.

Over the past week, he had tried again and again to get past her mental boundaries, but between the walls she threw up, and the persistent haze of pain medication, it was nearly impossible. A fact that both intrigued and unnerved him.

There was something about her that held him captivated. As battered as she was, she still had a spark, a mystique about her. He couldn't explain it. Her personality seemed as big as her body was petite, something he found ironic considering the weapons she carried.

Lily was undeniably beautiful. Her large, honey colored eyes were set in a soft, heart shaped face, and her skin reminded him of fresh cream, despite the large purple bruises. Her dark chestnut hair fell in a cascade of silk across her pillow, and her face and mouth were so expressive he found himself mesmerized just watching her sleep.

His body reacted to hers so powerfully, it stunned him. He was the hunter, the one used to call the shots. She was like a fire that promised both heat and danger—enticing yet unpredictable.

"Mr. Leighton," a voice called from behind.

Startled, he turned. "I'm sorry, Mary, I didn't hear you. What is it?"

"I'm sorry to disturb you, but Dr. Volkmann has been asking for you."

"Thank you," he said walking past her toward the private

elevators that led to the clinic two floors below. "I'll be downstairs if anyone else wants me."

"Yes, sir," she called after him as he disappeared onto the elevator.

The doors to the lift opened into chaos. There were patients waiting to be seen and nurses and administrative staff rushed around in triage mode trying to keep everyone calm. From the look of things, it was obvious the distressing news had spread.

"Leighton! I've been trying to get you all morning. We've got the preliminary results from the tests we conducted on the samples recovered from the attack site. I'm afraid it doesn't look good," Ernst Volkmann, head geneticist at the Leighton Research Facility stated gravely.

"Not out here, Doc. Let's meet in your office, in about thirty minutes. I want to make the rounds with the staff and then check up on Rissa and her daughter. Have someone call Mitch. We might as well let the Hunter's Council know where things stand."

Volkmann nodded and made his way toward the security doors that led to the restricted research part the clinic. He was a stout, little man who wore his lab coat like armor, but he was the best they had.

Sean waited, watching the doors click closed before heading through the double doors past admittance. Once on the other side, he climbed one flight to a bank of privately held rooms. Knocking quietly on the first door, he opened it as a soft voice called, *"come in,"* from the other side.

The room was brightly lit and looked more like a suite at a five star hotel than a hospital room. This morning, much of it was strewn with crayons, markers, and every conceivable kid's craft available as the television played softly in the background.

"Uncle Sean! Look what I made!" A squeaky voice said as he stepped into the living room.

"That's beautiful, Stephanie. You drew that today?" he asked, taking the multicolored image of a horse from a sticky little hand.

"*Mmmhhmm.* I just drew it. Will you hang it up downstairs for me? Mama says I shouldn't ask, but I like my horse and I think everyone else will too...it'll make them feel better, don't you think?"

"You betcha," he said, tousling her hair. "I'll hang it up for you but only if you promise to wash your hands and face. You look like a sticky mess monster!"

"*Grrrrrh,*" the little girl answered with a giggle.

Sean turned as a weak chuckle came from the large hospital bed tucked into the corner of the room. Walking over he took the woman's frail hand in his.

"How are you feeling today, Rissa," he asked gently stroking her pale skin.

"I'm a little stronger today. They think the virus has gotten about as bad as it's going to get for the time being. Now, it's just a waiting game," she said as she ran her other hand over the large mound hidden beneath the covers.

"The baby moving much these days?"

"Yeah," she chuckled and then grimaced a little in pain. "Dr. Volkmann thinks it's a healthy sign, but since there's no precedence for this, we're all just taking it one day at a time."

"Did they tell you we found Jerard?" By the tears that filled her eyes, he knew not only had she had gotten the whole story, but in much more detail than she needed in her condition.

"I'm so sorry, Rissa. If it's any consolation he died instantly," he paused, taking a deep breath before continuing. "He was stopped before he could hurt anyone else. You have my word, we did everything we could to try and bring him in first, but in the end, it wouldn't have done any good. He was just too far gone."

A thin trail of weak tears ran down her cheeks as she nodded. "I know, Sean. They told me. Is it true he injured a human woman, and as you tried to subdue him, she shot Jerard through the head?"

At her stricken face, he knew he had to tell her the truth. "No,

Rissa, that's not how it happened. Fuck, I hate gossip!" His voice was frustrated and angry, but he exhaled slowly, making himself calm down before he went on.

"I found Jerard in the woods not far from the Compound, and he was already in the process of attacking the human. He was intent on killing her, crazed with a kind of blood lust I've never seen. I called his name, but he didn't seem to hear. I pulled him off the girl...there was no recognition in his eyes...just blind rage.

"He was so strong. Stronger than ten hunters, and that's no exaggeration. I'm ashamed to say, he got the better of me. He would have killed me if the girl hadn't shot him. I can't attest as to why she was there, but it appears as though she was hunting something as well...maybe Jerard. She's upstairs in the main house. We plan to learn as much as we can from her before we decide what's to be done."

Rissa took a deep breath folding her hands over her swollen stomach. "Thank you for telling me the truth. I'm glad it was over quickly then, and that you didn't come to any harm. I don't think I could have lived with myself if anything had happened to you. You do so much for us all."

"Rest up, Rissa. If you need anything, just call, okay?" Nodding once, he kissed her forehead and started toward the door.

Stephanie ran up to him. "I washed my face, and hands Uncle Sean, now will you hang up my picture?"

Bending over he picked up the toddler, swinging her onto his hip. "If I promise, do I get a kiss?"

Squealing the little girl pressed her still wet face to his cheek and kissed it with a loud smooch. "There! Now hang up my horsey!"

A wide grin spread across his face as he put her down. "Yes, ma'am!" He gave her a mock salute. "Now be a good girl and help take care of your mother."

Sean watched her bound off toward the TV before glancing back at Rissa. With a half smile, he headed to his meeting with Volkmann and news that would only bring her more sorrow.

Volkmann's office was cluttered with medical books and papers strewn across the desk and in piles on the floor. He sat behind the mess, his glasses perched on top of his slightly balding head, and a grim expression on his face.

"The samples you retrieved confirmed what we suspected. Sean, your brother was infected with the pathogen we've been trying to isolate. It was just as you thought. His faculties were entirely compromised as the virus had already overtaken his mental and bodily functions. I'm so sorry."

Templing his fingers the doctor continued. "What we've analyzed from the information gathered, is the pathogen seems to have the ability to cross into actual DNA. It mutates a body's core genetics, while we originally thought it only wrapped itself around individual DNA strands, in effect holding them hostage."

Mitch Paris, Sean's second-in-command on the Hunter's Council, looked back and forth between his boss and the doctor. "What do you mean by 'holding them hostage', Doc? Are you telling us this pathogen has some kind of metamorphic capabilities?"

Volkmann's eyes were bleak as he looked at the two men sitting across from him. "Yes Mitch, that's what I'm saying. This virus has the ability to change our DNA. It seems to manifest itself over the course of a single moon's waxing and waning cycle. The end result is that the change in the DNA becomes clear when the infected individual phases at the next full moon. In effect, it causes them to lose all ties with the human side of their nature. They become utterly rabid."

"*Holy shit!* How do we stop the spread of this bug?"

Frustrated, Volkmann gestured with his hands. "That's just it. We don't know for sure where it was originally contracted or how it's primarily transferred. We know it's a blood borne pathogen. But we're not sure if it's coming from a food source or possibly from another creature killed or wounded during a hunt. It may even be something innocuous, something that only mutates when contracted by a supernatural host.

"We suspect it can be spread not only through the blood, but by sexual contact with an infected individual, as well. Hence the situation with Jerard's wife and her unborn baby. Rissa is only five months pregnant. Although she's tested negative so far, we won't know for sure since pregnancy compromises blood volume, and she's incapable of phasing while she's with child. We also won't know if the baby is infected until it's born. Right now, amniotic testing shows nothing irregular, but how the pathogen will manifest in an infant is yet another question. Will signs of the madness show right away or will it wait until the child reaches puberty and phases for the first time? We just don't know."

Stunned, Mitch shook his head before turning to look at Sean. "What about the human girl? She's still upstairs right?"

Sean nodded. "Yes, and according to the nurse's report she's healing pretty quickly. Considering how grave her injuries were, it seems to follow that her body siphoned some of Jerard's shifter traits when he attacked her."

"But you said there was no transfer of blood between the two?" Volkmann asked a little perplexed.

"That's right. As far as I know Jerard's blood never mixed with hers, but his saliva did. In his crazed state, he was drooling, and much of it dripped into her open wounds, not to mention the fact that he bit her. Of course, he was bleeding pretty badly himself, so anything's possible. Some of his traits must have transferred, there's no other viable explanation for how quickly she's healing—but we haven't run any tests yet to see if the pathogen transferred along with them."

Mitch and Volkmann looked at Leighton in shock. "Why not, Sean? If this girl is indeed infected, then she's a threat to us as well as to her own kind. You're the Alpha Council, why haven't you done anything about her yet? She should be taken out." Mitch scowled, his voice incredulous.

Sean put his hands up defensively. "Hold on a minute. Like the Doc said, we have no idea if this pathogen is something that's infectious only to us. Let's not forget, she's not dual-natured. And she's most probably not a shifter either. She may be immune.

"Besides, there's something different about her. I haven't had the chance to brief you yet, but she wasn't alone when I found her, and it doesn't seem to add up that she was there randomly. You should have seen the heat she was packing."

"Yeah, I heard some kind of crazy rumor she shot Jerard with a silver bullet. Stupid human myth! Have you interrogated her yet? Why was she out there armed to the hilt and so close to the Compound?"

"She's been unconscious for the past week, and I didn't *take her out* to use your turn of phrase for just that reason. I'm not going to kill someone when they are totally defenseless. Besides, we need to talk to her first."

"You said she wasn't alone. Do you want me to get a tracking party together to see if we can find her partner? It's been a week, and the scent will probably be obscured by now, but we should try."

Sean chuckled. "You could put your best noses on it, Mitch, but it wouldn't do any good. The person with her wasn't actually a person... or at least not any more...she was with a shade."

"A shade? As in ghost?"

"Yeah, if you can believe it. That's why I said there was something about her. She's certainly unusual, and I want to get to the bottom of it."

Ernst Volkmann cleared his throat. "I don't mean to interrupt your little strategy meeting, but can we get back to the business at hand? I have too much work waiting for me in the lab and not enough time to get it done. I want blood samples from the human drawn and sent to me as soon as possible. If she's absorbed enough of Jerard's traits, then she may very well be infected."

"How long before you'll know anything, Doc?" Mitch asked.

Volkmann took a deep breath. "It's been a week since the attack, so antibodies should have begun to form in her blood. It's still rather soon though, so we might have to grow the culture for a time in order to be sure. But it's certain we'll know without a doubt in a matter of days."

"I don't follow?" Mitch said his face puzzled.

Sean looked at his second-in-command, his face grim. "What the doctor means, is that in a week's time, it'll be a full moon. If she takes on the traits of a shifter and she's infected, then the virus will most likely do to her what it did to my brother."

"*Jesus*!"

"Don't worry, Mitch. Once we know what we're up against I'll have no problem carrying out my duty." The resolute tone of his voice seemed to satisfy his second-in-command, yet the idea of taking another life, Lily's life, left Sean utterly hollow.

Volkmann stood, pushing his chair back noisily. "Well, if there's nothing else then, I bid you good day, gentleman. Sean, I'll expect those samples as soon as possible. There's no telling what we'll find."

CHAPTER FIVE

Sean headed out of the clinic. He had given the nurse instructions from Volkmann less than an hour ago, but it seemed the good doctor was chomping at the bit for his samples. He had gotten a stream of messages from the man on his cell phone, the last one being nothing short of a dictate. *"Leighton! Check what's taking so long. I only wanted blood samples for pity's sake, not a biopsy!"*

"Talk about a textbook Napoleon complex," Sean chuckled to himself reading the man's latest text.

Mitch caught up to him in the hallway by the elevators. "Hey, Sean, got a minute?"

"Sure." His phone buzzed again. Holding up one finger, he motioned for Mitch to wait as he answered the call. "Okay. I'll be right up." Snapping his phone shut he pressed up for the elevator and turned back toward Mitch.

"That was the staff nurse I assigned upstairs. She's drawing the blood samples for Volkmann. He's such a persnickety bastard, wants me to collect them, myself. Says he wants to make sure they're not compromised. Come on, we can talk in the elevator."

The lift doors opened, and Sean felt the weight of Mitch's eyes as the doors slowly closed. "So, what's up?"

"Rissa."

"What about her?"

"Look, I know that Jerard was your brother and all, but it's no secret that he was, well let's just say it's common knowledge that he and Rissa weren't exactly the happiest of couples. If you know what I mean."

Sean's eyes narrowed, "...and."

"And she's got a tough road ahead of her now with the new baby and Stephanie barely out of diapers..."

"Get to the point Mitch. What do you want with my sister-in-law?"

"I want to know if it would be all right with you if I started spending some time with them, you know, to get to know them better." Mitch shrugged a little embarrassed by the question.

Sean just looked at him. "You truly are a mutt. I should tear your head off on principle. My brother's dead less than a week, and here you are already staking your claim."

"It's not what you think, Sean," Mitch shot back quietly.

Not knowing what else to say, they stood in awkward silence as the elevator climbed. Glancing over, Sean could see the muscle in Mitch's cheek working as he bit back on his wounded pride.

"Shit," Sean thought to himself. This was the last thing he needed right now. But Mitch was no fool. He was a good man—one he could rely on. And as much as he hated to admit it, he was right about Jerard.

Sean cleared his throat. "Look, I'm well aware of everyone's opinion regarding my brother. And you're right; Jerard wasn't exactly winning any prizes for best husband and father. Even I knew Rissa wasn't happy. But she's in a fragile state right now, and you know as well as I do what she's facing if things don't turn out the way we hope with this baby."

The elevator doors opened, and they stepped out into the main foyer. Mitch nodded. "I know," he said softly. "That's why I want to be there for her. It's going to be rough one way or the other, but maybe I can help. You know, be a shoulder for her."

Sean smirked. "Yeah, yeah. Just make sure your shoulder is the only body part you have in mind to offer, for the time being."

Mitch laughed. "Can't you give me a little more credit than that?"

"*Mmmhhhm.* Let's not forget, I know you and your reputation with the ladies. Rissa's different, Mitch, and I'm not saying that because she's my family."

"Don't you think I know that? Look, I may have been a player in the past, but Rissa...man, she deserves to be happy."

Sean took a long hard look at his second-in-command, wondering how Mitch would react if he decided to take a walk through the guy's mind. After a moment, he nodded, deciding to trust his gut.

"Okay, Mitch. If you were looking for my blessing you got it, but I hope you know, I will personally give you the beating of your life if you fuck up and hurt her. Just go easy man, okay?" Clapping Mitch on the shoulder Sean headed upstairs alone.

Stepping onto the top landing, Sean heard the sound of muffled yelling. As he crossed the hall, he recognized Lily's voice, the tenor of her complaints gaining in volume the closer he got to her door.

"Ouch! You know, I'm seriously starting to think you're enjoying this!" Lily said cringing as the nurse tried tapping yet another vein.

"And how are we feeling this afternoon?" Sean asked, closing the door behind him, but as he stepped toward the bed, he could already see that Lily's *I.V.* was gone, and despite the bloodletting, her color was better.

"I don't know about *we*, but I'm much better, thanks. I feel like a new woman. The bandages came off, and I was finally able to take a shower. Even *Nurse Ratchet* here is surprised I'm practically healed... Hey! ...come on! Take it easy with that needle; I'm not a pin cushion, you know!"

Biting his lip Sean tried not to laugh. "That's good."

The nurse taped sterile gauze to the inside of Lily's elbow "She's all ready for the lab, Mr. Leighton," she said, scribbling the last of Lily's information on the side of the glass tubes. She handed the box to Sean and ran a hand across her forehead, gathering her kit. "If there's nothing else then, I'll be downstairs. Just buzz if you need me."

Lily eyes threw daggers at the woman's back, and Sean had to stifle another laugh. Especially when she turned her attentions to him and the little white box, with vial after vial of her blood stacked neatly inside.

She picked at the surgical tape on her arm, shooting him a sullen look. "Twenty-four vials. Would you mind telling me why so much? What are you testing me for, Ebola?"

Arching an amused brow, Sean smiled. "You know, you shouldn't abuse my staff like that. It's not polite. However, to answer your question the doctors want to run a battery of routine tests."

The statement wasn't a complete lie. Still, in this situation there was no room for guilt. Sean continued to stare her down even as her eyes narrowed in suspicion. He knew she realized he wasn't giving her the whole truth.

Their gazes locked, and her eyes grew flinty as the first mental jab flew out at him. The second he felt her in his head he slammed down his own mental wall shutting *her* out this time. Did she actually think he was going to allow her to see what he wasn't telling her?

Eyes wide, Lily scrambled to the other side of the bed. "You!"

"Hasn't anyone ever told you how unattractive hysteria can be in a woman? You need to calm down. Perhaps, if you stopped trying to trespass inside my head, we could get to the truth of who you are, and what you were doing on the cliffs a week ago."

"I don't need to tell you anything! And I don't need to *trespass* anywhere to see you for what you are. You're the same as that thing! That beast that attacked me...that killed Terry!"

"It's unfortunate what happened to you and your friend. I have the coroner's report. As terrible a tragedy as it was, it still isn't anybody's fault."

"Unfortunate! I lose the closest thing to family I have left, and you call it unfortunate! Look, I may not have been in your head for long, but I recognize the thought patterns. Except for the fact that yours are coherent they are *exactly* the same. You're a werewolf as well—a supe—a filthy, beast. A monster that preys on humans!"

He studied her for a moment, saying nothing at first. "Is that what you think?"

Lily stepped away from the bed. "Give me a break! Do you have any idea who I am or what I do for a living? You already know that I'm psychic, but what you don't know is that I also investigate murders for the police! There's no way in hell you're going to stand there and hand me a load of crap. I *know* what you are! And you can forget trying to sell me on how innocent you *supes* are when I've seen your handiwork up close and personal!"

From her scent, Sean tasted her adrenaline flowing fast and furious. She was sweating and panicked. "Okay, so you work with the police. I'm sure you must have investigated plenty of cases that didn't involve the supernatural. So just for argument's sake, tell me, what's the difference between a supe, or whatever you call us, committing a murder and a regular murder?"

"Are you kidding me? I was there when that thing killed my best friend! And in case you've conveniently forgotten, it attacked me, as well! I've seen the ravaged bodies in the morgue—bloodless, torn to shreds or worse! There is no way in hell a human could defend themselves against any of you! At least with a human perp, they've got half a chance," she yelled.

Lily's hospital gown was open to the back, and she clutched it closed, tearing around the room pulling open drawers and closets. "Where the hell are my clothes?"

"What are you doing? I told you before, your clothes were ruined. Stop this before you reinjure yourself!" Grabbing her by the wrist, he tried to make her sit down.

She whirled around, kneeing him in the stomach, driving her elbow into his face as he hunched over. "I'm getting the hell out of here! You and your kind are all the same—vile, unnatural beasts!"

He struggled to hold her, curbing his own strength so as not to hurt her as she continued to fight. With blood trickling from his nose, he grabbed her other wrist and held them locked together.

Lily screamed in fury trying to break his grip. She fought him, trying to twist herself around, but only managed to wind herself further into his grasp. She struggled, but with his arms locked around her she was trapped. Sean felt his body tense and cock grow hard.

"I'm sorry Lily but leaving is out of the question. You probably feel as if you're being held against your will, but trust me, it is for your own good. If you want, you may walk the grounds with an escort, but I warn you, if you try to leave the Compound, you'll like it even less when I have you restrained."

Her chest heaved. Bottled up rage and despair rose to the surface and was spilling over onto him. Screaming turned to crying, her whole body shaking with grief and anger.

The room was saturated with her grief, and the taste of her pain washed through him. His own anger mounted as he listened to her sobs. She shouldn't be here. None of this should have happened. However, there was no way he was going to share his personal grief with a woman who'd just as soon shoot him as look at him. No. The Compound's safety and their secrets came first, regardless of how attracted he was to this hellcat.

Clearing his throat, he helped her to the edge of the bed. He picked up his cell phone, and as she crawled beneath the covers, he instructed the nurse to come back up and bring a sedative.

"Is drugging me truly necessary? Or am I that much of a threat?" She sniffed coldly.

"I don't know, are you?"

"You could have transferred me to the hospital in Portland by now. You're hiding something. I deserve to know what it is, why you insist on holding me hostage."

"You are not a hostage, Lily, you are my guest. An injured one at that. The purpose of the sedative is to help you sleep, and nothing more. It's for your own good, same as trying to keep you put. You're just going to have to trust me."

"And why is that?"

Sean didn't answer, they were at a stalemate. Finally, he looked right at her. "Because you have no other choice."

Lily looked at herself in the mirror brushing her teeth. No one would believe she'd been a hairbreadth away from death only two weeks ago. Impossible as it seemed, she was entirely healed. Truth be told, she felt terrific. That is except for the fact she was being held against her will and hadn't seen or heard from Terry since that night on the cliffs.

Rinsing her mouth, she dried her hands and face and put the toothbrush back in its fancy holder, along with the other toiletries Sean had sent up. He was certainly going out of his way to prove she was a guest, and not a prisoner. But she wasn't buying it. Guests didn't need big, burly guards following them about, and they could leave whenever they wanted.

Sean could sugarcoat the situation anyway he wished. She was still a prisoner, regardless of how gilded the cage.

Lily hadn't seen him much over the last couple of days. She knew there was something going on, and she knew that was one of the reasons he was making himself scarce. It was all connected. Her, Terry and what he was doing that night on the cliffs.

For a psychic, it should have been a piece of cake. A quick peek into any one of the minds around her and she'd have her answers. But it was as if someone had raised a smoke screen. She'd been cut off. Being in seclusion didn't help matters either.

Nonetheless, today she was venturing out, and it didn't seem plausible Sean could cloak everyone. She'd try her luck again, outside.

Lily pulled on a pair of cotton, drawstring pants and a matching pullover. Running a hand over the heather blue fleece, she reveled in its softness. They, along with a set of lacy undergarments had been waiting for her on the vanity this morning. Pulling her hair back into a knot, she had to admit it felt good to be out of the hospital drab.

Her guard was waiting for her by the window. "Ready?" he asked as she came out of the bathroom.

Lily gave him an answering shrug, but the truth was she couldn't wait to get outside. From her bedroom window, the grounds seemed enormous. It had finally snowed, and despite her circumstances, she wanted to enjoy its pristine beauty.

The young man stood waiting near the door, his expressionless face as cold as ice. Lily sighed. Did they seriously consider her that much of a threat?

Squelching the urge to throw her arms up and yell *"boo!"* She cleared her throat. "What's your name, soldier?"

"Lieutenant Jack Cochran, ma'am. I've been assigned as your escort."

Lily snapped her mouth shut. She may have been dripping with sarcasm when she called him *"soldier"*, but it was obvious he wasn't playing the part, regardless of his jeans and cowboy boots.

"In that case, Lieutenant, I'd like you to escort me home."

"Negative, ma'am. I can take you anywhere you wish, as long as it's within the Compound boundaries."

"Do you work for Mr. Leighton, Lieutenant?"

"Yes, ma'am."

"Then may I call you Jack, Lieutenant?"

"Yes, ma'am."

"Okay then, and will you please stop with the ma'am business. It's Lily, got it?"

"Got it, ma'am."

Grumbling, Lily picked up the jacket Sean had also sent up. She glanced at the Lieutenant and frowned. The boy's stance was so rigid he looked as if he would snap in the wind. Were all shifters that obstinate or just the ones connected to their pigheaded leader? Annoyed, she jammed her arms into the jacket's sleeves. Like everything else, it was a perfect fit, but that only added to her irritation. "Are you coming, or do I have to say *heel* first?"

Face impassive, the Lieutenant walked to the door and held it open. He let her pass, but growled a deep, loud, rumble as she went by. Lily shot him a dirty look but caught his stifled chuckle.

"Yuck it up, Lassie," she answered before turning on her heel, mumbling something about choke collars and obedience school as she stalked down the hall.

The Lieutenant caught up to her on the stairs and took her arm.

Lily slid her eyes sideways. The young man's face held an amused smirk, but at least it was no longer cold and hard.

She didn't know why, but she felt sorry for the guy. You didn't need to be a psychic to know the last thing he wanted to do was act as her babysitter.

"Look, Jack, I don't know why Sean is keeping me here, and I know you wouldn't tell me even if you knew. But as you can see, I'm fine. I'm perfectly healed, and I'd like to go home."

"Again, I'm sorry, but that just isn't possible."

They stepped into the foyer and Lily turned, exasperated, throwing her hands up. "Why then? I think I deserve an explanation, don't you? Sean had me just about convinced it was because of my injuries, but now that I'm healed there's no reason why I shouldn't be permitted to leave. Someone better start explaining and fast, or I'm going to find out myself. And you all know I have ways of doing that!"

"You're absolutely, right," Sean's voice answered from across the main hall. The Lieutenant snapped to attention as Lily whirled in the direction of the voice.

"At ease, Jack." Sean said offhandedly, his eyes traveling over Lily. A single glance told him what she said was true. She radiated health. A wash of dusky rose colored her cheeks as a result of her temper, and her scent was intoxicating. She was beautiful.

"I'm glad to see that you were able to make use of the things I sent earlier. You look wonderful."

"Thank you, I feel terrific, which brings me back to the point I was making. I want to go home, Sean."

Sean didn't answer. He looked to his Lieutenant and flicked his head sideways. "Thank you, Jack, but I think it's better if I escort Ms. Saburi this afternoon. You can go."

The young man left with barely a nod, but Lily remained, arms folded across her chest waiting for what Sean had to say. Grabbing a jacket from the hall closet, he opened the front door. "Come on, I'll give you the grand tour."

Arms still folded at her chest, she followed him into the snow. The grounds were a blanket of white, except where the late afternoon sun casted shadows in a deep, amber hue. It was perfect. *Or it would be if things were different.*

Sean was gorgeous. There was no denying it. And he affected her in ways she didn't want to admit—there was no denying that, as well. *You're weak, you're letting your body betray you. Betray Terry,* her thoughts admonished.

Yet, the more she fought it, the worse it got. How could her body want what she had vowed to destroy?

The snow crunched under their feet, leaving footprints five inches deep as they walked. Sean didn't say a word but led the way across the lawn toward a large greenhouse. The glass walls were frosted as if painted with intricate lace. Wrought iron benches lined the walkway, and there were stone urns with the remains of winter withered flowers, frozen in ice.

Stopping to clean the snow from one of the benches, Sean took off his jacket and laid it on the seat, motioning for Lily to sit.

"What about you, aren't you cold?" she asked.

"Nope. It's a shifter thing. Our bodies naturally run warmer than humans. I guess you might say I'm a hottie," he winked sitting down on the bench, patting his jacket again. "Sit down. I won't bite."

Lily sat with a huff. Did he have to sit so close to her?

"Pretty isn't it?"

"Yes, it is," she sighed. "Sean, I..."

"Tell me about Terry," he said cutting her off. Deftly redirecting the subject, he wanted to steer clear of her questions. "I've never encountered a shade before, and I'm curious. Has she been haunting you long?"

Lily pushed her legs back and forth digging deep grooves in the snow with her heels. She knew Sean watched, but she didn't look up. She also knew he deliberately changed the subject. "To answer your question, Terry wasn't always a shade. She was my best friend. We grew up together. Our families were extremely close, so when mine was killed in a car crash, Terry's family took me in."

Sean stayed silent. The wind had picked up blowing Lily's chestnut hair loose. He couldn't see her face, but he didn't need to. Her sorrow was in her scent. "I'm sorry, Lily. How old were you?"

"Ten. It wasn't too long after that my psychic abilities showed up." Lily exhaled sadly, looking out at the horizon. The sun was low in the sky, casting a halo of gold across the distant treetops. "Terry believed my abilities were a gift from God, a way for me to still see my folks. She was the only one who knew. That is until I started working with the police."

"But you're a bounty hunter? You hunt, and you kill. How does that fit in with helping the police?"

"Bounty hunter? I'm no bounty hunter, Sean. I hunt for one reason and one reason only. Revenge. And don't pretend you don't know why. Terry was murdered not far from here, by the same thing that almost killed me out on the cliffs.

I had been working a lot of cases. Mostly unsolved homicides and kidnappings. The sadness inherent in that type of case load became too much for Terry. You see, she was my business partner as well as my friend. Terry was tired. She wanted to take a break from our investigations, but I didn't. I had become immersed in them. The case here in Maine was supposed to be a compromise. A routine haunting. Easy."

A hawk cawed in the sky above them pulling her attention, but even its shrill sound couldn't drown out her guilt. *It should have been easy...it should have been effortless...it should have never happened, the little voice in her head accused.*

"Terry was outside taking baseline *EMF* readings when the beast attacked. It was more animal than human—hairy and grotesque, with an elongated jaw and razor-like teeth. Hearing Terry's screams, I ran out of the house, but I was too late. I couldn't face her parents after the funeral. Regardless of what the coroner's report said, I knew it wasn't a freak attack by some kind of animal. I'd witnessed too many extraordinary things in my life to discount the facts. It was a werewolf.

"Terry showed up in her current form about two weeks after her death. I had already started hunting. She said she was here to help me, but I don't see how. She's dead, and nothing is going to change that. I don't even know if she's still around."

Sean didn't know what to say, so he just stayed silent. The ramifications of what was happening in his world had just increased tenfold. He needed to let the Hunter's Council know, needed to up their patrols. As if on cue, his phone buzzed.

"What is it Mitch? When? Well, who's on it? Get Jack and his company out scouting the grounds, a.s.a.p.! This is no joke, Mitch. If he gets past the Compound boundaries, the chances of us finding him before he hurts someone are next to nil. We got lucky the last time. Just do it. I'm heading back to the manor now."

Sean's face was grim, and from the sound of what Lily heard at this end, there was a reason for it. "What's going on?"

"Nothing that concerns you. Let's go. I need to get you back to the manor. It's getting late, and it's not safe for you to be out here after dark."

"But I'm with you. I honestly don't want to go back yet, Sean, I've been cooped up all week."

"I'm sorry Lily, but I have to get back. There's something I need to attend to."

It was no use arguing with him. Tomorrow was another day, and maybe then she'd be the one to ask all the questions. "Wow, touchy, and the full moon isn't until tomorrow night!"

Sean shot her a look...if she only knew. The wind changed suddenly, and shouts came somewhere behind them. Sean raised his head and sniffed. A low menacing growl left his throat. “We have to go!” Grabbing Lily by the arm he yanked her up, all manner of polite chivalry gone. “Move your ass, Lily, and don’t argue with me! We have to get back to the manor, now!”

Jerking her arm away, Lily reached back and smacked him. “Don’t manhandle me! What the hell do you think you’re doing? What happened in the last two minutes to make you crazier than I thought? One minute you’re concerned and interested in me and my story, and the next you’re all Gestapo— what are you, a Good Samaritan or a Guantanamo Bay wannabe? Pick one, because you’re giving me whiplash!”

Sean tensed, ignoring her. It was too late. The air around them shifted, and even Lily felt the difference. A foul smell drifted toward them, and she gagged. It was the same stench she remembered from the beast on the cliffs. “It can’t be,” she whispered, the blood draining from her face. “It’s dead. I shot it!”

“Lily, get behind me and stay close. We’re going to back up slowly. Whatever you do don’t turn and run. Wrap your arms around my waist, slowly. We need to stay attached. This one may still be lucid. If it is, it will recognize my scent, and mine will mask yours enough to confuse it.”

Lily didn’t argue. She had no idea what Sean was talking about, but did as she was told, wrapping her arms around Sean’s waist, and pressing herself against him. A terrified giggle welled up her throat, but she swallowed it back. She’d fantasized plenty about wrapping herself around him, but this certainly wasn’t the circumstance she envisioned.

The two moved slowly backward. The beast came into view, rounding the corner of the greenhouse. It chuffed and sniffed, pawing the snow like a wild animal posturing before a strike. There were more shouts and the beast reared up. A spray of gunfire pierced the air, and Sean reached behind yanking Lily beneath him as they hit the ground.

The beast was surrounded as more shots were fired. A loud crash echoed against the trees as the beast flung itself through one of the greenhouse walls. Glass shattered everywhere, spraying shards like tiny pieces of shrapnel. A bloody trail smeared across the snow, steam rising into the air as it cooled, even in the dim light.

Sean got up, pulling Lily to standing. Brushing the snow from her jacket and legs he wrapped his arms around her. "Are you all right?"

"All right? Are you fucking serious? This is insanity, Sean, and I'm getting out of here right now!" She pushed him away and took off full speed toward the house.

Sean's men were still working, assessing the situation. He knew he had to take their reports, but he also needed to go after Lily. If she tried to leave, it would be bad. He flipped open his cell and pressed speed dial.

"Mitch. Get out here and take over for me. I'll take the report synopsis from you later. There's been a complication with the girl I need to attend to." Snapping the phone shut, he took off after Lily.

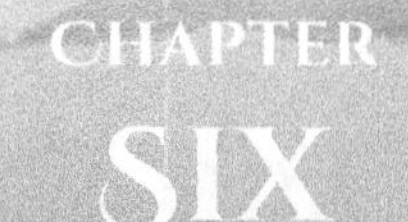

CHAPTER SIX

Lily slammed the door behind her. She knew she didn't have much time, so she grabbed whatever she could find—clothes, toiletries, any food she had, and threw it all into the clean, plastic bag she took from the wastebasket. Tying it in a knot, she slung it over her shoulder Santa Claus style.

She sent her senses out, trying one last time to get a read on the place hoping to smooth her escape, but all she got was the same damn static. *Shit!* Chewing on her bottom lip, she climbed out the window onto the narrow decorative ridge that surrounded the top level of the manor.

How the fuck did I end up in all this? Terry's right, I must be insane.

With her legs straddling the window, she scanned the roofline for a possible escape but nixed the idea, immediately. The pitch was too steep. Her only chance was to maneuver herself lower to the ground, so she dropped her bundle to the balcony below and inched around, turning her body to face the house.

On her toes, she carefully crouched down to grab the edge of the ridge on both sides of her feet. She got to her knees, one at a time and then gradually lowered her legs. *Thank God for all those pull-ups,* she thought as she hung from the ridge with her fingers gripping the edge of the decorative wood, a silent prayer on her lips that it didn't give way.

"You know, getting to the second floor is much easier if you just use the stairs," Sean smirked from the open window. He leaned nonchalantly against the frame with his arms crossed at his chest.

"Stay away from me Sean, I mean it."

"...and what exactly are you planning to do? Drop from balcony to balcony? Come on, Lily, tying bed sheets together would have made more sense than dangling like a deranged rock climber."

Without another word, Sean leaned over and grabbed her wrists, hoisting Lily onto the ridge. She landed against his chest with a faint *whoomph*, her soft curves pressed against his hard abs as he dragged her into the room, but this time she was too ticked off to register the sexy feel.

"Get off me!"

"Will you promise not to do anything else stupid, like try and scale the side of the house or run across the roof?"

Lily squirmed. "Let me go!" But Sean had her locked in his arms. As she fought, he chuckled, incensing her more.

"You think this is funny! You won't let me leave, but you won't tell me what's going on either. It's driving me insane!"

Sean breathed in her scent. "You don't like being out of control, do you, Lily? You like having the upper hand, especially with that psychic sense of yours. But that's all haywire now, isn't it? Why don't you just give in? Don't you think I can smell it on you? You're angry, that's for sure, but underneath all that piss and vinegar burns a fire that scares the hell out of you. You want me, but you'll never admit it, will you?"

Lily's eyes bore into his. Her face flushed with a combination of anger and embarrassment. He was right; she hated to be out of control. Oh God! Was she that obvious?

Keeping his arms wrapped around her, Sean let her slide down. He was careful to let her feel the full, hard length of him before he let her feet touch the ground. *Let the games begin.*

Lily hauled back to smack his face, but Sean caught her forearm. Sliding his hand into hers, he brought it to his mouth. Turning it palm up, he licked the inside of her wrist, teasing a couple of her fingers with his tongue.

He cupped her face, running his thumb across her bottom lip. It trembled as he leaned down and tasted her mouth. His lips were soft on hers, pushing her to open to him until he could smell the reluctant wet musk release between her legs.

Her scent was saturated with need, with want, but still, she forced herself to hold back.

Everything churned inside—her grief, her anger at Terry for dying and her own guilt at not being able to stop it. The emotions bit into her gut, worsened by the knowledge she was still weak from her injuries, and vulnerable without her weapons.

The shifter's touch sent tingles through her lower belly, and resentment bloomed at her body's betrayal, but it was as if she had no choice.

Sean's tongue danced along the edges of her mouth, breaking down barriers with each swirl, the rough, raspy feel, unlike anything Lily had ever felt. Drawing his tongue across the hollow of her throat, he worked his way back to her mouth. He pressed himself against her, pulling her body even closer, his hardness evident.

Sean slid his mouth over hers, urging her, pressing her further into her own uninvited need. She dug her fingers into his hair and bit his lip drawing blood. All her pain and anger, all her regret and unspoken need burst like a damn breaking, and she kissed him deeper and more urgently than she thought possible. She poured everything into that kiss as if she could smother every other emotion in a torrent of heat. As if she could burn away everything she felt with blind lust.

He was hungry for her. Stepping back, he grabbed the neck of her pullover and ripped it in two. Lily shrugged it off. Running his hands over her smooth skin, Sean traveled over the small of her back, his fingers trailing over the curve of her hip and delicately across her sensitive middle.

Lily whimpered and the sound jarred him, pulling him back. “Am I hurting you?”

“No, don’t stop,” she murmured reaching for him.

He growled sweeping her in his arms and carrying her to the bed. Gently, he laid her on top of the covers. Lily shivered as he ran his hand the full length of her body. Pulling the drawstring on her pants, he pushed them down, lace panties and all, and tossed them to the floor. He knelt on the bed and gathered her in his arms.

Starting at her shoulder, he kissed the path of the angry, pink scars his brother’s claws had made in her delicate skin. His tongue rasped over the sensitive flesh as if he could erase her pain, marking her as his own.

He trailed past her throat, over the full curve of her breasts, teasing with his fingers and the swirl of his tongue until her breath caught in her throat, her nipples hardening from their friction.

With a deft flick of his fingers he unclipped the front closure of her bra, tossing it to the floor, as well. Leaning over he took a single crested peak into his mouth and suckled, teasing the tender flesh with his teeth while his fingers worked the other.

Lily arched her back, and she moaned as he ran his hand past her stomach. He gently caressed the soft fuzz between her legs, letting his fingers graze her sensitive folds.

Sean stroked her slick entrance, deftly inserting first one, and then a second finger into her cleft. Gasping she rolled her hips under his hand. He teased her, leaving her breathless before moving his hand away and licking her musk from his fingers one by one.

She clamored to her knees and pushed him backward, her

honey colored eyes dark with desire and suffused with a commanding heat. Sean wasn't the only one who could call the shots. "Lose the clothes." It was her turn to growl as he rocked back, slightly.

Chuckling, he got to his feet pulling his shirt over his head. His stomach was flat and hard, and Lily leaned up, running her hands over the hard planes of his chest.

Her fingers nimbly unbuttoned his jeans, and when she started to push them off his hips, she smirked, realizing that beneath the denim, he'd gone commando.

"Nice," she purred running her fingers under the soft, blue fabric cupping his bare ass.

"I'm glad you like surprises," he answered, and stepping back he pushed his jeans to the floor.

Lily sat back and licked her lips. Prominent in a thick nest of black curls, above his strong, muscled thighs was his engorged sex—long and thick with corded veins that looked as if they would burst through his skin.

She reached out to stroke his flesh, wrapping her hand around his shaft. Moving back and forth, she stroked his swollen head till it seemed it would burst with each pass.

At Sean's sharp intake of breath, she smiled to herself and climbed off the bed. Raising her hands to his shoulders, she gently raked them down the length of his chest sinking to her knees in front of him.

With the tip of her tongue, she took her first taste of him, circling his head in languorous strokes and quick darts, luxuriating in the velvet feel of him on her tongue. Sean moaned and Lily smiled wickedly, sucking harder and deeper, taking him as fully into her mouth as she could. He growled and fisted his hands in her hair guiding her strokes.

Suddenly, he grabbed her around her waist and yanked her to her feet, kissing her with a kind of hunger she had never felt before. He rumbled deep in the back of his throat, and the sound was almost feral.

He laid her on the bed and Lily wrapped her legs around his back, urging him, begging for him. He raised and with one hard thrust entered her. Keeping his rhythm even and forceful, he drove his hips forward and she met him thrust for thrust.

His desire mounted, and he struggled to keep his wolf at bay as it snarled for release. His nostrils flared, and the scent of her desire pushed him to the brink. He was primal, predatory, and the whole of his body trembled with the feeling.

Lily moaned, her hips matching his tempo. As they climbed, he reared up and when he could hold back no more, he roared, shuddering, emptying into her as she screamed, clutching at him as she climaxed, as well.

They collapsed, exhausted but sated and Sean cradled Lily in his arms, holding her to his chest, breathing in her after-scent.

"Stop that. It tickles," she said, squirming a little.

"I'm just breathing in your scent. The way you smell now, right afterward. It'll make for a delicious memory."

Nothing will make me forget what we just did. Ever."

He inhaled deeper, nuzzling the back of her neck. "It was pretty amazing, even by shifter standards, and that's saying a lot."

"I wouldn't know about that, but humans can certainly hold their own. Maybe it was the combination that made the sex so explosive, you know, because you're a shifter and I'm human?"

"What?" he asked, putting a hand on her shoulder to turn her around. "Lily, do you actually believe we're all that different? That it's us *versus* you?"

She shrugged. "Well, yeah, I guess. This is all new for me. Especially since this is the first time, I don't have the urge to shoot you first, and ask questions later."

Sean rolled onto his back. He was quiet, but Lily could see the little muscle working in his cheek as he lay there.

"There's so much you don't understand," he murmured. Pushing himself up onto his elbow, he exhaled, reaching out with his other hand to tuck a stray curl behind Lily's ear. "So maybe it's time I showed you a little about what's been going on around here."

Lily tensed, eying him warily. There was an odd buzzing in her ears, and then an unexpected flood of emotion and thought poured through her mind. Her body rippled with recalled magic as Sean allowed her to feel his dual nature, sharing his memories of racing with the moon, his camaraderie with the pack. Lily watched his transformation in her mind's eye, stunned to see his majestic form, so different from the creatures she had seen. She saw his strength and his humanity, as well as his kindness and determination to do what was right for his pack.

Lily's warm tears fell to his arm as Sean let her see the waste and heartbreak brought by the sickness infecting his kind. He let her see his sadness at losing his brother to its devastation. Her breath caught in her throat when he showed her images of herself the night she was attacked and let her see just how close to death he, himself had come.

"I had no idea," she whispered.

Breaking their link, he relaxed, letting his arms fall to her waist. "Are you okay?" he asked, softly.

Lily nodded, not trusting herself to speak after all she had seen.

"I never intended to show you all this, but there didn't seem to be any other way to get you to understand."

Turning in his arms, she looked up into his dark eyes. "Terry tried to warn me, but I couldn't see past my anger and my own pain. Never once did I consider that it might be the same for you. I don't know what to think or how to feel anymore."

"You're a psychic Lily; you can see and talk to dead people. I think most definitions would qualify you as a bit of a supe, yourself. You see, we're not so different after all."

"I guess, but not really. I can't change my species, or god-forbid, have to drink blood to survive. But I see your point."

"What if you did—I mean what if you found out, through no fault of your own that you had been irrevocably changed. What would you do?"

Propping herself up on her elbow she just looked at him. "I don't know."

Leaning up he kissed her throat and the tender flesh beneath her jaw. "Maybe it's something for you to think about," he whispered taking her mouth again.

Lily closed her eyes, a satisfied smile playing on her lips as she replayed the last hour with Sean, over and over again in her head.

"I leave you alone for a while and look what happens... fraternizing with the enemy."

Lily's eyes flew open as she sat up. "Terry?" she said, looking around the room. "Where are you? Where have you been?"

Terry floated across the room and sat on the edge of the bed. She was still barely visible, but from her smile, it was obvious she was glad to be back.

"I haven't actually *been* anywhere. I was sort of floating in some kind of hazy nothingness. It was weird, kind of like floating in a cloud the consistency of Jell-O."

"Are you all right, I mean I can see right through you. Not that you weren't see-through before, but now you're *really* see-through."

She chuckled. "I'm fine. Though, I don't know if I'll ever be any more visible than I am right now. But it might be a good idea for me to lay off the ectoplasm thing, at least for a while."

Lily laughed. "God, I missed you! So much has happened. The guy that charged out of the woods he's the one that brought me here. But you already know that."

"Yeah, and that's not the *only* thing I know," she said a crooked grin spreading across her transparent face.

"What?"

Terry started fanning herself. "*No, don't stop...,*" she said mimicking Lily's breathless voice. "Things have gone way past hot and heavy with the werewolf, haven't they?"

"You were spying on me?"

"Let's just say I showed up at an inopportune moment. Just be happy I decided to be discreet and left the room."

Lily shot her a dirty look. "Thanks."

Terry put her hands on her shimmery hips. "Don't go getting all pissy on me; I'm glad you're hooking up. He actually seems to be a pretty decent guy and not to mention hung like a racehorse."

"I thought you said you left the room?"

Her friend shrugged mischievously. "Well, maybe I peeked a little."

Lily picked up her hairbrush from the nightstand and threw it at Terry's head.

"Nice try," Terry giggled. "You like him, Lil, admit it. And it's more than just physical, I can tell. You've got that sappy look on your face. The same one you always get when you're infatuated. That is until they get too close for comfort."

Heat rushed into Lily's cheeks, but she ignored it. "You're reading way too much into this. We had sex, big deal. It's been a trying few weeks. I needed the tension relief."

"Tension relief? Really? Come 'on Lil, you're the queen of one night stands because you never want to invest. I'm a Shade, remember? I have a decidedly different take on things than you. My perspective is just a smidge deeper than anything you can sense, even with your psychic abilities— which don't seem to be helping you much, by the way. I know you better than anyone else, and you feel something for this one."

Lily shrugged. "Maybe."

"So, what are you going to do about it?"

Lily's brows knit together. "What do you mean?"

"You do realize he's a shifter, right?"

Lily exhaled. "I know he's a shifter, Terry. Don't you think I'm beating myself up for allowing him to confuse me, tempt me away from everything I set my mind to since the night you were killed? I'm being disloyal—not only to you, but to myself and to everything I promised to set right—especially since it was his brother that attacked us both."

Terry floated up to stand. "His brother! Are you kidding me?"

"No, I'm not. But there's more. It turns out there's some kind of pathogen that's infecting his kind—some kind of a mutating virus or something. It takes ordinary individuals and turns them into crazed beasts. His brother had it, and supposedly that's the reason why you were attacked. Sean told me all about it, or rather he showed me."

"He *showed* you? How?"

"He let me into his head. I saw it all, Terry, how they live, how they are. They truly aren't so different from us, and they try very hard to coexist. In fact, they've been hunting infected shifters for months now trying to prevent the spread of this virus.

Terry's eyes narrowed, but her gaze was soft. "So, what now?"

Lily sighed. "To be honest, I truly don't know."

The Shade nodded her head, the small movement causing her hair to glimmer against her shoulders. "Yes, you do. I know you better than you know yourself, and this one's gotten to you. The minute he opened up and let you into his head, he had you hook, line and sinker.

No guy has ever shown you that kind of trust before. And don't kid yourself, he's smart—he knows who and what you were hunting that night, even if he hasn't pressed the issue. He's accepted you. And I happen to have found his last question both interesting as well as intuitive."

Lily shot her friend a look. "What are you talking about?"

"When he asked you what you would do if you found out you had been changed. But what you don't seem to realize is that you've already been changed, and I don't mean in an *American Werewolf in London* sort of way either and it's scaring the hell out of you."

"Don't say that. You're dead wrong, Terry."

"I may be dead, but I'm not wrong. Otherwise, you wouldn't be so upset."

"I don't want to talk about it."

Terry floated to the side of the bed. "Of course, you don't. That's half the problem. Why else would you be running around the woods in the middle of the night looking like a refugee from a terrorist camp? Every time something happens you react in extremes. Every time some guy starts to get too close, you cut him off at the knees. Of course, with the others it was only figurative; with this one, I'm not so sure." She reached out with her hand, and let it drop. "Tell me Lily, what's going on? Why are you too scared to go with what you feel?"

Lily crossed her arms in front of her chest. "I have my reasons."

Terry frowned, crossing her arms as well, mimicking Lily's defensive posture. "Is it just because he's a supe? Because let me tell you, having a shade for a best friend qualifies you for your own space on the weirdness meter. Lily, you've never been a coward before, so why now?" She wasn't going to let her friend off so easily.

Lily's arms unfolded in a huff. "Because! Everyone I care about always dies! Okay? Are you happy now?" she yelled, throwing her hands in the air. "First my parents in a car crash, then you—I refuse to let anyone else in, Terry. It hurts too much." Her voice broke along with her tears.

Terry sat down next to her on the bed, her hand outstretched. "You've got to let somebody in at some point or you're going to end up even more alone than you already are. It's no way to live Lily, and it's no way to die. Trust me."

Lily wiped her cheek with the back of her hand. "What do you mean by that?"

"I never let anyone in either. I always had you, always thought I had plenty of time. I was wrong. Too many chances passed because I was too busy chasing other things. The wrong things. Now I get to regret it, forever. Don't shut out a chance at love simply because you're too angry and afraid."

Lily looked at her friend, her heart breaking for both of them. "How'd you get to be so smart?" She sniffled.

"I died. But it's not a fate I'd recommend for you. You'll figure it out. You're a smart cookie Lil, except when you're being dumb. Why else do you think I decided to hang around?"

CHAPTER SEVEN

Sean leaned over and picked up the digital clock on his nightstand. Sighing in frustration at the glowing red numbers, he put it down. Five a.m. He rolled over and bunched the pillows up behind his head, but even its soft support couldn't ease his racing thoughts. He was torn, something he'd never been his entire life. His duty and doing what was needed from him was never a problem. Until now. He'd run each scenario, posed every *what if* he could envision. Yet it all came down to just one question. What if Lily was infected?

Sighing, he closed his eyes. He thought about Rissa and what she was going through, and also about the people in his clinic, terrified of the mandatory blood tests and what they might find. So far there had been only a handful isolated cases, but the virus was spreading quickly.

He knew he didn't have a choice, and he wondered how many others would be faced with the same dilemma as the sickness became epidemic. Volkmann's estimated half their population would be decimated if a cure wasn't found soon. The Hunter's Council was going to be hard pressed if it came to that—brother having to kill brother. It was a living nightmare, and it was just beginning.

Frustrated, he got out of bed and went into the bathroom. Turning on the shower, he stepped into the hot spray, letting the water jet on his shoulders, and back trying in vain to alleviate some of his tension. Lily's scent was still on his skin, and the steam swirled it like a caress, teasing his senses.

Leaning his forehead on the tile, he pictured her in his mind, the feel of her skin, the taste of her mouth. The images combined with her scent had his balls aching for release. He groaned, and his cock jerked as if in agreement.

With the water cascading over his skin, he wrapped his hand around his shaft and squeezed, running his palm along his corded flesh. Why did he want her so much? What was so different? His body tensed, his hand moving steadily over his sensitive head, over and over again 'til he came, one name on his lips—*hers.*

With one hand on the wall and the other still on his cock he knew the answer. He had fallen for her. Now the question remained, could he kill her?

Lily knew she was dreaming. She was in the woods but watching herself. She was alone, and it was dark; however, she seemed to know where she was going. The moon played behind the clouds, and its light dappled as it shined through the mists. It was cold, and she saw her breath as she moved, striding effortlessly through the underbrush.

The wind picked up blowing her hair, and she smiled, catching the scent of something warm. She ran toward a clearing, and as she stepped through the trees, a howl pierced the silence and a beautiful wolf walked out of the woods into the moonlight.

A slow smile spread across her face as she stepped toward the wolf. She knelt in the soft earth, and he sniffed her face and neck, licking her skin, a low growl rumbling deep in his throat. Reaching up she ran her hands through his thick fur, relishing its softness, and rested her head against his. She could see his mind, his love, his desire, and his pain.

Suddenly she knew. He howled, and the sound was pitiful. She got to her feet, but it was too late, the clearing was surrounded as other wolves closed in on them. The wolf at her feet turned to face the others, growling and snapping, teeth bared. He turned to look at her and in his eyes, she saw death.

Lily woke with a start. "Terry!" she yelled.

"What? What's the matter?"

"We've got to get out of here. Now. Right now! I saw everything. they're planning to kill me! They're just waiting to see whether or not my blood is of any use to them against their pathogen."

"Lily, you're overreacting. It's most likely a by-product of what we talked about last night."

"What, did they grant you some posthumous degree in psychobabble? I'm telling you. I *saw* it!"

"Maybe you'd better talk to Sean about this."

"Talk to me about what?" Sean asked as he stepped into the room. Walking straight toward the bed, he leaned over and brushed Lily's lips with his own.

She turned her face away. "Don't you ever knock?"

He straightened, looking at her a little perplexed. "And good morning to you to," he replied, clearly trying to read her reaction. "What's the matter?"

Crossing her arms in front of her, she huffed. "I'd like to go home. Today. Right now."

Sean shook his head, baffled. "Wait a minute. What happened in the six hours since I saw you last? What's going on here?"

Throwing back the covers Lily got up. She came around the edge of the bed and faced him. "I know all about it Sean. I *saw* it. I know you plan to kill me if I'm infected with that pathogen. All those vials of blood! It all makes sense now. Routine tests my ass! Go ahead, deny it. I dare you."

He stood there, his face a pained mask. "I can't," he answered quietly. "Though, it's not as cut and dried as it was, not anymore." His eyes locked on Lily's and held. "It's true I'm the Alpha, and yes, it is my responsibility to destroy anything, and anyone infected with this virus, and you're right that edict would include you too. But things are different now."

She glared at him. "Why? What's different? Haven't got the stomach to kill me now that you've slept with me?"

Sean exhaled softly, his expression calm despite Lily's defensive stance. "Will you sit down and listen to me? This whole situation isn't easy. I can't explain it, but things are different now. I'm different now."

Lily opened her mouth to retort but then froze. "How?"

He paused as if trying to find the right words. "Something has changed, and not just because we had sex. Hell, shifters are hot-blooded, almost perpetually in heat."

Giving her half a smile, he lifted one shoulder and let it drop. "I've never felt like this before, not with anyone. The truth is I'm not ready to let this feeling go." He reached out and ran his fingers gently across her cheek. "I'm not ready to let *you* go."

Lily stared at him. As his words registered, she sucked in a breath, the sound something between a choke and a whimper as she walked into his arms, resting her head on his chest. "Your timing sucks."

His hand came up to rest on her back, and she felt him chuckle. "This isn't funny Sean, what if I am infected? Will I turn into some kind of crazed beast like your brother?"

He sobered instantly. "I don't know. It could go either way. Our lab is supposed to have their latest results ready this morning. I'm supposed to be at a meeting in the clinic, but I wanted to see you first.

Maybe you should come with me, now that you know. You might as well hear everything from the doctor firsthand."

Lily couldn't help her nerves as they entered the clinic. Biting her lip, she felt everyone's eyes on her as she walked in with Sean's arm wrapped protectively around her shoulders. There were already five people in the reception area, including Mitch, Rissa, and Stephanie. The room was quiet, but the tension thick, as the doctor hadn't yet arrived.

"Uncle Sean!" Stephanie squealed running up to him. "You did it! You hung up my picture! See it! It's on the wall by the desk!"

"I know sweetie. I hung it there myself."

Stephanie looked up at Lily, her curious eyes noticing the way her uncle had his arm around her. "Who's this?" she asked.

Sean smiled down at the little girl. "This is my friend, Lily," he said, sliding his gaze sideways toward the woman tucked under his arm. "Lily, this is my niece, Stephanie."

Lily smiled, taking in the girl's pretty strawberry curls and inquisitive eyes. "Hi, Stephanie," she said. "Your drawing is beautiful. Horses are my favorite animal, too."

Tilting her head to one side, Stephanie studied Lily for a moment. Her drawing forgotten, she seemed to study the pretty dark haired lady standing so close to her uncle.

Lily stiffened. Waves of power flowed in and over her mind while clumsy, little jabs probed her thoughts like ten sticky, little fingers.

The sheer magnitude of the power Stephanie possessed was unbelievable. Too stunned to react, Lily scrambled, trying to close the little girl out of her mind. Lily's memories were hard enough for an adult to bear, let alone for a child. But it was too late.

Backing away, Stephanie's eyes filled with fear. "You're bad.

You're not our friend. Uncle Sean, come on, come on...she's bad...that lady hurt my daddy!" She tugged on Sean's arm, trying to pull him away from Lily.

The room went silent. "Stephanie!" Rissa scolded. "Apologize, this instant!" Mitch held Rissa's hand, his face hardening as he stared at Lily.

Stephanie's small lips trembled. She opened her mouth to do what her mother asked, but instead started to cry. Running back across the room, she buried her face in her mother's lap.

Rissa looked at Lily, the pain in her eyes obvious. "I'm sorry. Stephanie doesn't understand the gravity of what's going on, or what actually happened with her father." The woman's voice broke. "She only knows that he's gone. You'll have to forgive her, she's only four."

Lily couldn't bring herself to speak. There wasn't a hint of accusation in the woman's voice, only grace and sympathy. She had to blink back her own tears watching Rissa comfort her child and her heart broke for the two of them.

Terry shimmered next to Lily. "I guess I can stop holding my breath now, huh? You finally found one."

Lily nodded, tears running down her face. "I certainly did."

"Found what?" Sean asked a little confused.

"Another reason to stop hating," Lily answered squeezing his hand. Letting go, she took a breath and stepped closer to Stephanie.

Looking down at the mother and child, Lily's heart broke again watching the little girl's tiny shoulders shake in grief and fear.

Lily knelt down next to her. Stephanie hid her face while her mother whispered softly, rubbing her back. Mitch stood. His fists clenched at his sides. "Leave Stephanie alone. I think you've done enough damage for one day."

Rissa eyes locked on Lily's. "It's okay, Mitch. If Sean trusts her, then I do. She's not going to harm Stephanie. Let her speak." With a nod to Lily, she sat back, giving her room to get closer.

Lily didn't say a word. Instead, she laid her hand gently on the child's arm. *"Stephanie, I know what you saw in my head scared you, but please, I need you to listen to me. Your daddy was terribly sick, only he didn't know it. He didn't know what was wrong, or what was making him do the things he did. Your Uncle Sean tried to help him, but it was too late. I hope someday you can understand. I'm so very, very, sorry."*

She let Stephanie see how heartbroken she was for hurting her and her mother. She let her see her own grief, but also let her know she didn't have a choice in what happened, making sure to shield her from any further memories.

Slowly Stephanie turned her head, resting her tear-stained cheek on her mother lap. Her eyes found Lily's, but she remained silent.

Rissa's hand gently stroked her daughter's hair. As her finger glided through the soft curls, she glanced at Lily. "Because Stephanie is so young, we still share a mind link. I heard everything you said to her. I apologize for her intrusion into your thoughts. I've been trying to teach her that just because she can, doesn't mean she should. Her psychic gifts go way beyond that of simple telepathy— not unlike your own. She's just barely four years old, and it's a bit much to master."

Shrugging, Rissa exhaled sadly. "I'm afraid she doesn't quite get the concept of privacy. This entire situation has been hard on all of us, but your words did help, and for that, I'm grateful. Hopefully, Stephanie will understand more as she gets older."

Dr. Volkmann walked into the waiting room like a hurricane, oblivious to the tension already swirling around the room.

"Good, good, you're all here. The lab results are in. Let's talk in the examination room as there's too many of us to squeeze into my office."

Sean helped Lily to her feet. Winking at Rissa, he helped hand off Stephanie to one of the nurses before heading toward the examination room. "Doc, this is Lily Saburi, the girl whose blood you've been testing," Sean introduced them, trying to be delicate.

"Oh. I wasn't expecting to see you, my dear. Why don't you stay in the waiting room while I talk to Sean? I think you'll be more comfortable out here."

Sean felt Lily stiffen. "Doc, she already knows, so we might as well include her in the conversation, especially since it directly affects her."

Volkmann took a deep breath, looking back and forth between the two. "All right, this way then," he motioned, opening the door.

The room was a large examination suite. They filed in one after the other, pairing off on both sides of the tiled floor. Volkmann stood by the exam table against the wall, rifling through his papers, his wire rim glasses perched on the edge of his nose.

"Jesus, Doc, enough with the paperwork. What did the lab find?" Mitch asked impatiently.

"Yes, of course, I'm sorry," the doctor said clearing his voice. "There's just no easy way for me to say this, so I'm just going to say it. The results from the last round of tests were all positive."

Rissa buried her face in Mitch's chest, his jaw tightening as his arms went around her shoulders.

Stunned, Lily's breath froze in her throat. The little man in the white coat had just handed her a death sentence. One way or the other she was going to die, either by Sean's hand or by her own. There was no way she was going to allow herself to become some mindless, beast.

Sean's face was grim. There was no way out, now. In one day, Lily wouldn't be Lily anymore. He felt his anger rise, and clenching his fists he turned and punched the opaque glass separating the two rooms causing it to shatter. The people in the waiting room screamed as Sean growled, "Get out!"

Stephanie cried for her mother, her arms flailing as a nurse scooped her up and took her out of the room, mumbling something about ice cream while the rest of the patients fled.

"Leighton, please! I haven't finished. To begin with, Rissa's prognosis isn't as bad as it seems, at least not yet. Her being pregnant is actually a Godsend in more ways than one. It actually buys us time. Not only for her, but for the baby as well."

"What exactly are you talking about, Doc.? Are you trying to tell us you've found a cure?" Mitch demanded as Rissa looked up, sniffling. "Could you just spit it out? We're upset enough. If you can offer us some hope, then get to it and stop beating around the bush."

Volkmann nodded. "Of, course, of course." With a grim look, he peered over the edge of his wire rim glasses at Lily. "Rissa's hope is standing right over there."

Sean looked at the doctor in disbelief. "What are you talking about? You just said Lily was infected. How does that make her a hope for Rissa and the baby?"

"Her blood. The type of antibody it's begun to produce is highly effective and can be distilled into a vaccine. It won't cure *her*, but we can harvest her blood to provide a cure for us."

Incredulous Lily started to back away. "No! No way...*you're all crazy!*" There was no way in hell she was going to let them keep her as some kind of lab animal. Harvest her blood...no fucking way!

"Where are you going? I haven't finished yet," Volkmann barked after her.

"Oh, yes you have! Keep away from me! I'd rather die than let you use me like that." Panicking she ran for the door but couldn't get it open. She was trapped.

Mitch lunged for her throat. "You fucking bitch! If you won't help us, then I'll kill you and drain your carcass myself!"

Lily screamed. In a blur of speed, Sean phased, vaulting over Mitch. Teeth bared he stood between them. With a sneer, Mitch reeled back, phasing on the fly, as well. The two wolves hurdled forward, snarling and with jaws snapping, their large bodies colliding in mid-air as they fought, fur and blood flying around the room. The noise was deafening.

Sean grabbed Mitch by the throat, his teeth shredding skin and clothing, before sending him crashing into the side wall. Volkmann grabbed Rissa, pulling her out of the way, yelling for Lily to get down. Mitch reared back, the muscles in his hind legs coiling as he rebounded, lunging for Sean again, blood coating his massive chest.

Rissa covered her ears, her color draining with each snarl and yelp.

"Can't we stop them? They're going to kill each other, and it won't change a thing," Lily shouted her voice desperate.

The two wolves crashed into the examination table. The room was in chaos, papers, broken glass, and instruments everywhere. Volkmann ordered the women to the far wall, away from the frenzy. With the door blocked, his gaze flicked to the side cabinets and the only choice left.

As best he could, the doctor crawled across the floor and grabbed a tranquilizer gun from one of the smashed supply cabinet drawers. Fisting as many cartridges as he could hold, Volkmann loaded the cannon, praying Sean's presence of mind was still intact before he pulled the trigger, aiming for Mitch.

The large wolf reeled back before slumping to the ground in a silent heap. Sean's wolf froze. Sniffing the air, he growled, swiveling his big head in Volkmann's direction. Gun ready, the doctor tranquilized him next, and the alpha wolf chuffed out a soft whine before sliding to the ground, as well.

Volkmann's shoulders slumped, and he dropped the gun, the sudden quiet, unnerving. Lily glanced at Rissa who looked as if she would pass out at any second.

"I'm sorry, Rissa. I'll give the Doc as much of my blood as I can before it's too late. Hopefully, that'll be enough to help you, but I can't allow myself to be used as some sort of caged lab rat. I'll use my own gun on myself before I let that happen."

Volkmann stood up and brushed the debris from his knees, his eyes flicking between the two women. "Lab rat? What are you talking about? Who said we planned to cage you like an animal?"

"I was just being figurative, Doc. Nevertheless, I won't let you keep me alive in that crazed state just so you can harvest my blood."

Volkmann frowned. "That's why there's no place for this kind of emotion in my research lab. You didn't allow me to finish, none of you did before this craziness erupted! While it's true, your blood tested positive for the pathogen, for some reason you are asymptomatic. Your human blood is immune. All tests show your blood wouldn't allow the pathogen to alter your DNA. When Jerard bit you, he passed on some of his shifter traits, but not enough to activate the virus. Since you can't phase, you have the unique opportunity to have your own antibodies build to the point that even if you were to become a full shifter, you would never be at risk for infection."

Lily looked at him in confusion. "I don't understand."

"In this instance, your blood is like a fine wine. The longer it sits intact in your body, the better it will become. Preliminary tests have already shown it's a powerful antiviral. God willing, everything will turn out fine, for everyone."

Rissa sobbed openly after hearing what the doctor had to say, and Lily wrapped her arms around her in reassurance.

The little man smiled, patting Lily's arm. With a wink, he jerked his head toward the larger of the two wolves just starting to stir. "Just don't let him turn you, yet. Give it a year. That way we can be absolutely sure. After that...well, it's up to you to decide if you want to race the moon with him," he added with a shy smile. "So, will you help us?"

Lily laughed, heat rising to the tips of her ears.

"Of course, but can we stop these two from killing each other long enough to tell them the good news?"

CHAPTER EIGHT

"I can't sit here one more day, Sean. I'm going stir-crazy cooped up inside like this. I'm not an invalid! You were there when Dr. Volkmann gave me full medical clearance a week and a half ago. In fact, he said I'm better than ever."

"I know you're not an invalid, Lily, but it's not safe for you to go wandering around alone, yet."

"I think I'm capable of making my way to the lab and back unscathed. I think you know I can handle myself, yet you're the one insisting on my needing a handler. What are you afraid I'll do?"

The clock on the wall ticked, as if measuring out patience as well as time. "I'm not afraid you'll do anything. You've mentioned it yourself. Shifters are a fickle, unpredictable bunch. I don't need some hot head blindsiding you just because. Tensions are still high despite the encouraging results from all of Volkmann's tests. The community is still afraid. They don't trust this."

Lily turned from where she stood at the window and crossed her arms in front of her chest. "What you mean is they don't trust me."

"It's too soon, Lily. Too much has happened in recent weeks. You need to give them time. Give yourself time." Sean's voice was soft, but his meaning clear. This was going to be an uphill battle.

"Since the lab started its serum testing it's been either you or Jack escorting me back and forth." She unfolded her arms and stuck her hands in the front pockets of her jeans. "I get it, I do." With a quiet sigh she walked to the fireplace where Sean sat, legs crossed nursing a cognac.

"All I'm asking is that you loosen the reigns a bit, otherwise I swear I'm going to scream. I'm used to being on my own, Sean, not to mention I've put on at least ten pounds while atrophying in this asylum you call a Compound!"

His eyes scanned the lush curves of her petite frame and his body reacted, making him shift his legs to accommodate the sudden tightness in his crotch.

"Don't exaggerate. You look amazing. Besides, the extra weight you think you put on is just your body readjusting to the shifter traits in your blood. Trust me, it's all muscle."

"I wouldn't know that now, would I? There's so much I need to learn about you and this place, and I'm not going to learn a thing if you keep me in a bubble. I need to feel vital and more like me. I know I'm doing what I can at the lab, and Dr. Volkmann and his staff have been great, but despite everything I feel like a lab rat. Maybe if I got out for a run or something. I haven't trained or seen the inside of a gym since I left New York for Maine."

Sean put the cut glass tumbler on the small cherry wood end table and leaned forward, taking Lily's hand to pull her onto his lap. He knew exactly how she felt. At times the same restless urge grabbed him causing his skin to crawl with the need to shift. He didn't have the heart to tell her this was just one more present she inherited courtesy of his brother's bite.

Either way, he needed her safe—not just for the sake of the Compound, but for him as well. He was not going to lose her to a rogue shifter with a hard on for humans. Intel from his hunter's made it clear certain factions were not happy with him and his plans for leading the shifters, and derision was stirring. But Lily didn't need to know that. Not yet, anyway.

"You've sweat plenty in recent weeks, unless I'm very mistaken." he dropped his voice to a seductive growl, nuzzling the soft flesh beneath her jaw.

She wiggled off his lap, swatting at his hand as he tried to grab her around her waist. "Cut that out. That's not what I meant, and you know it."

He sat back, chuckling at the high color staining her cheeks. Lily was not the type to suffer embarrassment about sex or much of anything else. She had cabin fever with a tiny splash of moon fever thrown in just for kicks. There was no other explanation.

"If you want to get out on your own, I guess it would be all right, provided you let me have Jack show you around first. You may have been with us for about a month, but you've only seen the immediate area surrounding the manor. And let's not forget for most of that time you were either convalescing or in the lab with Dr. Volkmann."

Lily's eyes narrowed. "By show me around you mean give me the grand tour, right? Help me get my bearings. No babysitting."

He smiled. "No babysitting. The Compound is widespread and there are many out buildings beyond the four main houses, not to mention all the underground tunnels and bunkers. You have a lot to learn before you can set out on your own and not get lost. Just give Jack the chance to help without the risk of bleeding out from that sharp tongue of yours."

"I do not have a sharp tongue," Lily said poking out a petulant lip. She resituated herself on Sean's lap, sliding both arms around his neck."

"Perhaps," he whispered against her mouth, his own tongue tracing the bottom edge of her lower lip.

"No babysitter," she murmured into their kiss.

His mouth curved up as he slid his lips over hers completely shutting her up. *Babysitter? Not a chance. He'd need every hunter he had for that.*

"Three cups of coffee, Lil. You're nervous enough as it is despite that swagger you slapped on this morning along with your makeup."

"Terry, please. I'm doing this for Sean. I thought you'd be happy. He wants me to mingle, and you know I'm not exactly the mingle type."

Her ghostly friend floated onto the seat beside her. "That's the understatement of the century. Do me a favor and try to make the most of this, okay? Be polite and try to make some friends. You're going to need them."

Lily looked at Terry's translucent face. She scanned her friend's pale expression trying to decipher anything in her cool crystalline eyes. "Why? What's going on?"

Terry shook her head, her hair glittering as it floated back into place. "Nothing. It's just you can't rely on me for friendship. You need friends from the land of the living, too."

Lily made a face. "I know. I have Rissa. Right now, she's enough."

"Haven't you learned anything from all this?" she said, her shimmering hand skimming the outline of her body. "You can't keep putting all your eggs in one basket." At Lily's grunt of a reply, Terry sighed, and the sound was like the moan of a gentle wind. "I'm not wasting any more energy fighting with you. I'm tired, Lily. I'll see you later."

"Terry! Wait." Lily pushed herself back from the table, but Terry had already faded.

Lily chewed on her lip. Something wasn't right. Shades don't get tired. Do they? She shook her head. *No, it's just Terry doing what Terry always did when I'm being difficult.*

"Okay, Ter. You win. I promise I will make friends," she shouted into the empty air. "Happy now?" She waited a moment and then paced to the spot where Terry was last, her senses looking for anything, a sullen vibration of *I told you so*, or *I'll believe it when I see it.* But there was nothing.

Jack opened a heavy paned glass door off the hall next to the breakfast room. "Follow me." He gestured toward a series of corridors constructed completely of frosted glass brick.

He was tall and handsome, like most of the shifters Lily had seen, with dark hair and blue eyes and a set of shoulders that would make a linebacker cry. She chuckled to herself. It must be something in the water.

Jack was funny and didn't think twice about calling her out with her crap. Even without her psychic senses, it was easy to see he'd have her back if Lily needed someone, regardless of orders from Sean. If she wanted a brother, Jack would be him.

Lily followed, pulling her leather jacket tighter across her chest. "It's freezing in here, dude. Don't you people believe in central heating?"

He shot her a playful smirk. "Who needs heat when you're naturally this hot?" Lifting his arms with a flourish, he kissed his bicep earning a groan from Lily.

"Nice. That's something they teach you in Hunter School?" she managed between chattering teeth.

"Ugh, Lil...really?" he said, taking his jacket off and draping it over her shoulders. "God spare me from light weights. Better?"

She nodded. "Yeah, thanks."

Lily burrowed into Jack's lined denim jacket, at once surrounded by his clean masculine scent. It had that same underlying woodsy trace like Sean, and she sighed, closing her eyes as images of Sean's body tight and slick with sweat left her skin tingling with his unseen touch.

"Uh oh..."

Lily's eyes snapped open. One look at Jack's questioning gaze and enough self-conscious heat crawled up her neck to forego both jackets.

She glanced away, banishing the sexy images to the back of her mind and cleared her throat. "Are all shifters that much warmer than the average human or is it just the men?"

He smirked at her deft redirect and stuffed his hands in his pockets. "It's pretty much all of us, but then again I never really thought about it much. It's not that our temperatures run warmer; it's that we absorb heat and store it in a different way. Being dual natured helps, but it really has to do with species. I'm a wolf. It wouldn't be the same for say one of the Avians."

Avians. She knew Sean could shift into a bird of prey, she'd felt him in that form when they were both hunting Jerard, but she never equated birds as a species with the shifters.

"Just how many species of shifter are there?"

Jack lifted one shoulder and let it drop. "More than you would think— from big predators like wolves and big cats, to sea creatures to birds and everything in between. Why?"

Now it was her turn to shrug. "I'm just curious, that's all. There's so much I need to learn."

"I guess, but I wouldn't make myself nuts over it if I were you. There's plenty of time. And contrary to what Mr. Sunshine thinks, most people are glad Sean found you, otherwise we'd be up shit creek if you know what I mean."

Lily pushed at Jack's shoulder. "Mr. Sunshine. I'm going to tell Sean you said that."

"Tattletale."

She laughed out loud, and a lightness she hadn't felt in a long time, not since before Terry died, filled her chest. She reached over and linked her arm with his. "So, where are we going anyway?"

"These corridors connect the manor with many of the outbuildings, but we are headed to the primary training facility for new recruits. I thought you'd like to see where it all begins."

"Recruits?"

"Sean's hunters. You have to be called up."

Lily gave Jack a sideways look. "Called up. You mean drafted?"

He grinned. "No. We don't draft young shifters into service. Joining the ranks of the Alpha Hunters is voluntary, and you have to be recommended. There's a whole training program to be completed before the final test. It's not an easy task and not everyone makes it."

"Are there female hunters?"

He shook his head "None as of yet, although Sean is looking into expanding the program. We may even run into a few of the women already training in anticipation of the day they get the green light. Sean's father would never even consider it. In fact, Sean's sister Emily wanted to be a hunter and their old man nearly had a stroke."

Lily stopped mid-step, her hand jerking Jack's arm where they were linked. "Wait. Sean has a sister?"

Jack nodded. "Yeah. She's out west somewhere. California, I think."

"He never mentioned her." Lily looked at Jack, her eyes pressing him for more information.

"I wouldn't read anything into that if I were you. Sean has had a lot to deal with lately. There's much more change going on than just experimental shifter coexistence. Many of our traditions are being challenged— intermarriage between shifter species, intermarriage with single natured humans, marriage contracts...”

She cut him off. “Wait a minute. Contracts? As in arranged marriages?”

He nodded.

“Holy crap, Jack. Are you serious?”

The offended look on his face had her backpedaling, not wanted to sound as disdainful as she knew she did. “I’m not judging, Jack. I’m just taken aback. When I think of arranged marriages I think of things like Warren Jeffs and fundamentalist polygamy.”

“Lily! Jeez. Are *you* serious?” he said, turning her words on her. “We don’t marry children off to dirty old men. Marriage contracts are more tradition than anything else. Some families have bloodlines that go back centuries. They prefer to keep things status quo.”

“What do you mean status quo?”

“Undiluted.” He raised both eyebrows giving her a pointed look.

Lily winced at the unspoken inference. “You’re giving me the willies, Jack. I thought that kind of incest died with medieval royalty buying dispensations from the Pope to marry their cousins.”

“It may have a creep factor of one hundred and ten percent, but it is what it is. Emily had a contract set from the time she turned sixteen. The guy was from one of the northern packs near Montreal. In this instance he was a cousin, but distantly so. Emily wouldn’t have it, so skipped out the minute she turned eighteen. She headed out west. She was subsequently shunned, though her mother begged her husband to let her out of the deal. But old Jimmy B was a hot-head and stubborn to a fault.”

“Jimmy B?”

The corners of Jack’s mouth pulled down. “Sean’s father and our previous Alpha. James Boyd Leighton, hence, the nickname Jimmy B. Of course, no one called him that to his face. Jerard took after him in temperament, while Sean was always very much the opposite, more like his mother— levelheaded, tough as nails and gave allegiance to those who proved worthy. It's said Sean's mother, Caren, would have made a better Alpha than her husband, so it's no wonder Emily wanted to be a hunter."

"What about now that her parents are dead, and Sean is the Alpha? Can't she come home?"

He looked over his shoulder and then down the other end of the corridor as if making sure he wouldn't be overheard. "We're working on it. Mitch and I thought it would be a morale booster for Sean if Emily came home for Christmas. She knows Sean isn't like the others, but the problem is she never said goodbye when she left. She didn't tell anyone her plans—not even Rissa and they were best friends. That was five years ago. To say there were hurt feelings is an understatement."

Rissa had become a fast friend and didn't seem one to hold grudges, but the truth was Lily didn't really know the woman well enough to make that call, though her gut told her otherwise.

Lily didn't know what to say. She empathized with Sean's sister, and at eighteen would have probably run just the same. It was on the tip of her tongue to ask if the girl bothered to call or write, but Lily stayed quiet. Who was she to wonder? Thanksgiving had come and gone, and she still hadn't picked up the phone to call Terry's parents. A quick postcard was no substitute for real conversation, and suddenly the topic was a little too close to home, so she let it drop.

They turned left at the end of the corridor, neither saying another word. The complexity of their world and the dichotomy of the visionary combined with the antiquated were almost too much.

Jack opened another heavy door. "Ladies first," he said.

Instead of the polished wood floors, lush area rugs and rich décor she expected, the doorway lead into a wide lobby lined on either side with metal wire shelves stocked with jump ropes, yoga mats, towels, and cases of water. Corrugated rubber covered the floor, the same as you would see at the gym or in a locker room.

"Not what you expected, huh?"

She shook her head. "Not exactly. I know you said training facility, but I didn't expect this."

He pushed passed her, taking her hand in the process. "Come on, you haven't seen anything yet."

The lobby opened up into an area with tables and a juice bar that provided protein shakes and sandwiches. The pretty blonde behind the counter waved to Jack and blew him a kiss.

"Someone you know, Jack?"

He grinned. "In the biblical sense."

Lily snorted. "I'll bet."

Pulling her along, he stopped when the lobby narrowed into another wide corridor flanked on either side by indoor turf. The place was enormous, even bigger than the huge sports facility at Chelsea Piers in Manhattan.

Christmas twinkle lights blinked on and off along the half wall anchoring the safety netting to the edge of the turf, and the clean scent of pine from three large Christmas trees added a fresh edge to the underlying tang of sweat.

"We've got all the latest and best in here. The kids play football, soccer, and lacrosse during the winter months on the indoor fields. The weight rooms are located upstairs along with the cardio equipment and the spin and Zumba Eyesight fuzzy, everything looked and sounded far away. and Terry's voice sounded farther away than before.

rooms."

"Zumba?"

Jack shrugged. "Hey, it's not my thing, but the women seem to love all that booty pop, twerking crap."

"No, you did not just say twerking!" Mouth open, she laughed out loud.

"We may live in a communal Compound of supernatural beings, but that doesn't mean we're cut off from the rest of the world. I watched Miley Cyrus and her foam finger along with everyone else in the world."

"More's the pity." Lily added dryly. "So, what's downstairs?"

"Training rooms for the Hunters. The weapons room, the martial arts mat, and the heavy bags, although we do use the weights upstairs, too."

"Well, well, well. If it isn't Jack the Lackey," a snide voice said from one of the locker room doors.

Lily pivoted on her heel, the hairs on her neck and her guard shot up at the derisive tone. The only thing that surprised her was the fact it was female.

The holiday lights streaked splashes of color along the black rubberized floor, an odd counterpoint to the tension that erupted in the air.

"Delia. An unpleasant surprise as always."

The girl standing in the entrance was a statuesque redhead, nearly as tall as some of the men, with curves and long legs. She was dressed in workout clothes not leaving much to the imagination and what looked to be a permanent scowl.

She snorted. "Funny. That's not what you used to say when you thought I was the next alpha female."

Lily jerked her gaze from Jack to meet the woman's eyes. They were narrowed and glaring, and the daggers weren't for the tall, handsome shifter to Lily's left.

"When did you get back?"

"A few days ago," she replied, returning her attention to Jack. "I was running with a pack in northern Canada. There's nothing like the feel of ice under your paws and the taste of a fresh kill."

"If you love the raw life so much, what brought you back to the Compound?"

She turned an icy stare toward Lily. "Her."

Lily froze, jaw tight.

"Lily? Why?" he asked, his tone unconcerned, but Lily didn't miss the tense ripple that pulsed across her senses from him.

Delia snorted. "Because, Jack, she is threatening my place as Sean's Alpha female."

Lily's hands clenched at her side, and Jack put a staying hand on her arm.

"That was decided against you before you left for Canada. Sean rejected your father's offer. That is not the way the Compound is run anymore, and you know it."

"Since she obviously knows me, but I haven't a clue as to whom she is, I think you'd better introduce us." Lily clearly addressed Jack even as she kept her gaze on the woman.

As if reading Lily's mind, the woman laughed. "That's right, sweetheart. I was engaged to marry Sean before you came along."

Jack laughed, but the sound was mirthless. "That's a crock and you know it, Delia. Your contract to marry Sean was never going to fly. He may be all about honor, but there is no honor in forcing someone to do something against their will. He never loved you, and no sooner was Jimmy B in his grave than that contract was null and void. Lily is the new Alpha-Female-to-be, so I'd start practicing my courtesy if I were you."

Delia lunged, and before Lily could react Jack shifted his weight to the balls of his feet and slid sideways, just enough for the woman to overshoot her mark. A single shove sent her stumbling forward on her own momentum 'til she landed with an audible huff on her hands and knees.

With an angry growl she tossed her hair back, tearing a string of cracked Christmas lights from the half wall. She glared at Jack from over her shoulder, her chest heaving with unspent anger.

"Delia, when are you going to learn that rage filled outbursts make for a poor fighting strategy?" He crossed his arms in front of his chest watching her silent rant.

The woman slid her eyes from Jack to Lily, and in that moment, they flashed from hazel to a blazing yellow.

"Oh shit." Lily slid into a defensive stance, the expletive no more than a whisper. She instinctively reached behind her back for her 9mm, only to an empty space in her waistband. With another murmured oath, she brought her fists up. This was not going to be pretty.

"Enough!" Jack shouted, stepping between the two women. "Delia if you've got a problem with Lily, I suggest you take it up with Sean. In the meantime, she's off limits. Do you understand? The Compound needs her."

The woman's eyes flashed again but this this time they stayed hazel. Jack held out his hand to help her up, but she shoved him away.

"This is between her and me," Delia spat. "I'll decide when it's over."

She shoved her way passed, her shoulder bumping Lily's in the process.

"I look forward to it!" Lily called after, earning another dirty look before the woman stormed off.

Jack leaned against the half wall, his arms crossed in front of his chest and a smirk on his face.

"What?"

He shook his head. "You really are crazy, aren't you?"

She lifted her hand and let it drop. "What was I supposed to do, Jack? Cower? Apologize for living? Sean and I just got together, and I'm not going to let a wolf bitch with a hell hath no fury complex get in the way. I may not know a lot about shifters, but I do know a lot about people, and this goes a hell of a lot deeper than her getting knocked out of the marriage ring."

He snorted. "Good pun...marriage ring. But you and Sean are nowhere near that, right?"

A frown bloomed across Lily's face "I know I have the reputation for being rash, but give me a little credit, Jack. I'm not exactly the type to jump at something that comes with a lifelong price tag, at least not without a lot of thought—but that doesn't mean I'm not willing to fight for the chance."

He laughed, sliding his arm around her shoulders. "Come on Rocky...let me show you where you'll be training."

"Training?"

"Delia threw down a gauntlet, and whether you realize it or not telling her to bring it on means you picked up the challenge. I don't know when or where she'll pounce, so you need to be ready. I'll round up a few of the gals I know who have family members your blood serum helped. I'm sure they'll be more than happy to give you a hand."

She fell into step beside him. "Okay, but I think you know me well enough to know I can take care of myself."

He nodded. "Sure, you can. With humans. But can you fight shifter style?"

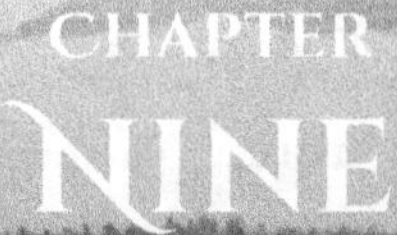

CHAPTER NINE

Sean stood pacing by the door to Lily's bedroom. "I don't like this, Lily. I won't allow it"

"You won't allow it? Come on, Sean. Do you think I want this?" she replied, tying her sneakers before she grabbed her duffel bag to check she had everything she needed.

"Delia challenged me. What would you have me do?" she asked zipping the black canvas bag.

He flung his arm out in a frustrated gesture. "Nothing. That's what. Delia is my problem. You should have left her to me to handle."

Lily placed her bag on the bed and sat down beside it. "You tried that, remember? Delia blew you off, and everyone knows it. Now it's only a matter of time before she challenges me in some way. I need to train."

"Then I'll train you."

Lily laughed, but the sound was soft and full of appreciation. "And how would that look? You're the Alpha. It wouldn't be right. Hell, I can't even let Jack help me even though he offered. It makes me look like I'm incapable."

"Jack should offer since he's the reason you're in this mess."

Lily got up from the bed and walked toward him. "Is that what's been bothering you about this?" Lily shook her head slowly. "I have news for you, Delia made up her mind about me way before she lunged. You may think Jack took things too far, but I think she deserved it."

Sean snorted. "Jack is a Hunter. He should know better than to get into a pissing match with anyone, let alone with a woman. He'll learn, though trust me."

Lily raised an eyebrow, not liking Sean's tone. "What did you do?"

Sean shrugged. "Nothing. The clinic is short staffed, and they needed a few extra hands with everyone coming in for treatments. Tensions are still high and raw nerves are causing issues at the clinic. I sent Dr. Volkmann some of my hunters to help out."

She looked at him. "That's all?"

"That's all."

She narrowed her gaze, her eyes searching his. "Okay, then," she said before turning to grab her bag from the bed.

"I'm so glad you approve."

With a wink she adjusted the duffle bag's strap on her shoulder. "I like Jack and he's been a big help, not to mention good company," she said before going up on her toes to give him a quick kiss. "Come meet me after my work out. We can grab some lunch,"

"If I have time. Who are you training with today?"

She shrugged. "Someone by the name of Shannon."

Sean burst out laughing. "Oh boy. I'll have the ice packs ready and waiting along with a big bottle of Advil."

Lily shoved his shoulder back. "Give me a little credit, will you. Who is she anyway?"

"Delia's sister."

Lily walked into the martial arts studio alone. The lights were on, but there was no one around and the mat was deserted.

"Terry?" she whispered, taking advantage of the solitude. "Come on, Ter. I'm sorry I was such a mouthy bitch at breakfast the other day. Talk to me."

With a sigh, she dropped her bag on the floor near the bench outside the training mat and sat down to take off her shoes. Since Shannon hadn't arrived yet, Lily grabbed her sparing gloves from her bag and slipped them on. A few rounds on the heavy bag would give her a good warm up, and from Sean's ominous chuckle it sounded as though she would need one.

"Here goes nothing." She bowed in a show of respect and stepped onto the mat. The large rectangular training area was lined with weapons and kicking pads of every kind. Hardwood nunchucks, bo staffs and short sticks were to one side, while blades of every shape and size flanked the other.

"This place reminds me of Dojo Dan's place off Christopher Street, don'tcha think?" Terry's voice was soft as a whisper.

Lily whirled around. Her friend floated between two of the heavy bags that marked either end of the mat suspended from the ceiling by thick steel chains.

"You haven't trained in Tai Kwon Do in years. What brought this on?"

Lily didn't answer, just finished straightening her gloves.

"What? You think I gave you the silent treatment, so now you're not talking to me? Come on, Lily. Don't be such a baby."

Terry's pale eyes narrowed. "You picked a fight with someone, didn't you? What did I tell you about making friends? I can't be your only lifeline to friendship, Lil! It doesn't work when that lifeline has no life!"

"Believe it or not, I didn't start this one. Sean's old girlfriend has something she wants to prove, and she wants to prove it all over my face. I'm just here to sharpen my skills." Lily stopped fidgeting with her glove and looked up, waiting for Terry to say something."

"Well?"

Terry shrugged, the motion sending sparkles cascading toward the mat. "Well what? Do you want me to haunt the bitch?"

Lily burst out laughing. "No, but cut me some slack, okay."

Terry studied Lily's face. "Are you okay to do this? I mean, you're well enough, right?"

Lily shrugged. "Let's find out." Feet apart, she perched on the balls of her feet. Fists by her face, she circled the bag, throwing jabs in a traditional front back punch. She slowly increased her pace, adding kicks and altering punches in different combinations.

Moving fast she pivoted for a spinning back kick, and as the bag swung out, she turned again, landing a jump round kick to connect as the bag rebounded back.

"Not bad," a woman's voice sounded from the side of the mat. "You're quite the flexible flyer."

Lily jerked around. At first, she thought the voice was Terry's, but her friend must have sensed another person and disappeared at some point.

An auburn haired woman not much taller than Lily bowed onto the mat and walked over. "You must be my new trainee," she said as she came to a stop about three feet from where the heavy bag swung back and forth like a pendulum. The woman inclined her head in a short traditional bow. "I'm Shannon."

Lily dropped her hands to her side and mirrored the woman's bow. "It's nice to meet you. I'm Lily Saburi."

"It looks like you know your way around the mat. Have you trained long?"

Lily shook her head. "Not in years, but I guess it's like riding a bike. You never really forget."

Shannon tilted her head, her eyes evaluating. "That depends on a lot, but it looks to me like you were taught well. You're quick and you stay loose. That's good. You'll need to stay loose, or Delia will chew you up and spit you out."

Lily's eyes locked on the woman. "So, you've heard."

Shannon laughed. "Who hasn't."

As if she could read Lily's unease, the woman put her hand on Lily's shoulder. "Look, I want to make one thing clear before we begin. I have no beef with my sister. It's true she and I are polar opposites—not just in appearance, but in demeanor and in viewpoint. I agreed to help you simply because I think Delia has overstepped herself. Sean made it clear to everyone he would never abide by any such contract. Our father's dealings ended the minute the old Alpha drew his last breath. Delia knew then. Hell, she knows it now. This business with you is nothing more than posturing to save face, at least in her own mind."

Shannon walked toward the low pegs on the wall and grabbed a pair of sparring gloves. "Dual-natured women aren't as hotheaded as our men. We're protective, but most of us can smell bullshit the same way we smell a storm coming. Too much has gone on over the past six weeks. Christmas is coming, and it's the time to end all this garbage, not add to it. The situation as is stinks enough." She slipped her gloves on. "So, are you ready to work?"

Lily nodded.

"Good. Get your mouth guard."

Lily moved passed her to grab her bag from the bench.

"Oh, and one last thing. Don't drop your hands or you'll drop and give me fifty."

Lily laughed. "I knew I was going to like you."

Lily groaned trying to sit up. "That woman is a goddamned sadist. Ouch! You and your evil chuckle. *Shit*! Ow! You weren't kidding, were you?"

Sean handed her a fresh ice pack. "You can't say I didn't warn you. Let's hope she doesn't tell Delia how sore you're going to be tomorrow. When do you train again?"

Lily gritted her teeth and pushed herself to a sitting position, wincing the whole way. "My abs are on fire, my legs are like noodles and I'm going to be covered in head to toe bruises, and you want me to train with her again?"

Sean reached for a cup of water and the Advil. "Stop being a baby. I spoke with Shannon. She's impressed at how well you did. She said you were one tough bitch, to quote her exactly," he said handing three gel-caps to Lily.

"That's nice, but I still want my .45 and 9mm back. If I have those, I'm good. No one is going to blindside me then."

"You can have them back whenever you like. I never said you couldn't have them."

Lily's mouth dropped open, and even that caused physical pain. "Well you could have told me before I put myself through Samurai training."

He laughed out loud. "Give it a day or so. You'll be back to normal faster than you think. In the meantime, I think it's time we made you a full member of the Compound."

Lily winced. "Sean, I'm not ready for this. It's too soon--"

"I'm not talking about making you a full shifter." The scent of her adrenaline made his nose burn. "I know how you feel about that—for now."

She raised an eyebrow at his little addendum but didn't comment.

"I'm talking about having the clans officially accept you into the Compound. It's a ceremony that takes place only a few times a year, and it has to be at the full moon."

Lily still didn't say a word.

"What, no good?"

She hesitated, not wanting her words to be misconstrued. "It's not that. I'm honored, but are you sure it's the right time for this?"

"Lily, do you know how many people at the clinic have benefited from the work you are doing with Dr. Volkmann? It's time, so what do you say?"

She nodded. "Just tell me when and where."

Lily opened her eyes to the sound of the phone blaring. Who would call this early? There was only one person perky enough for that. *Rissa.*

Rolling over, Lily picked up the receiver, her muscles screaming in protest. "Good morning, Rissa," she croaked.

"Good afternoon is more like it. How are you feeling?"

Lily squinted at the clock radio. *Two p.m. Ugh.* "I'm okay. A little sore, but nothing a hot shower won't cure. How are you? Aren't you supposed to be at the clinic today?"

"Already been and done. Listen, why don't you take a shower and then meet me for a late lunch? I'll meet you in the conservatory in say, one hour?"

"Ris, I don't think so."

"I'm not taking no for an answer. If you don't show I'm coming to you."

Lily sighed, flopping back onto her pillow. "Okay. One hour."

The conservatory was a large room with three glass walls overlooking a large duck pond. Even this late into the season, swans glided majestically in the cold water giving the snow covered landscape an ethereal yet regal feel.

The room had a gas fireplace built into the center of one of the walls, with a floor to ceiling rock mantel separating the panes of glass, giving the hearth a freestanding feel.

"Lily!" Rissa called from one of the chairs near the fire. "Over here."

"Hey," Rissa said, giving Lily a quick peck on the cheek. "You look pretty good for someone who went ten rounds."

"Hey, yourself." Lily looked around a little more. "Not exactly what I expected when you said meet me for lunch. This looks like it should have a chamber quartet playing."

She chuckled. "This isn't where we're eating. I just wanted you to meet a few of my friends." Rissa gestured with her hand to a handful of women standing near the bar at the far corner. With a smile she waved them over.

Lily smiled keeping her cool, not wanting Rissa or anyone else to see the anxiety clutching at her stomach. She hated surprises, especially ones that required social graces.

"Lily, I want you to meet Gillian Albright, Celia Wegman and Heather Snow."

Lily inclined her head. "It's a pleasure to meet you all."

Celia sniffled, fishing in her purse for a tissue. "No, Ms. Saburi. The pleasure is all ours—I mean mine."

The woman dissolved into tears, and Lily glanced at Rissa, not knowing what to do.

"Cel, pull yourself together. You said you wouldn't do this. I know how you feel but we're supposed to be letting go and having fun today. Remember?" Rissa said patting the woman's arm.

"I'm sorry, Rissa. I'm just so relieved. I got a call right before we got here. Kevin is going to be all right. They were able to reverse the damage the virus did, he's going to recover. He may have some spotty memory loss, and they will have to give him something to prevent him from phasing for a while, but he's going to be okay...and it's all thanks to you, Lily..."

Celia melted into sobs, throwing her arms around Lily's neck nearly knocking the petite woman over. "Thank you for saving my son."

"It's okay, Celia, I'm glad I was able to help." Lily replied rubbing the woman's back. "That's what I promised Rissa and Sean I would do."

Rissa and Gillian helped peel Celia off Lily's shoulders. Heather handed her another wad of tissues, and then glanced at Lily.

"Rissa invited us today so you could meet other dual-natured women. We know that besides us, the only other women you've met are Delia and Shannon Monroe. Shannon is a good friend. She's as sweet as she is a bad ass, and I think the two of you are probably cut from a very similar cloth—especially after hearing how you went toe to toe on the martial arts mat." She paused, for a moment. "Delia on the other hand, well...you saw for yourself."

Lily gave the woman a half smile. "Thanks Heather, I appreciate that. I like Shannon, too."

Heather shrugged. "It is what it is, but things are changing, and we wanted you to know we don't all resent you. Personally, I think it's kind of romantic the way you and Sean got together—I mean, besides Jerard and the attack and all."

"Heather!" Gillian's voice was a harsh whisper, and she shot an apprehensive glance across her shoulder at Rissa.

"It's okay, Gillian. I happen to agree with Heather. Sean has been waiting a long time for someone like Lily. I think we all have," Rissa said linking arms with her new friend."

Lily raised an eyebrow, and gracefully removed her arm. Putting both hands up, she tamped down on the self-conscious heat blooming in her cheeks

"Okay, everyone. I appreciate the vote of confidence, but enough with the mush. My reputation as a bad ass is in jeopardy of damage beyond repair."

They all laughed.

Heather sat on one of the plush couches. Why don't we order drinks and then go into town for lunch? I'm in the mood for lobster at the Oarweed in Perkins Cove.

"Sounds good to me. Who wants what? I'll treat first," Lily said.

Celia shook her head, pulling Lily down onto the couch next to her. "No way, you're our guest of honor." She turned to the plump blonde standing to her left. "Gillian you do the honors."

The blonde fished in her bag. "I still can't believe you survived an 'A' level training session with Shannon...Where the hell is my phone? I have a notepad app on it somewhere... Anyway, my brother is training to be a Hunter and she threw him off the mat. He couldn't take it. You must be very determined." She paused, glancing into her purse again. "Got it. Okay order up ladies."

"'A' level?" Lily glanced at Rissa questioningly.

Gillian lifted her hand as if showing height. "Oh yeah, 'A' level is way up there. Most Hunter trainees start at level 'C'. I heard Shannon keeps a private diary of all the hunters who vomit on her mat after their first class."

"I do no such thing."

Everyone turned at the sound of the woman's voice. She was sitting in a high back chair with her back to everyone. Sitting to her left was Delia.

"Shannon!" Gillian got up, her face pale. "I didn't know you were sitting there."

"Obviously," Delia muttered from behind the chair's leather wing-back.

Lily got up and moved around to the front. "Hello Shannon, good to see you again." She smiled at the woman, and then shifting her gaze to her sister, she nodded once. "Delia."

Delia snorted back. "Gold-digger."

Shannon put her drink on the small round table between their two chairs. "Delia, this is what I'm talking about. You just don't get it, do you? Either that or you just refuse to accept it."

"What I don't get is how my own sister could spend her time and her expertise on a single-natured human."

"Dee, I'm sorry things didn't work out for you the way you hoped. I'm sure everyone here feels the same. But that's just the way that one went. Lily had no part in Sean's decision to annul the contract— and I've got more news for you— I will teach her every counter move, every trick I know if you follow through with this immature notion of challenging her."

She paused, her face both frustrated and sad. "Think about it, Delia. Don't you think all your time and effort would be better spent in some other way? A more productive way? Maybe then you might actually meet someone who will appreciate you for who you are and not what our family can give them. Sean never cared about political gain, but if that's all you think you're worth, all you value, then I'm sure there's a guy who will sniff that out and use it, and you."

Delia stood. She towered over her sister and Lily and half the women present. She smiled, but it was cheerless. "Maybe you're right, Shannon. Maybe I have been setting my sites too low."

She glanced at everyone, pausing to glare at Lily before she nodded to her sister. "Shannon... ladies. Have a nice lunch."

Shannon exhaled watching Delia walk out. "Why do I have a sinking suspicion I made things worse."

Rissa put her hand on her friend's arm. "Come on, forget it. Everyone knows Delia's a psycho."

Celia sucked in a breath, her eyes moving between Shannon and Rissa, waiting for the explosion.

Shannon smirked. "Relax, Celia, I'm not about to take out a pregnant woman simply because she speaks the truth. Dee may be a psycho, but she's also my sister. All I can do is muzzle her, so no one gets hurt."

Lily laughed out loud. "See, I said it before, and I'll say it again. I knew I was going to like you. Listen, I don't know where they're taking me for lunch, but I'm sure it involves a lot of alcohol. You in?"

Shannon grinned and picked up her purse. "Just pour the way, ladies."

CHAPTER TEN

Sean stood by the open window waiting for Lily. An early winter breeze carrying the scent of snow drifted past. Filling his lungs, he exhaled. The moon had crested, and it paced back and forth behind the clouds mirroring his impatience. "What's taking you so long, Lily? You already know almost everyone on the Hunter's Council. Tonight, is just a formality."

The statement was true, despite the grumbling from a few traditional dogmatists. The Compound had its share of detractors, there was no denying that—still, no one in their right mind could deny the service and sacrifice Lily had given the community of shifters. She deserved this honor, and everyone knew it.

"Relax. It's not like they can start without us. Besides, I'm almost done," Lily called from behind the bathroom door. "Don't you want me to look nice?"

Sean grunted. "That question is as loaded as one of your guns. I'll tell you this, though, if you don't hurry it up, I'm coming in and carrying you out over my shoulder."

"Hmmph," was her only response.

Time had gone by in a blur, so much so Sean could swear he had vertigo. Lily had gone from unknown quantity to a possible threat, to lover and savior in just two short moon cycles. Adventure and miracle all wrapped in one petite woman.

As much as Sean hated gossip, this time the rumor mill had worked in his favor. There was no way he or his hunters could have spread the word that quickly. A test vaccine had been developed, and the initial results were remarkable, even Rissa and her unborn baby were responding well.

Thanks to Lily, this typically volatile community had found a way to rally. So far, so good. Of course, he and Mitch would never live down the havoc they caused in the clinic that day. Volkmann and his staff would certainly see to that.

Even so, people viewed Lily as a godsend, so it was only fitting the Hunter's Council acknowledge that. Tonight, they would hold a blood rites ritual—an ancient act of initiation and acceptance. Originally used to unite different clans in kinship, today it was more symbolic, a traditional ceremony used to honor and acknowledge those who had been of great service to the pack. No one had actually demanded a true bloodletting in ages.

Lily opened the door. Sean's eyes swept the full length of her petite frame. "You look beautiful," he said, swallowing back the comment he had waiting for her on how long it took.

She had traded her standard black leather pants and biker jacket for a creamy cotton sweater dress. The knee length, clingy knit hugged every lush curve, while a low, square neckline dropped from her shoulders to skim the top of her breasts, tiny ruffled edges highlighting her cleavage. Her dark hair was curled and pulled back, falling softly to her shoulders, and high-heeled, winter white boots replaced her usual shit-kickers.

"Too much?" she asked, doing a little twirl.

"No. You look fabulous. But who are you and what have you done with Lily?"

Without batting an eye Lily pivoted, landing a perfect spinning back kick to his solar plexus, the point of her heel nailing him dead center.

Pivoting back around she stood, head cocked to one side and her hands on her hips watching him recover his breath.

"Who's afraid of the big bad wolf?" she teased.

Sean's hand shot out like lightning, grabbing her around her waist and pulling her down in one fluid motion. Dipping her back, he growled low, licking her throat from her cleavage to her ear. "You should be."

At the raspy feel of his tongue, Lily shivered but gritted her teeth. "You're the one who told me to keep training with Shannon. Don't presume there's no fist in the glove just because it's made of something soft."

Sean straightened, keeping her body close. "So dangerous," he whispered into a kiss, deepening his fervor until its heat threatened to take them over.

Breathless, she broke away. "I thought you wanted to get going? You've been sitting around grousing for an hour that people are waiting for us."

Throwing his head back, he laughed. "Okay killer, after you." Releasing her waist, he stepped aside, smacking her butt in the process.

Lily rubbed her backside in feigned disgust. "Just like Terry...has to have the last word!"

The two walked into the great hall. The room was enormous, big enough to host twice the two hundred guests invited this evening.

Holly and pine boughs decorated the hall, giving the room a festive air and a crisp, clean scent. Christmas was only a week away, yet the atmosphere was more than just merry as people laughed and talked; it was hopeful.

While Sean busied himself with greeting guests, the polite banter was lost on Lily. Wide eyed she surveyed the room and all its regalia. The ceiling was beamed by rough-hewn boughs dotted with large, iron chandeliers. Two stone hearths graced both ends of the room, each immense and fully ablaze, yet it was the center table that held her fascination.

A great round slab of carved oak sat in the direct center of the room. Nine wooden chairs surrounded it, each adorned with the crest representing the dual nature of the hunter elected to that seat.

"Close your mouth, Lily. You look like a codfish," Sean said from the corner of his mouth.

"I can't help it. This place looks like something from another time. I'm surprised there aren't rushes on the floor or half-dressed serving wenches carrying trenchers of food."

"Read Harlequin much?"

"Shut up. There's nothing wrong with romance novels. You could learn something from them, you know."

Sean's mouth curved into a slow, seductive grin. He let his fingers drift casually along the side of her arm, deliberately grazing the edge of her breast. "Could I now?"

Lily's breath caught in her throat. She opened her mouth to retort but was interrupted by the sound of beating drums.

Trumpets sounded, and nine people cloaked in red and gold robes entered through an ornately carved door to the side of the far hearth. The room fell silent.

"The Hunter's Council," Sean breathed in her ear.

"Shouldn't you be with them?"

He shook his head. "I'm the Alpha Council. I sit at the head, but matters are decided amongst the nine. Only during a stalemate do I get involved. My job is to preserve the safety and security of the Compound and to protect our anonymity. It is my wish that you be recognized tonight. That's why I'm standing here with you, instead of with them."

Lily didn't know what to say. The council members approached the table, each carrying a long lance. Sean explained they were the traditional weapons used to hunt shifters centuries ago. Each had an extraordinarily long spearhead thought to be spelled. It was believed the spearheads kept the souls of each shifter whose heart it pierced. He went on to say the council now carried them in remembrance of ancestors who died at the hands of human superstition and fear.

Lily gulped. *Human superstition and fear?* What about her human intolerance and hate? Suddenly she was sorry she had chosen to girl-it-up tonight instead of wearing her usual armor.

Sean wrinkled his nose at the quick spike in her adrenaline. "Relax. You have nothing to worry about. These people owe you their lives. We wouldn't be here tonight otherwise." He squeezed her hand. "*Besides, I have my own personal reasons for wanting this,*" he added whispering through her mind.

A stunned grin spread across Lily's face. Picking up on his thread her smile grew. "*You never said we could actually speak telepathically! I thought it was just imprinted memories and residual images.*"

"You never spoke to anyone else this way, not even Terry?" he asked.

"No one, never...this is great! Now I can keep a smile on my face even if I'm yelling at you!"

"Ha. But you'd better watch what you say. I'm not the only one with this talent, you know. It's just stronger between us because we've..." Sean

trailed off growling low in the back of her mind, sending her explicit images to make his point.

Lily's face grew hot as the sensation pinked up to her ears. "Cut that out!" she hissed.

The nine were seated, and Mitch Paris, Sean's second-in-command stood. "Sean Leighton, Alpha Council of the Brethren," he paused rapping his lance on the floor three times, "Make your request."

With Lily in tow, Sean approached the table. In a loud voice, he addressed the hall. "As Alpha Council of the Brethren and Protector of the Compound, I formally ask that Lily Saburi be initiated as an ally and honored member of our ranks. She has shown true compassion for our kind, even at the cost of her own sacrifice and suffering. She is a companion-at-arms and a friend to the pack."

The room erupted into cheers. Even Mitch had to stifle a smile as he rapped the end of his lance calling for order. Shouting over the din, he tapped the lance again, "What say the council?"

Eight council members stood, sending eight resounding ayes echoing through the great hall. But when the room quieted, all eyes turned to the still seated and silent ninth.

Lily held her breath feeling Sean stiffen at her side as Edward Parr, ninth council, stood and faced the hall.

"I, too, acknowledge this young woman's sacrifice and her help. Let it be recorded that for those reasons I, too, am grateful. However, everyone here knows what our traditions allow and what constitutes sedition. It is no secret I was not in favor of this council when it was formed. Over the centuries each shifter group had its own method of governance, separate from the other. Now we are thrown together for reasons of necessity as some believe. But, I for one, believe that our individual traditions and rituals suffer by it.

"I acknowledge that centuries of change in the human world have led us to where we are now, yet I cannot and will not agree to flout tradition so much so as to allow a human to join our ranks. It has never been done, and as long as I draw breath it never will."

Sean stepped forward with a nod to Rissa to come and stand by Lily's side. "I can appreciate your reluctance, Edward," he began. "However, Lily Saburi stands as an exception to our tradition. She has shifter blood flowing through her veins, the same blood that has provided us with the cure for the disease that would otherwise lead to our slow, but certain extinction. While it's true the amount is small, it still gives my request validity."

A hushed murmur spread as people debated among themselves. It grew to a dull roar as dissent broadened. A gleam of triumph glinted in Parr's eyes, knowing that council members would never vote with such unrest and indecision swarming throughout the community. He turned toward Sean. "Of course, there is a solution to this dilemma, but you already know that. It is the only acceptable one for many of us. You must turn her."

In a clatter of books tumbling to the floor, Doctor Volkmann stood with a look of shock and disbelief on his face. "That's not possible! How could you even make such a request? We need her to stay intact, at least until we have a vaccine that is fail-safe."

Volkmann pointed his finger at Parr. "You are a calculating madman, sir. By demanding this, you risk the health of every shifter in this community, including Ms. Saburi's. We will self-destruct. But perhaps that is your intention!"

The little man's voice trembled with anger. Everyone knew the consequences, not only for the shifters, but for Lily, as well. The event of a premature conversion increased the likelihood of Lily's blood becoming tainted, and the end result was unthinkable.

Parr's eyes held a sly glint as they narrowed. "I know full well the risks, doctor. Then again, what good is our future survival if we have nothing anchoring us to our past?"

The room exploded as factions splintered. Fights broke out

between rival groups. Old grudges and slights long buried were once again unearthed, and chaos ensued.

Sean howled, a long piercing sound that brought the room at once to order. He looked at Parr whose white teeth flashed momentarily in triumph. His adversary had managed a stalemate, a decision needed from the Alpha Council. Parr's smile said it all, this had happened just as he wanted. Delia appeared in the crowd and moved to Parr's side. Her smile was punishing, and as vengeful as Edward's was cunning.

Sean knew he had been set up. He should have expected this, but he thought for sure the security and health of the community at large would supersede any past disputes or personal vendettas.

Now he knew he was wrong. Personal gain and power was at the root of this—as if they weren't up against enough.

He howled again, but this time the pitch was higher, resonating in multi-timbres. The community fell to its knees in shock. It was the timbre of the Alpha, and its significance unquestionable. Sean was pissed. "This meeting is recessed 'til midnight." Storming out of the room, Sean left every shifter trembling in his wake, but he didn't care, he needed time to think.

Lily went to follow, but Rissa held her back. "No Lil. He's in Alpha mode, and he needs to be alone. This is serious. He needs time to weigh everything, and your presence will only make matters worse. It's going to be hard enough for him to be impartial, without adding to it. Why don't you let Mitch and me walk you back?"

Lily shut her bedroom door, slumping against the jamb. She hadn't said a word the entire way back, but Mitch and Rissa were just as quiet, neither knowing what to say. They were just as stunned. As she stood in the dark, Lily couldn't help but wonder which way Sean would decide. Maybe Parr was right, and she didn't belong here.

"Why are you standing alone in the dark?"

Lily whirled, snapping on the light. "Terry! For Chrissake! Where have you been? You've been gone for a week."

"Giving you a little space, that's all."

"Space, really? You have no idea what happened. I could have really used someone on my side tonight."

"I gather it didn't go as Sean expected."

"To say the least." Lily exhaled, flopping down on the couch. "Sean honestly thinks this can work, but I don't know, Terry. I'm starting to think I don't belong here after all. Maybe we should go home, perhaps Sean will decide to come with us."

Terry didn't answer. She looked at her friend, a bittersweet expression on her face.

"What's the matter? Don't you want Sean to come? I thought you liked him."

Terry laughed, her eyes shining with unshed tears. "Oh, Lil, I love Sean, and I know whatever happens, you two will find a way to be happy. It's just," she paused, struggling to find the right words. "It's time for me to say goodbye."

Lily sat straight up. "Goodbye? What do you mean goodbye?"

"I finished what I stayed to do, Lily. You don't need me anymore; you're going to be all right."

Lily was speechless for a moment. She didn't need this bull right now. "You're full of it, you know. What could make you spew such garbage? If tonight proves anything, it's that I certainly *do* need you. Don't be an idiot, Terry, you're not going anywhere."

Her friend smiled sadly. "You don't understand. You've grown so much, and you don't even see it. You've learned to let go, Lily. You've gotten past it all and learned to forgive. Especially yourself. You're going to be okay, no matter what."

Lily sat, stunned. "You're right, I don't understand. Where are you going, then? Does Sean know?"

"Yeah," she nodded. "I told him this morning, but I asked him not to say anything to you. I wanted to tell you myself...say goodbye just the two of us. It's funny. I thought sticking around was my choice, but it looks like God was in on it the whole time, and now I *have* to go. So you see, I'm not actually going anywhere, I'm just moving on to where I should have gone in the first place."

Lily finally understood. She'd heard all the clichés about spirits going into the light, but in all her years as a psychic she'd never been witness to it. A deep ache squeezed her chest, and she suddenly couldn't breathe. Standing, she gripped her own arms against the pain. It was like losing Terry all over again. "When?" Her words were barely a whisper.

"Anytime, now."

The door to the bedroom opened quietly. "I figured you might need me right about now," Sean murmured, walking toward where Lily stood hugging herself in stunned silence. She looked so fragile he slid his arms around her shoulders as if trying to hold her together.

Soft tears trickled down her cheeks. "It's not fair," she mumbled burying her face in Sean's chest.

"I'm sorry, Lily. I know the timing sucks," Terry said, her voice echoing with regret, but she had no more control over this than anyone else.

The air in the room changed. It sparked as if suddenly overflowing with static electricity, and a tiny light winked into existence, swirling swiftly behind Terry.

It grew in its brilliance until she was entirely immersed. Divine radiance filled her as she took her first step into the vortex.

"Terry, wait!"

She looked back, her translucent hair whipping silently around her. "I can't sweetie, even if I wanted to," she said, with a shake of her head. "Only happy tears for me Lil'...this is as it should be. Remember, I love you...always," she whispered and then was gone.

Lily stared at the empty space where Terry had been, and an even emptier feeling crept across her heart.

"You okay?" Sean asked, wiping her cheek.

Blinking back the rest of her tears, Lily shook her head. "Not really. She had been trying to warn me for a couple of weeks, telling me to make friends and fit in. I guess she felt this coming. Maybe that's why she chose to stay away so much."

Sean pulled her close. "Terry's right, you know. She's where she should be, and it's a better place than you or I will ever know here on Earth."

Lily's breath hitched in her throat. "You're right, and I know it's true. It's going to take some time for my heart to catch up to my head."

Taking a deep breath, she closed her eyes and rested her head on Sean's chest. This had been some night, but upset as she was, she wasn't giving Sean lip service. Terry was right. Though her heart was breaking, she knew she was going to be okay. Six weeks ago, she would have either fallen to pieces or beat the crap out of someone—probably both.

Lily sighed and snuggled further beneath Sean's arms. She loved his strength, and how he made her feel when they were together, like she'd never have to put up a wall again.

With everything happening in his world tonight, it meant so much that he thought to be with her, even though she knew he would have to leave again. More than just her fate lay in the balance, and the weight of the heavy burden was clear in the air around them.

"Aren't you supposed to be somewhere else? It's almost midnight."

"I knew you needed me."

"I do," she admitted wrapping her arms around him tighter. She inhaled, waiting for the familiar suffocating feeling, but it didn't come. Being able to confess that she needed someone, so easily, and without the usual self-loathing, stunned her. Terry was right, again. She'd learned to let go. Only problem now was she didn't want to let go of Sean, afraid if she did it would be the last time she'd hold him like this.

Neither one spoke, but his tension was clear, nonetheless. *"You should probably get back; they're all waiting for you,"* she whispered along their shared mind path unable to speak the words out loud.

"I know. Lily, whatever happens tonight..."

Lily opened her eyes to stare up at him, putting her finger to his lips. She shook her head slowly. "I know you'll do what's right. Not just for me, but for everyone. Do what you have to, and don't worry. I'll be fine."

Through the window, they heard the sound of the drums. Their cadence slow at first, but as it increased in urgency, Lily clutched the back of Sean's shirt. They were out of time.

Resting his head on top of hers, he murmured, "It's time."

Beneath his chin, all she could manage was a nod. Squeezing back tears, she opened her mind, flooding his with love and reassurance. *"Whatever you decide, I'll never regret this... or you."*

Sean stepped back, and it struck her how his eyes searched hers. "You sure?" he wondered aloud.

With a steadying breath, she smiled bravely. "Surer than anything else in my life."

Sean didn't say a word. He kissed her instead, leaving quickly without saying goodbye. Standing at the window, she watched him cross the courtyard, keeping her mind linked with his until he closed the door between them.

Anger boiled in Lily's mind, knowing this whole thing was nothing more than a ploy orchestrated by Edward Parr. But why?

In her frustration, she wanted nothing more than to send the bastard a mental bitch-slap. A rueful smile tugged at Lily's lips at the thought, but she knew it wouldn't serve their purpose, regardless of how much she'd enjoy it.

Delia. She was another pointless complication in the entire mess. An ugly sound crept from Lily's mouth at the part Delia had played in all this. Parr was the perfect vehicle for her to exact her revenge without needing an actual challenge. Stupid bitch probably slept with the smarmy bastard to fuel his ambition with her own malice.

Lily snorted. The two deserved each other and whatever consequences came their way. Special delivery, courtesy of my boot up their ass.

With an aggravated sigh, she watched Sean disappear into the great hall, his shoulders squared for battle. He was the Alpha Council. All she could do was wait and pray he'd find a way to make this work. If anyone could, it was Sean.

CHAPTER ELEVEN

Sean opened the door to the bedroom, boots in hand. Across the room, Lily slept, or at least that's what she wanted him to think. A small smile crept across his lips at the narrow lump beneath the covers. She had been through so much in such a short time, and now this. How was he going to explain? Well, you see, sweetheart, shifters are a fickle bunch and as a group no better than sheep to the slaughter, laughing the whole way about how smart they are...

"Jesus, help me," he sighed, silently. There was no getting around it. Politics were politics. Since the beginning of time, there was always someone trying to feed Kool-Aid to the masses. In this case, it was Edward Parr.

The clock ticked on the desk next to his walk-in closet, with Lily's rhythmic breathing keeping pace. Her dark hair fanned out against the white cotton sheets, and what remained of the moonlight peeked through the curtains accentuating her creamy skin and the swell of her breasts above the sheet.

As tired as Sean was, a pang of desire swept over him, but he squelched it. On so many levels, it had been a long, trying night for both of them. Terry may have moved on, but here on Earth nothing had yet been accomplished. Nothing significant, anyway.

He yawned, wanting to crawl into bed and feel Lily's warmth beside him, close his eyes and not think about the mess he had to deal with.

The hunters were not happy with him, especially Mitch, even though Sean managed a hard won moratorium. Tonight they tried to convince him to force the issue with Parr. To reestablish dominion and the power of the Alpha and set the ruling, regardless of dissent. Even now, Sean shook his head at the idea. The whole point to the council of shifters was for diplomacy to reign, not the will of one man.

Sean's elected position to Alpha Council of the Brethren wasn't done by committee. The process had included everyone. One man, one vote—though his bloodline made him the obvious choice in the eyes of the wolves, a point his hunters made abundantly clear this evening.

For the Compound to be considered a success, a resolution of this kind had to come from a majority rule. Otherwise, what was the point to the experiment of species? If they couldn't agree on something as cut and dried as the situation with Lily, then how could they ever hope to overcome the serious issues facing them in the future—land rights, food resources, the freedom to hunt, etc.? It all hinged on how they worked together now. Parr may have forced a stalemate, but the battle was far from over.

Sean placed his boots on the floor by the foot of the bed and unbuckled his jeans. He slid his shirt over his head and tossed it into the wicker hamper before heading into the bathroom. In the mirror, he took inventory. Dark circles and frown lines. Christ, this job was aging him fast.

He turned on the tap to rinse his face and brush his teeth, and then slipped out of his jeans and hung them on the chair next to his desk.

"Hard run?" Lily asked from the bed.

"I wish," he answered, snapping off the light and then climbing into bed. "Believe me, I'd much rather have raced the moon than argued all night with Edward and his cronies. At least then, I wouldn't have a headache."

Lily shifted, turning onto her side to let him spoon behind her. Sean slid his arm over her waist and pulled her close, her warmth sinking into his tired limbs.

"You're the softest thing I've held tonight," he murmured, kissing the top of her bare shoulder. "Aren't you cold sleeping in the nude like that? You know you're not a full shifter, yet."

She chuckled, pushing herself further back into his warmth. "That's what I have you for."

"Hmmm."

His sex grew hard against her wiggle, but he didn't push the issue. As if she knew something else was up besides the obvious, Lily turned in Sean's arms to face him, her eyes narrowing. "Are you too tired to tell me what happened, or are you stalling because it's bad news?"

"Stalling?"

She nodded, but kept her eyebrows raised. "You heard right.. Stalling."

With a sigh, he rolled onto his back.

"Sean."

He rubbed his face with his palm, muffling an exhausted sigh. "There's not much to tell. Parr's antics tonight were entirely premeditated. He was too schooled, too prepared in his arguments afterward for it not to be. He pushed, but I pushed back. As alpha, the hunters wanted me to force the decision as is my right, but I declined. I have to be clever about how I handle this, Lily. For both our sakes.

The handwriting is on the wall. Parr will make this about me and the object of my affection, if I give him the chance."

"Object of your affection?"

The side of Sean's mouth quirked up in a crooked smile. "That's how Edward refers to you when he's showboating."

"And..."

"And nothing. I suggested a postponement."

Lily pushed herself up on one arm, her brows coming together nonplussed. "A postponement? Why? What for?"

Sean turned on his side to face her. "Because, Christmas is in a week, and for shifters, the holiday season extends from Christmas Day straight into January and ending at the Wolf Moon. Traditionally, festivities last the length of a single moon cycle.

"Parr timed his coup well, knowing everyone would opt for a quick decision just to wrap things up in time for holidays. I threw a monkey wrench into his plan by suggesting we wait. From the look on his face, he hadn't counted on that."

Lily chewed on her lower lip, thinking. "Okay," she murmured with a slow nod. "You know the situation better than me... so we wait."

She sank down against Sean's chest, resting her head in the crook between his arm and his shoulder. He glanced across his chest at her still chewing on her lip. "What?"

She shook her head, absently. "Nothing," she replied. "I was trying to remember something I read once about the Wolf Moon. It's Native American, right?"

Sean nodded. "Sioux, although some of our academics say the term originated from the Algonquin. Either way the name refers to a time when winter is at its worst and the wolves came howling, looking for food. Among the Native Americans, my kind was revered, celebrated as living examples of nature's magic. Folklore was passed down from generation to generation about how we protected the tribes. It wasn't until the white man came that shifters became feared and hunted. The Wolf Moon is our way of remembering, of keeping tradition. Edward just loves to throw monkey wrenches during festivities, stirring up nostalgia for our glorious past."

Lily pushed herself up on her elbow. "Then postponing the decision on my acceptance to the pack can't be good. There are only a couple of weeks until the Wolf Moon. If Parr spins this the whole time, won't that make things worse for us?"

Sean lifted one shoulder and let it fall. "It might, then again it might not. That's why it's crucial for you to be front and center at every holiday event. We need for people to see you, to get to know you better. This way when Edward tries to label you a mere human, it won't resonate with thc Compound. By then you'll just be Lily, a real person with a real face and a real heart."

Lily exhaled, concern etching her eyes.

"What? Too much too soon?" he asked.

She shook her head. "No, I'm okay with being on display, but I think I need to go shopping. Everything I own makes me look like a Hell's Angel biker babe."

Sean burst out laughing and pulled her on top of him. "You can buy anything you want," he said, sliding his hands down the curve of her waist, his fingers brushing the side of her breasts. "Except pajamas."

He crushed his mouth to hers, and she answered his need with her own. Neither was getting much rest tonight.

Lily walked into the breakfast room, squinting from the sun glinting in through the large portrait windows facing the expansive back property.

"And how are you feeling this morning?" Rissa asked, looking up from putting two silver dollar pancakes on Stephanie's plate.

"Better, I guess," Lily answered, pouring a cup of coffee from the silver carafe on the sideboard. She stood between the table and the spread of food long enough to feed an army. "I still can't get used to this communal living. Don't you ever want to be alone?"

"We do pretty much everything together. You'll get used to it, I'm sure."

"All I can say is I'm glad you don't all sleep together."

Rissa snickered. "I'll bet."

Lily looked up, the creamer in her hand halfway to her cup. "What's that supposed to mean?"

Rissa shook her head, a huge grin on her face. "Nothing, really. It's just you smell... happy."

"Lily frowned pouring the cream into her coffee cup. "I don't think I'll ever get used to what you people can and can't smell. By happy, I'm assuming you mean as in X-rated, right?"

Rissa just laughed

"Mommy, what's X-rated?" Stephanie asked, looking up from making swirls in her syrup.

Rissa's head whipped toward her daughter. "It... it means a... a grown up thing," she stammered over herself.

"Oh," the little girl said, glancing over at Lily. She sniffed, and then glanced back at her mother, a curious expression on her face. "Mommy, you smell happy like that too, sometimes. Whenever Mitch has a sleepover."

Lily choked, spewing coffee everywhere.

"Who's having a sleepover?" Mitch asked, walking through the breakfast room door.

Rissa got up to help Lily mop up the table and wipe down her shirt. "Nothing, Mitch. Forget it."

"Mommy and Lily smell the same when they're happy," Stephanie said through a mouthful of pancakes.

Mitch looked at both women, his nostrils flaring slightly. His eyes widened. "Oh, for the love of Pete!" He cleared his throat and grabbed a mug from the shelf.

"I think I'm going to go upstairs and take another shower." Lily muttered, not making eye contact with either of them as she threw the wet napkins in the trash.

"Don't leave on account of me," Mitch teased, grabbing an English muffin from the tray. "Shower's not going to help much anyway. It's a shifter thing," he added with a shrug.

Cheeks flaming, Rissa's head jerked in his direction, her expression mortified. Lily didn't comment. Sean made it clear people needed to like her, so it was best she didn't say a word.

She leaned against the sideboard and plucked one of the sausage links from the tray next to her. Finger sized, she bit it in half, chewing while she watched Rissa compose herself enough to pour more syrup on her daughter's plate.

"Are you coming to the Wolf Moon Ball?" Rissa asked, noticeably changing the subject.

Lily shrugged. "I suppose. Sean said there were a bunch of holiday do's during the next month."

Mitch laughed. "That's putting it mildly."

"Are you two planning to go? I mean, are you up to it?" she replied, indicating Rissa's burgeoning belly with the second half of her sausage link.

"Ha! Not if Mitch has anything to say about it. That man would have me in bed with my feet propped up being spoon fed if he could manage it," she shot back with a huffy laugh, her eyes warm as she touched the big wolf's shoulder. "But yeah, thanks to you, I'm good. The baby is growing, and I'm healthy, and were both glad I'm back to being a full time mommy. Aren't we Stephie?"

The little girl looked at Lily over the rim of her double handled cup. Her blue eyes crinkled, flashing a quick smile at Lily.

Surprised, Lily glanced at both Rissa and Mitch.

"We've been telling her about you, about how you're helping everyone here get better. How you helped me and the baby, especially." Embarrassed, Rissa picked up a napkin and busied herself with wiping one of Stephanie's sticky hands.

Stephanie nodded, putting her cup down next to her plate. "Are you coming to our house for Christmas?"

Lily looked at the adults again, not knowing what to say.

"Of course, she is, sweetie. Uncle Sean wouldn't have it any other way." Rissa answered for her. "That is if you're not going home for the holidays," she added.

Lily shook her head. She had a hard enough time facing Beverly and Carl Hess after Terry's funeral and on the days that followed. She'd already missed Thanksgiving, as Terry didn't want to go home in her ethereal state, not trusting herself to be around her parents.

It was distressing enough that Terry felt their grief; she didn't want to see it firsthand. At the time, Lily was relieved, even grateful, especially since she was caught up in vigilante mode.

Beverly was already on the brink of a nervous breakdown. Having to watch Lily walk around like a character from the movie *Death Wish and* overhear her talk to her dead daughter's ghost would have certainly pushed her over the edge. Terry's parents knew Lily well enough to realize she needed to be away, that she needed to grieve alone. They'd understand.

"No. I don't have any plans for Christmas, and New York is just too sad a place for me, right now."

"I know, honey, and I'm sorry for that. Sean told us about Terry. You shouldn't be alone. Why don't you come for Christmas? We all have something to grieve, but we also all have something to hope for, to be merry about."

Lily smiled, but it was tinged with a sad, empty feeling. "You're right, and I'd love to come. I guess I need a little help in getting to the merry."

"Mommy, I'm done. Can I go outside now?" Stephanie asked, pulling on Rissa's sleeve.

Rissa turned toward her daughter. "Sure." She nodded. "But only for a little while and only if Nanny goes with you."

"Yay!" The little girl slid out of her chair and hugged her mother and then bounced out the breakfast room.

"Bundle up!" Rissa shouted after her, and then bent to clear her plate. "If only I had her energy," she chuckled.

"I'm heading out, too," Mitch said, putting his cup next to the large coffee carafe and giving Rissa's cheek a peck. "I'm running drills with the new recruits, so I'll keep an eye on Stephie." He grabbed his jacket from the end of the sideboard. "And don't worry about finding the merry, Lily. Sean's great at directions."

Lily grinned after him as he walked out the breakfast room. Who would believe two months ago he wanted to rip her throat out.

"So, new recruits and holiday parties. Exactly how busy is it going to get around here?" Lily asked, topping off her coffee.

Rissa straightened, grimacing a bit, one hand going to the small of her back. "The festivities start right after Christmas with the Yule Hunt. It's pretty exciting, and it's the first hunt for many of the adolescent shifters. Sort of a rite of passage. After that, the Hunters host a massive game dinner where the men actually cook whatever they caught."

Lily's brows hiked up. "Game? As in deer?"

Rissa nodded, carrying Stephanie's dishes to the sideboard. "Deer, elk, bear..."

"Bear?"

A large grin spread across Rissa's face. "Don't look so shocked.

Bear is actually pretty good, and before you ask, the answer is no, we don't eat it raw! You'd be surprised how gourmet-ish the recipes get. After that, it's New Year's and there are too many parties to count. We give it a few days to let everyone recover before starting the next round of events, but the biggest one next to the Yule Hunt is our Ancestor's Dinner, which is followed by the Wolf Ball at the end of the month. We try to have the ball coincide with the Wolf Moon, but sometimes the calendar doesn't cooperate."

Lily slid into a chair, her fingers tapping the edge of her cup. Sean wasn't kidding when he said there was a need for her to be front and center. From what Rissa described, over the next month Lily would literally meet and greet almost everyone in the Compound.

She glanced up from her cup. "Sean told me a bit about the history behind the Wolf Moon. Sounds like a remarkably rich and poetic story."

"It's a long standing tradition, and it truly helps solidify our heritage, especially with the kids," Rissa replied, pouring a cup of decaf. She slid into a chairs across from Lily. "Although, there are some blowhards who like to use the event as a soapbox for their agendas. You know, like celebrities sometimes do at the Oscars."

Lily didn't comment, but Rissa's face told her exactly who she meant. Edward Parr. She wondered if the man's posturing was part of his everyday persona.

"The Oscars, wow. That's some comparison. I guess it's safe to assume you plan on going, then, huh?"

Rissa chuckled. "I'm going, whether Mitch likes it or not. All I have to do is find a dress flattering enough to hide this bump," she said tugging on her maternity top. "I wouldn't miss the Wolf Ball for the world." A shadow found her eyes, and Lily caught it before Rissa blinked it away.

"You okay, Ris? Did something else happen?"

A roll of the eyes followed a tired exhale. "Not something. Someone." She paused. "Cecily Paris is coming for a visit. Mitch's mother. She doesn't like me much."

"Have Mitch tell her not to come. You just started feeling better. Why would he put you through that kind of stress?"

"He wouldn't. It was me. I insisted. If Mitch and I are to make a life together, I need to get ahead of the biggest obstacles. His mother, for one."

Lily watched her clean up crumbs. "For one. What else is standing in your way?" She hoped to God it wasn't Jerard's memory, or worse, the unborn baby she carried.

"Technically, Mitch is the blood alpha of the Abenaki. A clan in northern Canada." She brushed the crumbs from her palm into a napkin. "He came here after his father died. It was the man's dying wish to help him deal with everything and finish his training."

"That doesn't sound unreasonable."

Rissa smoothed the front of her shirt. "Except that was almost ten years ago." Her eyes met Lily's gaze. "Mitch never really went back."

"And you think that's why Cecily doesn't like you?"

A shrug was Rissa's only reply.

Lily put down her cup and leaned her elbows on the table, her hand clasped. "Ris, anyone who judges you for what you've been through, or holds you accountable for someone else's decisions, needs a steel toed boot where the sun doesn't shine. Sean said he wants me front and center this season so the Compound can get to know me. If that means running interference for you with the wicked witch of the north, then I'm happy to help."

A small grin tugged at Rissa's mouth. "Well, maybe if you promise to where flats or slingbacks, then yeah. Let's save your steel toes version for when I really need them."

"I can do flats. I can even do heels. Whatever you need." Lily paused, glancing out the window to a sky that threatened snow. “Since you’re feeling better and you said you needed a dress, how about a little retail therapy? I think we could both use a day out.”

Rissa beamed. “How soon do you want to leave?”

CHAPTER TWELVE

"What's all this?" Sean asked from the doorway.

Lily followed his gaze to the bed and the spread of clothes lying across the fleecy duvet. "Rissa and I went shopping. I told you I needed a few things."

"A few things? I think this qualifies as an entire wardrobe." He chuckled.

With a sexy smirk on her face, Lily walked to the bed, sweeping her black sweater up and over her head and depositing it on the pile. She picked up a silky tunic style top with a plunging neckline and slipped it on, the clingy fabric hugging every curve and leaving little to the imagination.

"You're the one who said people need to get to know me," she answered, modeling the garment or him.

In two strides he was in front of her. With a practiced hand he glided the sexy blouse from her shoulders and tossed it back onto the bed. "They don't need to know you *that* well," he murmured, his lips finding the soft hollow beneath her jaw.

Standing in her black bra and leggings, she shivered, but the cold winter air had nothing to do with it.

"Sean... Rissa and Mitch are waiting for us."

He feathered kisses along her collarbone and down the deep plunge of her décolleté. "Let them wait."

"Sean."

He picked his head up and sighed. "And so it begins."

"Ha. You're the one who suggested we be at every function this season. With the political climate among the shifters the way it is, it doesn't help if people think I'm distracting you from your duties. Edward Parr is maneuvering against me, and you. You said I need to be front and center, so his spin doesn't gain any more momentum. You're the Alpha Council of the Brethren, Sean. Not a horny teenager."

A low rumble echoed from the back of Sean's throat, and he gave the swell of her breast a little nip before he straightened.

Lily chuckled. "Famous last words, huh?"

With a throaty growl, Sean grabbed her around the waist and threw her on the bed, straddling her hips. "It's not my fault your scent is irresistible."

Heat crawled up her lower belly at his sensuous tone, but there was more at stake than Sean being a horny wolf. She tucked her arms behind her head, watching his eyes. "Argumentative and stubborn is usually my thing. What gives tonight? Why are you hedging about going to Rissa's dinner party?"

Sean's expression was somewhere between annoyed and admiring. "That mind of yours. Someday it's going to save my life or kill me." He laughed, detangling himself from her legs.

Lily rolled to her side, her gaze still watching his face. "You're still being evasive. What's going on? Is Rissa sick? Has the virus relapsed?"

"No, nothing like that. The vaccine Dr. Volkmann distilled from the antibodies in your blood is working wonders, and both Rissa and the baby are doing fine."

If the serum the doctors at Leighton Research developed failed to work, Edward Parr would have a field day. Her place in the pack and at the Compound would be finished.

"Rissa is, what? Almost five months pregnant?"

Sean nodded. "I think so."

"Does this have anything to do with the fact I was the one who killed her husband after he attacked us on the cliffs?"

"You would think that, but no. Everyone knows Jerard was no longer Jerard when he charged. The virus had turned his brain to mush. He was a base creature by that time, and as hard as that is for me to say, it's the truth. His fate was his own making."

Lily shook her head, perplexed. "I don't understand. People catch viruses every day. What did he do?"

"Jerard and Rissa were separated long before he degenerated into what you witnessed on the cliffs outside Ogunquit. He had practically disowned Rissa and Stephanie. Even going so far as to claim his wife was pregnant by another man. Everyone knows that's bunk. Rissa got pregnant in one final attempt at saving their marriage. Unfortunately, because she's found happiness with Mitch, tongues are wagging that Jerard's claims are valid."

Lily sat bolt up. "That's ridiculous! Christ, you shifters are a fickle bunch."

Sean lifted one shoulder and let it drop. "We're no different from humans, Lily. People are people and they love gossip. The juicier the story, the better, regardless of the truth or who gets hurt in the crossfire. Jerard had become addicted to prescription drugs. He was badly injured in a fight with a rival pack after we formed the Compound. You know quite well not everyone approves of the experiment to unite all shifter species."

He exhaled, and Lily reached over to brush her fingertips across his cheek. The topic was exhausting.

"Jerard's addiction spread to intravenous use, and that's how

Volkmann thinks he contracted the virus. He was always a womanizer, and not exactly the best husband and father, but he was my brother and I loved him."

Lily chewed on her bottom lip, and Sean raised an eyebrow. "Whenever you nibble on that luscious lip of yours it invariably means trouble for me."

"I'm just processing everything you said. Rissa commented she and Jerard weren't the happiest of couples. Talk about an understatement. If it were me, I would have cut off his balls and served them to him on a plate."

Sean winced. "Now *that* I believe." He smacked her on the butt before getting up from the bed. "The reason I'm so hesitant about tonight is that Rissa is trying to bring her family and Mitch's family together with this dinner. Mitch's mother is the matriarch of the Abenaki. They're an allied pack, and she can be, well...hard. I need to be there for Rissa and Stephanie, but I guarantee Mitch's mother will not only have her sights set on them, but you, too. I guess I should be grateful my sister isn't here. Emily's not exactly a favorite of the Abenakis. But that's a story for another time."

"Rissa mentioned the Abenakis. They're somewhere in Canada, right?"

"Exactly. Along the northern Canadian border."

A pensive shadow crossed Sean's eyes, and Lily hated he had this extra burden on top of everything else. "You're a good man, Sean, but you don't need to worry about me. I can take care of myself. Believe it or not, I can be a seamless mix of polite passive aggression when needed. I know you're not enthused about going, but Rissa needs you. Needs us."

Lily reached her hand up, and when Sean took it she gently pulled him onto the bed. Sliding one hand behind his head, she trailed the other down his chest, stopping at the base of his zipper.

"Just so the evening isn't a total loss—" she whispered against his lips but was cut off mid-tease when he crushed his lips to hers.

"Lily, I think we should put a napkin at the center of each dish. They're folded exactly like we saw at the Williams Sonoma store in the mall," Rissa called from the kitchen.

From his vantage point by the fireplace, Sean chuckled, giving a sharp salute in the general direction of the kitchen.

"Stop that." Lily whispered, sparing a glance for the kitchen door. "Can't you see she's a nervous wreck?"

He poked at the logs on the grate to get the fire burning. "You women are nuts. It's just a table setting for Chrissake."

Lily snuck another look, watching Rissa hand Stephanie a spoon to put into the sink. "Did you or did you not just bribe your way into my pants a little less than an hour ago by telling me how hard this was going to be once Mitch got here with his mother?"

"I..."

"I nothing. Let's not forget you have yet to meet my family and considering I'm all Beverly and Carl have left since Terry died, it's not going to be the piece of cake you expect."

Lily bit the inside of her cheek. Big talk from someone who couldn't bring herself to call the only family she knew. She cleared her throat, mollifying her guilt with a silent promise to call them soon.

"I may find you irresistible, but that doesn't mean they will. The same holds true for Rissa and Mitch. Only she's got it worse because of Stephanie and the baby. Not to mention all the gossip you mentioned earlier."

Sean answered, putting his hands up in surrender.

"Good." She punctuated the word with a sharp nod. "We are in defensive mode and here to run interference, so put your Alpha on and let's get this party started."

Lily walked back to the table, deliberately swinging her hips a little more than usual. "Wow. Look who's bribing who now," he said, with an appreciative whistle.

"Let's just say it's incentive," she replied, leaning over to fix a napkin on a far place setting, giving him a lacy preview.

The doorbell rang and a dish clattered to the floor in the kitchen. "That's got to be them. You answer the door and I'll make sure Rissa remembers to breath." She shooed Sean toward the foyer.

With a wink he shot her a crooked half smile. "Operation Mistletoe Minefield is now a go."

"We're here," Mitch called from the hallway. "We made good time, considering the holiday traffic."

Mitch walked in just ahead of Cecily. The women stood in her coat, holding her purse like an undiffused bomb. She followed Mitch toward the living room but didn't enter. Instead, she gave the place a onceover and a loud sniff.

"The house smells wonderful, don't you think?" Rissa moved past Lily to greet the older woman. "It's the balsam fir. Mitch got us the tree for Christmas tree, and the fresh scent lingers all over the house."

An awkward silence was her only reply, but Rissa held out her hand anyway. "It's a pleasure to finally meet you, Mrs. Paris. I'm Rissa Leighton."

The older woman still didn't respond. She just sniffed again, ratcheting the tension in the room up another notch. "*Uhm*, why don't you take your mother's coat and hang it in the closet?" Rissa glanced at Mitch for help.

"And how about I get everyone a drink?" Sean suggested, drawing the focus away from Rissa.

"I'm way ahead of you, babe." Lily winked, earning a cough from Sean and a raised eyebrow from Mitch's mother.

"It's nice to see you again, Sean," Cecily said, peeling off her coat and handing it to her son. "Though I do wish it was under better circumstances."

At Sean's questioning gaze, the woman's eyes came to rest on Rissa before lowering to the younger woman's belly bump. "Such sad news about your brother. My condolences to you both."

Lily walked in carrying an aperitif tray. Five sherry glasses circled a small silver bowl filled with cashews. Four people took a glass, even Rissa, leaving just one short, stemmed glass on the tray.

"Mrs. Paris, won't you join us in a welcome toast?" Rissa asked.

Cecily looked at the proffered drink. "A welcome toast is it?"

"Of course, Mother. Rissa and I both want to make sure you feel welcome in our home."

The smile on the older woman's face was stiff enough to crack. Was her game just intimidation or was there more to her ice crusted courtesy?

Lily's grip tightened on the silver tray. There was one way to find out for sure. Ignoring Sean's side eye warning, she focused her senses and took a peek inside the woman's head. No harm, no foul, right? Although foul was the perfect word considering the bile coating Cecily Paris's thoughts. Rissa had been tried and convicted before the woman stepped through the door.

"Mother, please." Mitch gestured to the drink still on the tray.

With a grudging nod, the woman took the thin crystal glass and then held it in front of her chest, her eyes glancing between Rissa and Lily.

"Forgive me, Mrs. Paris. Where are my manners? This is Lily Saburi. Sean's girlfriend."

"Yes, I've heard tell about you."

Lily smiled, putting the empty tray on the table. "And I know plenty about you, too."

Sean coughed again, trying not to laugh as the Cecily's eyebrows shot to her hairline.

"Relax, Mother. I haven't told them any of our family's deepest darks, so set yourself to defrost and try to enjoy the evening. Take it easy, though. I wouldn't want you to strain yourself."

The woman was not amused. "I don't find any of this appropriate, Mitch. And that goes for you too, Sean. I don't appreciate this cozy quartet greeting me at the door. It's unseemly."

Sean clapped his hands. "That's because it's too drafty this close to the hallway. Why don't we sit by the fire and get to know each other?" He swept out his arm, ushering Cecily into the living room.

"Oh, there's a chill all right." Lily murmured under her breath. "You could freeze water on that woman's ass."

Rissa pinched her friend's arm. "Behave yourself."

"I will if she will. You've got to know the odds are stacked against, you Riss. She's judge and jury, and had her mind made up before she crossed your threshold."

"I know that, but I'm doing this for Mitch. At least no one can say I didn't try."

Rissa's determination made Lily's heart ache. Cecily Paris would never accept her, at least not without a miracle. Either way, she'd run interference for her friend until the old bat flew north again.

CHAPTER THIRTEEN

"You look awful." Lily stared across the stack of cups and saucers on the end of the sideboard to where Rissa sat at the table. "I thought pregnant women were supposed to look radiant. Please tell me you weren't up all night sick."

"No. I just didn't sleep very well."

Lily snorted, pouring herself a cup of coffee from the silver carafe. "I can't say as I blame you. Your future mother-in-law is a piece of work."

The breakfast room was awash with sunlight pouring through the large portrait windows facing the expansive back property. The cheerful light, a poignant counterpoint to the tense atmosphere of the night before.

Rissa spooned up a mouthful of oatmeal and brown sugar. "Tell me about it, but Cecily isn't my future mother-in-law. Mitch would have to ask me to marry him first, and so far, he hasn't said a word."

"Yet," Lily interjected. "He hasn't asked you yet. I gotta say, though, with a hard ass like her for a possible mother-in-law, I'd have second thoughts if I were you."

"This from a woman who repelled down the side of the manor house to get away from a possible love relationship with Sean."

"That was different. Sean was still deciding whether or not to kill me."

Rissa choked, spewing decaf halfway across the white linen tablecloth.

"Now that's class." Trying not to laugh, Lily handed her a napkin. "You should have done that last night. Cecily would have peed her pants."

Still coughing, Rissa wiped her mouth on the white linen. "You forget I'm not you. The mortification alone would have *me* repelling down buildings to escape."

Lily carried her coffee and a croissant to the table. Chafing trays filled with eggs, sausage and bacon, biscuits, fresh fruit, yogurt, and hot cakes lined the long sideboard table. Enough food to feed the army of shifters living in concert at the Compound, and for a loner like Lily, it was a harder concept to accept than the existence of the dual natured.

"At least Mitch had your back. A lot of men would cave if their mother sniffed at their girlfriend like that."

Rissa made a face. "Literally."

"What's up with that anyway? Is all that sniffing a shifter thing or was that her being rude?" Lily placed her mug on the long dining table and pulled out a chair.

"What sniffing?"

"The sniffing Cecily did when she walked in the door. It was like she hoped to find something nasty lingering in the air just to stick it to you."

Rissa sighed. "Both. By nature, shifter mothers are very possessive, and when you've been an alpha-female your whole life, and then acting alpha while waiting for your son to reach maturity, control can go to your head."

Lily blew on the steamy edge of her coffee cup, holding the warm porcelain between her hands. "I think her control issues have nothing to do with being a shifter. Did you hear the way she spoke about her pack?"

"More than once."

"The Abenakis are a proud clan whose history and tradition are as deep and plentiful as the Canadian wilderness from whence we came." Lily mimicked the woman's snotty tone, and then made a face. "Listen, Ris. I'm all for being proud of who you are and where you come from, but her damned condescension! She could have used that long nosed stare to stir her extra dry martini. With three olives, if you please..."

Rissa shrugged. "What other choice do I have? I love Mitch, and I absolutely have to make peace with his mother, or she'll use it against me."

Hmmph. "Seems to me like she'll use anything she can against you, regardless. Absolute power corrupts absolutely, and she's got it bad."

"Again, tell me about it." Rissa pushed her plate away with a disgusted sigh. "This has thrown a monkey wrench into everything I have tried to build with Mitch over the past six weeks. I know Sean told you everything about the unknown virus attacking the Compound, and how fast it spread among shifters, but what he didn't tell you was how many lives it took, driving others to madness.

"I was sick well before you came and agreed to help. All I could think about was who was going to take care of Stephanie if I died. Jerard was gone from my life long before the madness took him onto the cliffs where you and Sean found him. Mitch was there for me even then."

Rissa looked down at her lap, her hand smoothing over her rounded belly in a comforting caress. "God help me. I can't stand that woman! I know I'm pregnant and all, but she made it sound like I was ready to drop this kid any minute. The size of my belly! Ha! She should talk."

Lily laughed at Rissa's sudden vanity. "You know what I think you need?"

"Should I be afraid?"

"Depends."

"Out with it then. What do you think I need?"

"A night out with the girls."

Rissa snorted. "Lily, I know you mean well, but I think that's the last thing I need."

"Come on, Ris, it's just what the doctor ordered! Of course, we'll make you the designated driver since you're pregnant and can't drink, but that doesn't mean you can't have a good time."

"Who says she can't drink?" a feminine voice questioned from the doorway.

Both women turned to find a tall statuesque blonde standing in the entrance to the breakfast room. The young woman had sandy hair and blue eyes, just like Sean. She was tall and slender, and when she turned there was no denying the family resemblance.

"Emily!" Rissa squealed and jumped up from the table. "I thought for sure it would be another five years before we saw you again!"

"What are you talking about? I told you I'd be back." Emily laughed, giving her friend a squeeze.

Rissa beamed, her whole demeanor changing from exasperated to delight. "Yeah, that's what you said the last time, and it took Mitch's threats of flying out and dragging you home for you to agree to come for a visit."

Emily pulled back, holding Rissa's arms out, her eyes sinking to the pregnant woman's belly. "Looks like I've missed more than I thought!" Emily's face sobered and she wrapped her arms around Rissa again. "Thank God you're better. I was so worried about you."

Rissa slid her arm across her friend's shoulder and gave her a small squeeze. "Yeah, me too, but that's all in the past now. I'm as healthy as a horse thanks to this one over here and all the help she's been at the clinic." She gestured toward Lily. "Em, This is Lily. Sean's girlfriend."

"From what I hear she's much more than just my brother's girlfriend." Emily made bunny ears with her fingers.

Lily's mouth dropped, but she snapped shut, regrouping enough to stand and extend her hand. "It's nice to meet you, Emily."

The young blonde took three steps forward and wrapped her arms around Lily's shoulders. "From what I've been told, you helped save the entire Compound, not to mention putting Delia Monroe in her place."

Emily let go of Lily's shoulders and stepped back, taking Lily by the hand. "That girl and her family have given my brother endless hell. I may not have been around much over the past five years, but I heard the gossip. Delia must have shit her pants when you stepped up willing to meet her challenge."

Lily's hands were still locked in Emily's, so all she could do was shrug. "It didn't amount to anything, though. Delia decided to align herself with the Compound's naysayers instead, trying to punish Sean by using me. Never in a million years would I have thought being human was such a liability."

Emily's face softened. "It's not, so don't think that."

"I don't. And I don't have patience for people trying to use my single-natured status to manipulate your brother, either. Some days I have to bite my tongue until I taste blood, but I only do so to help Sean."

"Either way, you brought joy back into my brother's life," she said pulling Lily in for another hug. "It hasn't been easy for him. Especially with me purposefully staying away, and Jerard, well... being Jerard. I'm grateful."

Self-conscious, Lily gave the woman a small squeeze and then stepped back, clearing her throat.

Switching gears completely, Emily steered Rissa to the table and deposited her in her chair. "Now, about to this plan of yours. A girl's night is a terrific idea, but you know what's even more terrific?" Eagerness glittered in Emily's eyes. "A girl's night out in Boston!"

Neither Rissa nor Lily said a word watching Emily pace back and forth between them like a party planner on crack.

"Don't be such a pair of old wet blankets," Emily said, stopping behind Rissa's chair. She rested her hands on her friend's shoulders, leaning sideways so could look at her face. "It'll be fun, I promise."

Giving the top of Rissa's arm a playful squeeze, Emily let go and walked to the end of the table, her arms crossed lightly in front of her chest. "Tonight, is the first night of the full moon, and unless things have really changed since I've been away, that means the guys will be out for their monthly howl. Sean and Mitch are going to enjoy every second since they'll be caught up in council bullshit soon afterward. Which means we girls are free. Come on. Say you're game."

Rissa shook her head. "If we head to Boston that means we'll have to stay overnight. Besides I don't have anything to wear."

Lily laughed. "Yes, you do. You cleaned out the mall when we went shopping. You have tons of stuff."

Rissa leaned back, molding her hands to either side of her belly bump. "That was before I became a pop queen."

Lily threw a piece of croissant at her. "That is Cecily Paris talking and you know it. You look wonderful. So, you've got a bump. So does half of Hollywood these days. Pretend you're a Kardashian and flaunt it."

Emily burst out laughing and with the way her eyes crinkled, the resemblance between her and Sean was obvious. "Cecily is a miserable bully in a too tight girdle. Believe me, she's the original panties in a wad prototype. I'm not surprised the old witch got in your head, but Sean told me Mitch put her in her place. I think a girl's night out is just the ticket to put a little strut back in your step before you start to waddle."

"Hey!" Rissa made a face, but her eyes twinkled. "That's not nice. You're home for what, five minutes and already conspiring with Lily to get me into trouble? I'm responsible for more than just myself you know."

Unconcerned, Emily waved her off before walking to the sideboard for a cup of coffee. "I hope by now you know I will never let anything bad happen to you. And based on what I've heard, Lily can more than handle herself and anything else that comes up. We're golden, and I won't take no for an answer. So what if we have to stay overnight? One thing I learned from being in exile is life is too short to not enjoy yourself when you can. It's time you provincial wolvettes lived a little."

Lily cracked up. "Wolvettes?"

With an answering grin, Emily's small white teeth sparkled along with her eyes. "Beats being called a bitch in heat!" Emily lifted her coffee cup, gesturing with it toward Rissa. "You're the one who wanted me to come home, so humor me. Okay?"

Rissa groaned, slumping forward onto her folded arms. "I can see it now. The two of you are going to tag team me until I give in, right?"

Emily grinned. "Pretty much. So, what do you say?"

Groaning, Rissa nodded. "I am in so much trouble."

CHAPTER
FOURTEEN

The moon was bright in the sky, the air frigid. A ring of pale winter grass circled each of the four bonfires, the heat from the tall flames melting the snow to reveal the green sleeping beneath the white frost. Each bonfire was lit in positions representing the four directions, and at the center was a single Yule log, burning with pinecones, holly, and cinnamon.

The Hunters gathered around the ritual fire to offer thanks to Mother Earth for the animals the clans would claim tonight during tonight's Yule Hunt. Young shifters hung about the perimeter, their excitement snapping in the air along with the crackling wood on the fires. For these boys, it would be their first hunt with the men.

"This is amazing." Lily whispered into the cold night, her breath puffing out in silvery clouds. Eagerness for the chase and delight in the season brought everyone to the forest clearing tonight, and more than a few people greeted her with a warm welcome.

"See, I told you people would come around." Sean said, wrapping his arm around her shoulders He kissed her temple, inhaling her scent. "You smell wonderful."

She smiled up at him. "Just soap and water. Nothing fancy tonight."

"Maybe I'll sneak back and leave all the hard work to the boys tonight." Anticipation rumbled deep in his throat.

She bumped him with her hip but peeked across her shoulder in a flirty sideways glance. "After."

"After," he repeated in low, sexy whisper. "I'm holding you to that."

Lily's hand shifted to her stomach where her lower belly jumped at the images Sean sent along their shared mind path. The fact they could communicate in such a veiled way still left her breathless. It was sexy and so intimate it felt a little wicked.

"Uncle Sean!" Stephanie ran across the snow, her face barely visible inside her pink snowsuit with its white faux fur trim.

"Hey there, peanut. Ready to watch the Parade of Flags?"

She nodded, the brim of her hood flopping into her eyes even more.

"I can hardly see you in there. Are you hiding on purpose?" he asked making her giggle as he swung her up onto his hip.

"Stephanie!" Mitch called, from the edge of the clearing with Rissa bringing up the rear.

"I'm over here, Mitch. With Uncle Sean and Lily!"

The two joined them, Rissa bringing up the rear, panting from a combination of exertion and worry.

"Stephie, don't you ever do that again! Running ahead of us in the dark is not safe!" she said trying to catch her breath.

"Sorry, Mommy. But I was okay. I have eyes like Uncle Sean that see best at night." She growled putting her hands up like claws.

Sean chuckled. "And an answer for everything just like your dad," he mumbled. "Okay, little wolf, do you promise to stay here with your mother and Lily while Mitch and I get the Hunters ready?"

She nodded her head.

"Good. That's my girl." He gave her a quick peck before handing her off to Rissa.

"Looks like we've got a great turnout," Mitch said scanning the crowd.

"It's cold but dry and the moon is full. Perfect conditions for the hunt."

Sean turned to Lily, giving her a solid kiss. "I won't be too late," he said with wink, and then motioned for Mitch to follow him to the center of the ring of fire.

It was time to begin.

The council of shifters gathered on either side of the ritual fire. Every clan was represented, each sending two elected men to hunt alongside the Alpha and his Hunters to help with the younger shifters.

Drums beat in a steady fashion. Spectators rounded the outer perimeter of the fire ring, forming circles within circles until everyone was in position. The drums changed tempo and began a rhythmic beat, slow and methodic. People stepped to the side in time with the metrical pulse, and soon each of the circles moved in unison around the fire, some going left, others going right.

People began to sway and chant, and the drums picked up their cadence, until suddenly they stopped. Trumpets blared, and Sean walked into the center with Mitch and Jack flanking him.

"Welcome, everyone, and a Blessed Yule to you all!"

The crowd erupted in cheers, and Rissa reached for Lily's hand and gave it a squeeze.

"Another year has come and gone, and we have much to be thankful for. As we end the old and prepare for the new, let us take a moment to bow our heads and remember those who are no longer with us, and give thanks for the ones that still remain. Make your offerings to the universe and to the Earth for the bounty they will bestow on us tonight."

In that moment, the forest grew silent, and a single hoot owl echoed in the distance. The trumpets sounded again, and Sean raised both arms. “I give you the Parade of Flags! Let the Yule Hunt begin!”

Each clan was represented. Each species of shifter residing in and around the Compound. Chosen hunters carried standards, each with clan crests and colorful depictions of their dual natures.

The flags were spiked into the ground circling the ritual flame like a Shifter United Nations, and after thundering applause, Sean called for quiet.

“Alpha Hunters take your positions.”

The Alpha Hunters splintered off, each group taking up their position by each of the bonfires.

“Elected Hunters, take your positions.”

The clan’s elected did the same, each group taking their adolescents with them as well.

Lily looked at Rissa. “What now?”

She flashed Lily a smirky smile. “The get naked.”

Lily laughed. “No way. In front of all these people and kids?”

“Lil, you’re playing by our rules now, and we don’t have the same protocols about nudity as the single-natured. How else do you expect them to phase? It would cost the council thousands of dollars to replace all the ruined clothes if they didn’t ask them to strip first.”

Lily guffawed. “Streaking for the sake of economics. You gotta love it.”

Sure enough, each one of the men and boys stripped down to nothing, piling their clothes next to the bonfires where their families could retrieve them.

A single trumpet blast signaled it was time. Sean stood in all his naked glory, the last one to phase. His eyes found Lily’s, and with his fingers to his lips is a loving solute, he then dropped to all fours and in a snap of ozone, bone and muscle stood a majestic black wolf. He bobbed his big head once, and then vaulted after the others, a howl of communion on his lips.

The crowd roared again, applause and cheers as the howls and screeches echoed through the forest.

"We really needed this," Rissa said. "There's nothing like the holidays to bring people back to what's important."

Lily looked around at people talking and laughing, others pouring libations into the fire as offerings for the night. She glanced back at Rissa, a smile spreading across her face. "You're right, and I'm sorry I didn't come for Christmas dinner."

Rissa squeezed Lily's hand. "I didn't mean to make you feel bad. We missed you, of course, but I understand needing to be alone. I'm just sorry you missed Sean's sister. She's been gone for a long time."

Lily nodded, noting the wistful melancholy in her friend's tone. "Jack told me how he and Mitch were working to bring Emily home as a surprise. It was part of the reason I chose to stay behind. I wanted you both to enjoy her visit to the fullest without having to worry about me. Sean was great about it, too. It was as if he read my mind."

"You're joking, right? You do realize he can read your mind."

Lily snorted. "I found out the night of the Blood Rites fiasco, and oh boy can he read my mind—and send me pornographic images and things I'd rather not tell you about. Still, the best part of it is I can read his, too."

"Ack! Don't go there, please!"

Lily laughed. "Don't worry, I won't."

The two walked toward the path leading to the manor, each holding Stephanie's hands and swinging her between them.

"Where's Emily? I thought she'd be here for sure."

Rissa shrugged. "I don't know. Emily is as unpredictable as they come. She got to know you a bit at our girls' night, but she's still as curious about you as you are about her."

She raised one eyebrow at Lily's snort of disbelief. "You can make all the noises you want, but I think I know you well enough to know how your mind works." Rissa winked at her friend. "Not to worry, though. Emily will show up again at some point. If not tonight, then at the Wolf Ball. She's as nosy as you are."

Lily half smirked, half laughed at Rissa and her insights, but didn't say a word. Sean mentioned other shifters had the gift of telepathy. She already knew Stephanie was both psychic as well as telepathic, and she had a strong suspicion Rissa was as well. Not that she minded. It was comforting to know she was no longer the only one.

The temperature had dropped, and away from the bonfires the night seemed suddenly empty and a little forbidding.

Lily stopped and looked at the sky, focusing her senses on a ripple that made her skin tingle—and not in a good way. "Something is wrong."

Rissa picked Stephie up and swung her onto her hip. 'What's the matter?"

"I don't know, but something is out there with the men that shouldn't be."

Rissa glanced from the path to the woods and listened. "I don't sense anything."

Lily shook her head. "It's there, trust me. Something is watching them. Planning. I need to warn Sean, so he can warn the others. There are too many people here for me to sense anything more. Take Stephanie back to the manor and then wait for me in the great room by the fireplace. I'll be quick."

Lily ignored Rissa's protests and took off running toward the bonfires. She passed Celia walking with a teenage boy. The two waved, but she didn't stop, just yelled over her shoulder that she would catch up with them later.

As she ran, she tried their shared mind path just to warn Sean of the possible threat, but all she sensed was the wind and the cold. Crap. He was deep in wolf form and couldn't hear her.

When she got to the bonfires there were still people milling around, but not enough to stop her from running into the woods along the same path the men had taken.

She crouched down, skirting brittle branches and winter bare shrubs looking for a place to settle and send her senses out fully.

Finding a spot near a moss covered boulder, she crouched down into the leaves. She focused, casting her senses out in a net. The trace was dual-natured, but it was whole and coherent. She exhaled a tense breath, relieved it wasn't another rabid shifter. But who then, and why was it tracking the Hunters? The feel was calculated with definite ill will. But why?

Could Edward or Delia be out there stalking Sean or even Jack, knowing Lily had a soft spot for the young hunter? Lily tracked the mental trace for Edward and found him in his quarters. She did the same for Delia and surprise, surprise; she was with Parr in his rooms, as well. Ha. The two were having a little post Yule hookup. Lily slammed the door on the trace, not wanting to eavesdrop on something that might turn her stomach.

Damn. She couldn't track the pulse without disrespecting Sean and the Hunters by having a female in the woods during their ritual hunt. No way. After everything that happened, she was not going there.

Lily made her way back to the bonfires, picking her way carefully through the leaves and shrubs. Her scent would be there, regardless, but the least she could do was try to keep it to a minimum. If she had to, she'd explain to Sean when he got back.

Rissa was pacing back and forth in front of the fireplace when Lily walked into the great room. Celia, Heather, and Gillian were waiting on the couch as well, and Shannon stood by the window, drink in hand.

"What did you do? Call a conclave? I told you I'd be right back." Lily said, put off at having a jury of her peers sitting in wait.

"That was an hour ago. I didn't know what you were up to. You make a statement that there was something out there in the woods, something that shouldn't be, and then you take off like a bat out of hell. What did you expect me to do? Sean is gone, Mitch and Jack, too. They are deep into the animal, so there is no contacting them. I called in the girls, instead."

"You could have shared that bit of shifter info before I went traipsing off into the woods, you know," Lily replied, brushing leaves and debris from her pants and jacket."

Rissa put both hands on her hips, her jaw dropping to her chest. "I tried, but no! You had to go running off full steam ahead."

Lily pursed her lips at Rissa's defiant stance, but she couldn't help the smile that twitched at the corner of her mouth. Rissa was such a mom.

"Okay, I know. I'm rash and impulsive. We know this, but I swear there was something out there that shouldn't have been. Whatever it was, it was tracking the men, and it wasn't a bear or a big cat. It was duel-natured, and it was completely coherent and calculating."

Shannon looked at Lily pointedly. "Who do you suspect?"

Lily lifted one shoulder and let it drop. She itched for a cigarette, but Rissa was pregnant, and smoking was a no-no around her, so she grabbed a piece of hard candy from the bowl at the center of the coffee table.

"I don't know." She shook her head, running a hand through her dark hair. "I followed the trace into the woods, but I couldn't get anything more on it, not even if it was male or female."

Lily glanced at Shannon and met her eyes. "I know it wasn't Delia." She shifted her gaze to Rissa. "It wasn't Edward either, to answer your unspoken question."

"Sit, you need a drink." Heather said, pouring Lily a glass of white wine.

"Maybe you're getting a little paranoid," Gillian added, but at the look on Rissa's face, she backpedaled adding, "...not that anyone could blame you."

Lily chuckled. "Ris, you don't have to glare daggers at your friends for speaking their minds. It's okay. I'd rather people be upfront with me. And you know what, Gillian has a point. I need to lighten up."

"Hear, hear," Celia interjected raising her glass. "Me too. I need to lighten up."

"Who was that handsome boy with you I saw when I went racing past. I'm assuming that's Kevin?" Lily asked.

A sheepish grin bloomed across Celia's face. "Yes. That's my son... and he is handsome, isn't he?" she nodded.

They all laughed.

"Lightening up is a good thing, especially since Kevin will be old enough for the Yule Hunt next Christmas. So, are you going to let him go, Cel?" Heather asked.

Celia blushed high color and laughed out loud. "If Sean will take him, then absolutely!"

Lily patted her new friend's knee. "If I'm still around to influence him one way or the other, I'll see that he does."

Shannon coughed. "Well, if I have anything to say about it, you will not only be a match for our Alpha, but anyone else who comes along."

Rissa raised her glass. "To influences."

Every glass touched. "You bet!"

CHAPTER FIFTEEN

Time flew by in the blink of an eye. Christmas and New Year's had come and gone, and though they were cheerful for the most part, a somber note lingered at the core of holiday events. Too many people had lost loved ones to the virus over the past months to ignore.

Decorations gracing the great hall had been taken down, along with the twenty foot Christmas tree that held the spot in front of the vaulted windows where a full orchestra now warmed up for the Wolf Moon Ball.

Streamers in bright, jewel tones replaced the holiday décor; the colors signifying each shifter assemblage represented at the Compound. Standards had been hung from the beamed rafters earlier that day, each one depicting a different group's crest, and the great hall looked regal.

Two hundred people milled as they had two months earlier at the Blood Rites ritual. Only this time, everyone knew more than just Lily's face and name. They knew her.

The ball was set on such a grand scale that dozens of round tables had been arranged along the room's perimeter to accommodate the crowd. Each table was decorated in red and gold, the primary colors of the Alpha Council of the Brethren. The gesture was a nod to Sean and his leadership, but also to Lily. On the whole, things looked encouraging, but then again, the night was young.

The room sparkled. From the blood red tablecloths to the long tapered candles and crystal vases filled with sprays of holly and winter flowers. Gold trimmed dinnerware gleamed in the candlelight, as did the crystal champagne and wine glasses at each place setting.

"The room is just beautiful!" Lily exclaimed as she and Sean walked in hand in hand through the arched entry, her eyes scanning the expanse and the stunning decorations.

"No. You're beautiful," Sean replied, his eyes glowing with pride and unspoken desire as they swept Lily's petite frame.

Lily squeezed his hand, and then lifted onto her tiptoes to touch her lips to his. "I'm glad you think so."

Mitch and Rissa stood toward the center of the dance floor. He chatted away with one of the hunters while Rissa scolded Stephie for turning cartwheels in her party dress.

"Would you look at how cute that kid is," Sean said with an expression as soft as butter.

Lily met Rissa's frustrated plea as Mitch caught Stephanie by the arm, swinging her up onto his hip. "I'm not so sure Rissa would agree with you at the moment."

"I bet that kid would have done headers off the Council table if we hadn't moved it earlier," he replied with a chuckle.

Lily laughed as well. "I don't think she'd stand much of a chance, not with Rissa fussing and Emily standing in as her second."

Emily's gaze was nothing short of appreciative when she lifted her champagne glass and winked, giving Lily a nod and a smile.

Sean's gaze tracked to where Emily stood, his earlier lightness dulled by a sudden sadness in his eyes.

"She looks just like you. Lucky girl," Lily said, trying to bring him out of this unexpected melancholy.

He shook his head, a wistful smile touching his lips. "She looks like our mother." Lifting his own glass, he waved Emily over.

With a smile, Emily nodded before leaning over to whisper something in Rissa's ear. An ear-to-ear grin spread across the pregnant woman's face, her eyes bright as she bobbed her head hopefully. Patting Rissa's arm, the young woman walked across the floor toward where Lily and Sean stood, her sapphire dress floating along her lithe body as she moved.

"You look beautiful, Em." Sean's eyes skimmed his sister's face.

"Thank you, Sean. And you clean up pretty good, yourself." Without a word she snuck one arm around her brother neck and kissed his cheek, resting her head for a moment against his jaw. "It's good to be home."

Her words were no more than a whisper, but Sean's jaw tightened, and he blinked away the wetness shining in his eyes.

"It's good to see you again, Em," Lily interjected, taking the pressure off Sean so he could compose himself without scrutiny.

Emily's broad smile met Lily's, and she took the woman's hand in hers. "Same. I feel like I've known you forever."

"Likewise," Lily replied.

They stood in awkward silence before Emily snagged two glasses of champagne from a passing waiter, handing one to Lily.

"So, this place never changes, though I see you finally decided to move that monstrosity," Emily said, indicating the immense council table with the edge of her glass.

The large table had been cleared, and its crested chairs moved to the wall, each resting under its matching banner.

"I still can't believe you moved that massive slab. I'd have sworn it was a permanent part of the décor based on its sheer size alone," Lily added.

Sean grinned. "Though I'd love to take all the credit, I did have some help. Shifters have been hefting that table for years, so we've got it down to a science."

Lily took a sip from her glass. "Wouldn't it be easier to leave it and use it as a high table or maybe decorate it?"

Sean glanced at Rissa watching them intently from the other side of the room. "Your new best friend over there would never let me hear the end of it. She claims it gets in the way of dancing."

"Dancing?" Lily coughed, nearly choking on the word.

"Yup, and that means you and me. I'm the Alpha of the Brethren, and we open the ball with the first dance."

Lily swallowed, not wanting to seem like a baby. "I thought that was just at weddings?"

"Nope," he shook his head, enjoying her discomfort a little too much. "The unflappable Lily Saburi, afraid of a little waltz around the dance floor. Who would have thought?"

"That's not fair, Sean. You never said a word about being the opening act," she huffed.

He laughed. "Why else would I be wearing a monkey suit? Have another glass of champagne and relax. It'll be fine."

"You haven't changed a bit, Sean. I love it!" Emily laughed.

He reached out and tweaked her nose. "Yes, I have, squirt. I'm older and I'm wiser, and I'm glad you're home."

Rissa was right when she compared the ball to Oscar night. Everyone was dressed to the nines. Sean was gorgeous in a classic black tux. The athletic cut tailored perfectly to highlight his broad shoulders and narrow waist. As always, he was clean-shaven, yet his standard military hairstyle was slightly longer on top, giving him a sexy mussed appearance.

Butterflies winged around Lily's stomach as he kissed her hand and excused himself to speak with a few of the guests. He was stunning, and he was all hers, even if it meant she had to do an impression of *Dancing with the Stars* to prove it. Emily, too, had gone to talk to a few people she knew, leaving Lily on her own.

"What's the matter, opening night jitters or leftover indigestion from Mitch forcing you to taste everything at the game dinner?" Jack Cochran asked as he came to stand beside Lily.

She shot him a look. "Does everyone know I'm the entertainment tonight?" she said, feeling herself blush at the lieutenant's put-on.

"Nah, I just wanted a chance to talk to you. Besides, Sean's never been able to do the first dance before. By law, it's got to be with his mate, or at least someone in the running. Be happy. It says a lot about your relationship. Speaking of which, how have you been holding up? I've missed hanging out."

"Pretty good, I guess, but I'd have thought you'd be tired of me by now."

He shrugged. "Not entirely, although I was getting pretty good at babysitting the alpha's lady, even if it isn't my dream job," he stopped and looked at her thoughtfully. "But then again, I've never met anyone so game for anything."

Lily's stomach churned at the word game. "Again, with that word. That dinner was an experience I never want to repeat. I know Sean wanted me to get up close and personal with everyone and everything, but that was pushing it."

Jack snorted, giving her a lopsided smirk. "That's not what I meant, and you know it, but come on, you didn't enjoy the Elk Parmesan? What about Mitch's Bear Fricassee?"

"Quit it, Jack." Lily said, smacking him on the shoulder. "You're going to make me lose my lunch, and velvet isn't exactly easy to clean!"

His eyes swept her face and her dark curls, his gaze appreciative as he trailed her cranberry colored gown and every curve, lingering on the deep v-cut of her off-the-shoulder bodice in a smooth once over.

"I guess I wouldn't want to do that, now would I?" he murmured.

"Ha! Nice try, but you can sell the smolder to someone else tonight. I'm taken, and you know it. You wolves are all the same. Horn-dogs at heart!"

He sniggered. "I know, but you can't blame a guy for trying." He paused, a genuine smile replacing his trademark smirk. "Don't be a stranger...okay?"

She gave his check a peck. "Not a chance."

"Not a chance at what?" Sean asked, stepping to her side as Jack walked away in route to a statuesque blonde by the bar.

"Nothing," Lily said, smiling up at him.

"Is he behaving himself, or do I need to remind him who's the boss?" Sean said with a smirk, and Lily knew he had seen Jack flirting with her.

"Jack certainly likes the ladies, huh?" she added, gesturing with her drink in the young wolf's direction. "But he's harmless enough. At least with me. All bark. If you know what I mean."

Sean followed her line of sight, a deep chuckle rumbling in his throat. "The blonde is one of Volkmann's nurses. If you believe the chatter around the Hunter's barracks, this one's got him wrapped around her finger."

"Really?" she replied, impressed anyone could tame the irreverent wolf.

Sean smirked. "Really." His gaze stayed on Jack, but his face sobered a bit.

"What?" Lily asked, not liking what she was reading from him.

He shifted his eyes back to Lily. "It's nothing. Remember I told you I sent some of my hunters to help out at the clinic?

She nodded. "And?"

"Well, he and a few of his bunkmates weren't too happy about being reassigned, but with Parr stirring animosity at every turn; I needed people on the inside to protect Volkmann's research. With the vaccine proving itself to be a success, the last thing we need is sabotage."

She glanced at Jack and then back at Sean. "Parr trying to discredit us is one thing, but he wouldn't stoop so low as to endanger everyone's lives? Would he?"

Sean sighed. "I certainly hope not."

From the corner of her eye, she caught Edward standing off to the left of the bar and staring at Jack with his eyes narrowed.

"What's the matter?" Sean asked, concerned.

She shook her head. "Nothing. But it looks like putting Jack in Volkmann's backyard was a smart move after all," she added, gesturing toward the man's dagger-eyed stare.

As if Parr knew he was being discussed, he turned his scowl on Lily, her skin prickling from the weight of his gaze. "He gives me the creeps," she muttered, making a face as she broke eye contact.

With a smile and a nod, Sean raised his hand giving Parr a little wave. "That's okay. If he wants to play political dodge ball, then bring it on."

"Sean—"

But before Lily could say another word, the conductor stepped in front of the orchestra and tapped his baton. Sean licked his lips, obviously changing focus. "That's our cue, love," he said, grinning at the look of panic on Lily's face.

As the overture to Gershwin's, *Our Love is here to Stay,* poured from the bandstand, Sean tucked her arm in his. Wide-eyed, she walked with him to the center of the floor, mumbling, "This is going to be a disaster," under her breath, but loud enough for him to hear.

He led her in a circle to the sound of the crowd's applause, showcasing his beautiful partner.

"I don't like this, Sean. I feel like a show dog." she protested through a forced smile.

Flashing a predatory grin, he slid one hand around her waist and pulled her close enough to kiss her cheek. Trust me," he murmured, and with his fingers splayed across her back, guided her around the floor.

Cheers echoed through the room as Sean twirled her around the floor, her gown swirling in a rush of velvet. Rissa's faced beamed, and Mitch shot her two thumbs up. The music swelled, and Lily relaxed into Sean's arms, letting the beautiful strains take her, when in a sudden disharmony of instruments, the music stopped.

Edward approached the podium, and all eyes followed as the man took center stage.

"What's the meaning of this, Edward? Explain yourself." The alpha demanded.

"Oh, it' not me who has to explain— it's her," he said with his finger pointed emphatically at Lily.

Sean took a step forward, his displeasure with Edward's effrontery seething beneath his surface calm. "Edward, this is neither the time nor the place. Any debate involving Lily has been adjourned until after the holidays. Look around, does it look like our festivities are over with?"

Edward sneered. "Yes, yes, the council is in recess. I know. But this is a matter for everyone, something each and every shifter should be made aware about the woman you've paraded for the past month. She is a murderer."

Sean inhaled, letting his breath out slowly. "Everyone knows Lily's the one who ended Jerard's misery. That's no secret, Edward. So, why are you rehashing this?" The room was quiet enough to hear a pin drop while everyone waited for Parr's next move.

The politician shook his head, his expression the perfect

affectation of both saddened and hard, but Lily could see the smug satisfaction lurking beneath his faux concern.

"This has nothing to do with your brother's unfortunate end, and everything to do with the vigilante you brought into our midst." Parr swung his hand out, gesturing for someone in the crowd to step forward.

An unkempt man burst onto the stage, his face red and blotchy, and his movements awkward. He pushed past Edward, nearly knocking him over. "That's right. She killed my boy in cold blood," he cried, pointing at Lily. "Murderer! You murdered my boy!"

The room erupted in shock, and Lily looked at Sean in just as much confusion. "I've never met this man before in my life," she responded, clearly taken aback.

The man was undeniably drunk as he stumbled across the stage, belching into the microphone. "You never met me, but you met my son in Central Park, didn'tcha? You shot him dead in the head, you murdering bitch! Just because he was a shifter."

The man collapsed in a flood of boozy tears, and Parr slid his hand around his trembling shoulders in a perfect show of compassion.

Lily's eyes flew open as the memory of that night flooded back. Every eye was on her, watching closely, including Sean. She shook her head, taking a step back.

"Your son was attacking a jogger! He had the poor woman pinned against an outcrop of rocks. She was trapped and screaming, so I shot him as he lunged for her throat. She ran before he reverted to human form. It was done in defense of an innocent."

Sean nodded once, putting his hand out in a show of solidarity. Lily clasped it, stepping to his side, but her eyes never left Parr.

Sean raised his other hand for silence. "Edward, this poor man is drunk. It's apparent he's chosen to drown his grief in a bottle, and while our hearts go out to him for his loss, he is not from our Compound. We know nothing about him, his situation, or his pack."

The alpha turned his attention to the man, keeping his tone even and calm. "Sir, can you tell us who you are and where you're from?"

The man belched again, causing Parr to jerk his face away, earning a few nervous chuckles from the crowd and a scowl from him. "This is no laughing matter, you cretins!" Parr hissed.

Sean held his hand up once more. "Please, sir, I ask you again. Who are you and where do you come from?"

Marcus stepped forward. "I know who he is, boss." Stunned, all eyes turned toward the burly computer-tech assigned to the Hunters.

"His name is Angus Flanders. He's from a pack near Indiantown, Florida. A swamp shifter," Marcus continued.

The room buzzed, and Lily glanced around at the frowns and stares, not sure if they were aimed at her or at Parr's unfortunate pawn.

"You're a long way from home, Mr. Flanders," Sean said, addressing the man directly.

He nodded, brushing his greasy hair back with his palm. "Yesssir. I am… but I need to set things to right. She killed my boy, and where I come from it's an eye for an eye. I want my due."

"And what is that, exactly?"

Parr opened his mouth to speak, but Sean interrupted him. "Let the man say his piece, Edward. That's why you brought him here, isn't it?"

Angus Flanders nodded, wiping spittle from the corner of his mouth before taking the microphone from Edward. "I want my due. That's all. My boy's dead by her hand, and his mama died of a broken heart because of it. That girl owes me for the loss of my loved ones. You give her to me, and we'll call it even."

The room exploded. Sean raised his hand for the third time, quieting the crowd to a hush.

"While I'm sorry for your loss, Mr. Flanders, Ms. Saburi is no more a vigilante than you or I. She acted in defense of another." Sean glanced at Marcus, and the young man nodded his beefy head, stepping forward.

"That's right," Marcus verified. "I hacked into the NYPD record archives when I compiled Lily's dossier. Defense of an innocent, definitely. She's telling the truth."

"The jogger filed a complaint with her local precinct later that day about being attacked by a wild dog in the park. The location and time all matched with the body the police found the next morning. The NYPD treated it as two separate incidents, but we know better."

Edward fixed the husky young hunter with a stare. "You don't know all the facts, young man. How can you when Leighton keeps you shackled to fatuous internet searches."

At the look on Marcus's face, Sean exploded. "Enough! You're responsible for bringing this drunkard into the heart of our holiday festivities. You interrupt the opening dance and cast aspersions once again on a woman who has done nothing but help us. For Chrissake, there are children in the room, man!" He paused for a calming breath. "I think you should leave, Edward, and take Mr. Flanders with you."

Parr shot Sean a withering look. "I'll leave, but only after we take a consensus vote. Your postponement of the inevitable ends the day after tomorrow, and I would remind everyone here that facts are facts. Our tradition and laws remain steadfast.

"This man lost his son, killed in cold blood by *her* hand. A human against a shifter. What say you, people? Do we accept a woman capable of such crimes into our world, or do we close ranks? Giving her your back in a public shunning will be sufficient for me. Do you agree, Alpha Council of the Brethren?"

Sean's lips pressed together in a grim line. He had no choice. If he disagreed, he would look altogether partisan and strengthen whatever argument Parr had waiting for him.

At that moment Lily knew she wasn't paranoid the night of the Yule Hunt and was sorry she thought better of telling Sean what she sensed. The man on the stage with Edward was the one stalking the woods that night. She was sure of it. This was all part of Parr's plan—the calculating malice she had sensed in the air.

"Sean..." Lily touched his arm, shaking her head gently. "You don't have to do this. Don't make this an issue over me. If I'm not wanted here, I'll go. I'll just disappear."

His gaze was soft but edged with resolute determination. "It's not about whether you're wanted or not, love. It's gone way beyond that. And if you left, I'd find you," he said, giving her hand a squeeze.

Letting go of her hand, he turned to face the crowd. "With a show of backs, who would turn on the woman who has vowed to help us? Hasn't there been enough sickness and death? Enough fear? Haven't we moved beyond rumor and innuendo? Moved beyond suspicion? Show yourselves and your choices, now."

Low murmurs grew steadily louder as arguments erupted in the crowd. Lily watched in dismay. The scene was complete déjà vu from the night the Blood Rites Ritual.

Mitch waved, letting Sean know he was taking Emily, Rissa, and Stephanie to safety in case the room exploded into chaos, but before they got to the door, Parr called for quiet and a consensus.

One by one, two hundred people picked sides and in the end, half had turned their backs on Sean and Lily. The lines were drawn.

Parr flashed his Cheshire cat smile. "In two days' time, our deliberations will resume. It's clear I am not alone in my interpretation of the law and what's best for the shifters." With a nod to Sean, he flourished a mock bow to Lily, mouthing the words, *until then*, before sweeping from the hall.

The ball was ruined. People either went home or gathered in small clusters, their whispers and furtive glances causing Sean's hunters to stand in protective formation around their alpha and Lily. Only the few friends Lily made over the past few weeks remained, arguing loudly with the naysayers.

With an aggravated sigh, Lily pulled the bobby pins from her hair. She shook out her curls, running her fingers through the dark mass until it fell softly to her shoulders. "Sean this has gone too far. I didn't sign up for this when I fell in love with you. I know it's supposed to be for better or worse, but not when the worse affects so many people's lives," Lily's eyes searched his, and then dropped to stare at the tips of her black velvet shoes.

Slipping his finger beneath her chin, he lifted her face so their eyes could meet. "Parr wants something. I haven't figured out what it is yet, but I will. I haven't given up hope on the intelligence and determination of the shifters I've come to know and love. I have to trust in that. They know what's right, and can usually smell bullshit miles away, but Parr's rhetoric is confusing the obvious. I can beat him at his own game, Lily. I have to bide my time and let diplomacy do its work, but I promise you, if forced I will restore the power of the Alpha and its absolute rule to protect you. You're my life, and nothing and no one will stop me from having you at my side."

Lily chewed on her bottom lip, words failing her.

He chuckled, even though his eyes were severe. "Whenever you start nibbling on your lip, it's never a good thing. Are you with me?"

Lily slipped her arms around his waist, crushing the soft crimson velvet of her gown against his chest. "I shouldn't have doubted you. Of course I'm with you."

"For better or for worse?"

She tightened her grip around his waist. "For better or for worse. Let justice be done, though the heavens fall."

"I like the sound of that. Make you even more the perfect storm. Beautiful. Intelligent. Dangerous... and Just. Parr won't know what hit him." Sean pressed a kiss to Lily's temple, and then gave the order for his hunter's to escort her back to the manor.

"I don't need a babysitter battalion, Sean. I've proved I can take care of myself." She cocked one hip. "Perfect storm. Remember?"

"Do it for me, then. I need to know you're safe under my roof. No one, not even Edward, would risk an attack there."

At the resolute look in his eyes, she gave him a reluctant nod and then left the great hall with a cadre of hunters. Parr had agreed to a two day truce before his next onslaught of accusations. A good leader prepares for all contingencies, and if nothing else, Sean Leighton was a good leader and he had work to do.

CHAPTER SIXTEEN

"Sit down, Lily! Your pacing is making me as nervous as a cat."

"I can't," she sighed, shoving her hands into her pockets. "They've been at it for days now, Rissa. Aren't you even the slightest bit concerned?" Lily exhaled sharply, itching for a cigarette.

The fire crackled alongside the soft swish of Lily's leather pants as she walked back and forth. Black leather jeans and a matching, formfitting jacket, zipped to just above her cleavage was her armor of choice. With what she faced at the Compound of shifters these days, she was leaving nothing to chance. She might look like a porcelain doll dressed in biker gear, but God help anyone who assumed she was easily broken, or worse, easily manipulated. If pushed, she would fight. She'd done it before, and she'd do it again. Hell, with her background and skills, half the shifters here still thought her a vigilante against their kind. Ironic, considering she turned out to be their salvation.

Rissa put down the half-done blanket and skein of baby blue yarn covering her growing belly. "Of course, I'm worried." She winced, adjusting herself on the couch, wedging a pillow behind her back for support. “What happens behind those doors affects me as much as it affects you. I have more to worry about than just myself,” she patted her belly.

“Pulling the baby card, Ris? Really?” Lily winked.

Rissa smirked back. “You bet your fine, leather clad ass. Sean can hold his own regardless of what Edward Parr throws at him. Besides, Mitch is with him, so need to relax.”

Lily’s eyes softened. Her life wasn’t the only one turned upside-down since she crashed into Sean Leighton, Alpha of the Brethren of shifters. She’d known about the supernatural since her best friend died at the hands of a rabid werewolf. Terry’s death brought her to Maine that fateful night almost three months ago. Hunting the beast that killed her friend was an obsession, until the creature nearly killed her, too. Sean saved her life, and now that bold, stubborn alpha *was* her life… and vice versa.

At least that’s what she hoped.

Her life, and the life she and Sean wanted together, were inescapably twined with the lives of those at the Compound of Shifters. His kind had become her kind. Or at least that how she viewed things. The question remained, would they let her stay? She was human. Though her senses told her the matter went much deeper than that.

The fireplace filled the comfortable room with warmth. Rissa’s idea to curl up in here was a nice try, but a hot tub and a trained masseuse wouldn’t ease Lily’s urge to pace.

Or punch someone.

She walked to the window and pushed the delicate curtains from the paned glass. Across the frozen landscape, smoke circled the manor’s four chimneys where Sean was deep in debate. February in Maine was brutal, but the waiting worse.

As she gazed at the building’s gabled peaks, it wasn’t hard to imagine Edward Parr’s smug grin. The debate over her humanity was his doing. A supernatural web to trap Sean, with Parr sitting dead center like a spider in wait.

One month. That's all it had been since Sean led her into the blood rites ritual that would have sealed her acceptance into the pack. Into his world. Until Edward Parr threw his curveball.

That night was one to remember. Hopes high and her heart full, she walked into the sumptuous room on Sean's arm. Everything was perfect. From the soaring ceiling and intricate tapestries to the intricate wooden doors at the entrance to the Great Hall, each carved with scenes from the shifters' long and complicated history.

That night the place held otherworldly awe, but tonight it was a war room. A place of division where a split council pitted member against member for the first time in a century.

From her place at the window Lily watched the smoke curl, silently wishing there was a message from Sean hidden in the wisps. *Black smoke...no. White smoke...yes.* Like when the Vatican chooses a new Pope.

With a sigh, she tucked the curtain back in its place. "It's been too long, Ris. Something's not right. I can feel it."

The pregnant woman raised an eyebrow, looking up from her knitting. "Is that a gut feeling, or are you eavesdropping again?"

Lily glanced over her shoulder, her lips curling to half a smile at her friend's suspicious face. "No, Miss Maternity Pants. Sean made me swear I wouldn't snoop."

"Well, can you blame him?" Chuckling, Rissa folded the blanket. Rolling the yarn and knitting needles carefully before stowing them in her sewing bag. "With your temper, and that nasty psychic habit of stomping around inside people's heads, he probably figured it was safer that way."

Hmmph.

"Lily, listen to me. Sean is the Alpha Council of the Brethren. The shifters sitting at that table may be politicians, but they aren't stupid.

They know which side their bread is buttered on, or at least I hope they do. What's more, Sean's hunters are with him. That's not to say the big wolf couldn't take care of things himself if it came down to it. Edward Parr is manipulative, but he's not foolish enough to start something he knows he can't win. It's not his style. Parr is far too smooth to put himself in a position where he'd have to fight, especially if it means a fair fight."

"Smooth? I think you mean cowardly." Lily snorted, folding her arms. "When it comes to Edward Parr, smooth just means slick, and not in a good way. Parr's already forced one deadlock, so you can't blame me for worrying what else he's spinning his way."

With an aggravated sigh, Lily moved to the hearth, hoping its warmth would chase away her worry and the hostility pummeling her mind from across the lawn. Sometimes being psychic sucked. Her stomach churned from the hot-tempered arguing rather than civilized debate happening behind those closed doors.

"Sean's lucky I promised to stay out of it, or I'd kick the doors in over there and take Parr out myself." A private grin touched her lips. "The man makes my knees go weak, and he knows it. Hottie bastard."

Rissa laughed. "Give it up, Lil. Hot or not, you love that gorgeous wolf."

"Am I that obvious?" She sighed. "I can't help it. He's got such big hands and a big—"

"Oh, no you don't!" Rissa lifted a hand cutting her off. "T.M.I., girly. You want to throw the pregnant woman into premature labor? I don't need a verbal play-by-play from your plentiful sex life, thank you very much. The walls in this house are thin enough."

Lily laughed. "What? Is Mitch falling down on the job keeping you *happy*? You shifters aren't the only ones who can pick up on heat."

"That's none of your business." Rissa's wide grin softened. "Seriously, though. I don't need psychic powers to see you two belong together. That's been apparent for a long time."

Lily snorted again. "Then why is your stupid council still arguing the point?" She flung an arm toward the window.

"You already know why." Rissa looked at her. "Delia Monroe wants to get back at Sean for nullifying their marriage contract. In her eyes, you robbed her of being alpha female. She's the reason Edward forced this debate. She persuaded him to make you the human scapegoat for everything: the virus, Sean choosing a human over one of his own, etc."

"That's just smoke and mirrors, Ris. Parr wants power and Delia's butthurt charge was an easy excuse to use. I'm the *cure* for HepZ, remember? My blood. So I don't understand why the council fell for Parr's bullshit call for this debate. The same virus that has already killed hundreds, still threatens your people. My blood is the only thing standing between shifters and certain death.

"For months, this nightmare of disease went hand-in-hand with fear over who would be next. Sean and his hunters did everything they could to keep panic at bay." Lily made a face. "Until Parr got involved."

A frown tugged at Rissa's lips. "You're preaching to the choir. Parr used me and my unborn child, as well. The moment news hit I had contracted the virus it was game on.

"We still don't know why it affects mostly males, yet people don't seem to care."

"Memory is short-lived when headlines matter more than the facts, Lily. The same is true in your world, as it is in mine."

Lily threw up a hand. "Can't they see Parr deliberately skewed the conversation away from what's important. It is crap cloaked in politics, Ris. Edward Parr has an agenda, and both Sean and Mitch know it." She looked at her friend. "My gut isn't wrong. Parr is dangerous."

"But to what end?" Rissa questioned. "I mean, what is Parr's game in this? Sean is the Alpha Council of the Brethren. No one has proved more loyal to our kind. Especially over the last few months."

Lily turned her back to the fire and raked a hand through her long, honey-colored hair. She liked her new look, despite Sean's grumblings. He preferred her natural dark chestnut, but with all the waiting around, she needed something to occupy her mind and her time. Rissa suggested a salon day, and Lily jumped at the chance. After all, blondes have more fun, right? Based on tonight, not so much.

Lily exhaled sharply. "Parr's an oiled snake winding his way through council members and the community. I know his game, Ris. He wants to pressure Sean into making me a full shifter."

"He can't. Everyone knows it's too risky."

Lily held her breath for a moment. "What if he convinces the council to force Sean's hand? To turn me against my will. Against medical advice. Doctors warned I need a year for the virus in my blood to go dormant before risking transformation."

She ran her fingers along the deep scars beneath her jugular. The physical wounds that nearly took her life had long since healed, but the memory of sharp canine's was still fresh in her mind. Jerard's sharp canines.

"I know Jerard was your husband, and Sean's brother, but Rissa, I saw what this virus did to him. I was in his head. He had no memory of the man he was, or the people he'd killed in his feral state."

Lily swallowed hard, before continuing. "When he attacked me on the cliffs, his brain was mush. Ruled by base bloodlust. I won't allow the virus I contracted from his bite to become active through a forced transformation. As for Sean, the fact he hunted his own brother for the good of the Compound should prove his loyalty beyond any doubt Parr could sow— but no— the council opted for long ass summit to decide something that's common sense."

A shadow of unguarded grief crossed Rissa's face, but it faded before Lily shut up. Rissa didn't utter a word. She sat with her eyes trained on her folded hands on her belly.

Guilt bit into Lily's chest. "I'm sorry, Ris. I didn't think."

The pregnant woman offered a tired smile, but its warmth didn't quite reach her eyes. "I'm exhausted, Lil. I'm going to turn in."

Lily cursed herself and her big mouth. "Don't leave because my brain-to-mouth filter is malfunctioning. I shouldn't have brought up Jerard. This waiting is making me crazy."

"You mean crazier than usual?" Rissa's soft chuckle was a balm against the underlying tension. "And you have *no* filter. Malfunctioning or otherwise." She held out her hand for help off the couch.

Lily grasped her friend's hand, and at the simple touch Rissa's emotions flooded her mind: Her sorrow at losing Jerard. Her guilt at finding happiness again with Mitch. Worry over the future for her four year-old daughter, Stephanie, and for the baby she now carried. Lily's grip tightened on Rissa's hand, and her heart clenched.

"You're a crazy-ass bitch, Lily Saburi, but I'll show you crazier if I catch you feeling sorry for me." Rissa got to her feet, her hand moving to rub the small of her back. "Still, it's your crazy that brought you to us, and one of the things I love most. You're strong. Even if you do need to grow a serious filter."

Rissa winked, motioning for Lily to bend for her sewing bag. "I *am* bone tired, though. Enormous as I am, it's a wonder I don't fall asleep where I stand." She patted her swollen belly. "As for the rest," she shrugged, "it is what it is. I have to accept there was nothing anyone could do to save Jerard. We weren't the happiest of couples, but we did care for each other in our own way. I have to let what happened go, but sometimes—" Her voice trailed off. "One day at a time, right?"

"Ris—"

Rissa wrinkled her nose, and the uncomplicated gesture said it loud and clear. Drop the subject. "Don't stay cooped up in here much longer." Ris waddled for the door with her knitting bag. "You look like you could use some rest yourself. Or at least some relief." She turned with a sly grin. "You might make use of those *toys* in your night table drawer."

Lily's mouth fell open. "Oh, my God! How could you possibly know that?"

"Thin walls, remember?"

"Ack! How can you expect me to relax now? Sean and I will definitely have to move." She glanced toward the window, again. "If we ever get the chance."

Rissa opened her arms for a hug, and Lily stepped in as tight as her friend's big belly allowed. "Once way or another, you'll both figure it out. Even if the answer takes a different path than the one you expect."

Lily watched as Ris closed the door behind her. A different path? Right now, their situation felt more like a maze with no way out. The whole thing sucked. Three months ago she had a normal life. Until everything changed. She had gained, and she had lost. She may have found the love of her life in Sean, but she had lost her best friend. And while she knew she wasn't responsible for what happened to Terry, she wasn't about to lose Rissa simply because she couldn't remember to keep her thoughts to herself.

What did Terry used to say? "Girl, you've got constipation of the brain and diarrhea of the mouth," Lily murmured into the quiet.

Yup. That just about covered it.

The living room was silent, except for the sound of crackling logs and the hum of her own racing thoughts. Glancing at the closed door, she frowned, angry with herself again. She was lucky Rissa was the forgiving type. Like Terry.

With a sigh, she walked toward the window again. Terry had always been there for her. Lily's throat tightened. No matter how much time passed, she would never quite get over her death. Terry was the only one Lily could count on to help keep her eye on what mattered most. She was a touchstone. The one to make her to see the truth about herself, whether she wanted to or not.

Lily smiled to herself. Terry would have liked Rissa. They were different personalities, but somehow, they both brought out the best in her. "Maybe I should try the love is patient, love is kind, thing, too," she murmured, half-expecting Terry's snort of laughter at the idea. Yeah right. That from the poster girl for shoot first and ask questions later.

Even as a ghost, Terry had been there for her. Conquering death just long enough to force Lily to face her fears, and ultimately her love for Sean. To put aside her guns and her vigilante need for revenge and learn to forgive. Starting with herself.

Lily blinked back the wetness pricking at her eyes. She hadn't cried in a long time, and she wasn't about to now. Only happy tears. That was the last thing Terry said before moving on into the light.

Move on.

Lily lit a cigarette and took a drag. Blowing smoke through her nose, she flicked the ashes into the fireplace as she looked through the window across the frozen landscape again. "Would she and Sean be able to move on or would Parr derail that, too?"

CHAPTER
SEVENTEEN

Lily rolled onto her side. She cracked one eye open, staring blankly at the window across from her bed. It was well past three a.m. and still no sign the council had come to any kind of a decision.

With a sigh, she shoved a pillow beneath her down comforter, and wedged it between her knees to get comfortable. Not that it helped. Sleep wasn't happening tonight, no matter what she did.

Why had she agreed to let Sean handle this alone? She kicked at the duvet, sending the down blanket puffing out around her. Lily promised she wouldn't interfere, and as much as she hated to admit it, Sean hadn't given her much choice.

Stubborn was certainly one way to describe Sean Leighton, Alpha Council of the Brethren. As was Mitch Paris, his second-in-command, and the rest of their team. A disgusted sigh left Lily's mouth. If it were up to her, she would give Edward Parr two shots behind the ear without batting an eye or ruining her mascara.

As tempting as that idea was, she had to keep her cool. For whatever reason, Sean was trying his hardest to remain politically correct. There was something hidden behind this or why else would Parr risk so much? On that point, she couldn't argue with Sean. The status of her humanity wasn't a strong enough case to merit all this uproar.

She stretched her legs, and her feet brushed the cold edge of the sheets. The Alpha's bed was large and comfortable, but without Sean to fill the emptiness, it was nothing more than a vast sea of lonely blankets. There was no soft snoring or wide, warm back to cuddle against. Not when the large wolf that should have occupied the other side of the bed was still out playing with pack politics run amok.

According to tradition, the Alpha's word was law, but this situation was different. It required finesse. She snorted to herself. *Finesse*. That was the word of the day. Sean held the right of Alpha in his own wolf pack, but the Compound wasn't just comprised of wolves. Many different species of shifter had joined Sean in an unprecedented experiment to unite their world. They elected him Alpha of the Brethren to stand for all shifters, and then gifted him with abilities from each species.

If the Compound failed, the shifters would splinter into traditional groups, and steps taken toward the dream of one cohesive Shifter State would be lost forever. Even before the viral epidemic, Sean had been on the verge of uniting the normally volatile groups, but facing near extinction brought the factions together and they rallied. At least that had been the case until Edward Parr had had his fifteen minutes of fame.

She frowned. Parr's political spin not only upset her acceptance into the pack, but it also succeeded in driving a wedge between her and Sean. As if a relationship between a human and a shifter wasn't hard enough.

She sighed.

So what if she was human? She had shifter blood in her veins, courtesy of Jerard's rabid attack. Lucky for her, she was asymptomatic. Even luckier, her antibodies were the key to curing this mystery illness.

Enough was enough. Sean had closed the door on their shared mind link, but as the Alpha, he had no other choice. He needed a clear head, especially since Parr would use any excuse to discredit him.

Chewing on her lower lip, she sent her senses out. shifters were tricky to read, but all she needed was one person with their guard down and she could be the proverbial fly on the wall.

It only took a moment to sift through the barrage of thought from across the lawn. Bingo! She found an opening and slid easily into the unsuspecting mind. Her vision was hazy, as she had no clue as to whose eyes she borrowed, but she sensed an underlying fear radiating from the host mind. Whoever this was, they'd rather be anywhere but there.

Sean's voice rang above the din, bringing all eyes to him. One leg crossed over the other, his hands rested casually on either arm of the Alpha's chair. His relaxed pose was a complete contradiction to the tension echoing through the room, and Lily guessed it took major effort on his part to appear that composed.

"Let's be reasonable. Every blood test, every lab report generated over the past month, states unequivocally that Lily's blood needs to stay constant. Would you risk everyone's life for an archaic law? Would you risk your own?" Sean's gaze traveled across the room, fixing Parr and his allies with an icy stare. "This virus affects everyone. Or did you think status would spare you?"

Parr stepped forward, his robes swirling for effect. Lily snorted from her vantage point. Poser! Couldn't they see how smarmy he was despite his theatrics?

"Once again our illustrious Alpha proves his contempt. What more does this council need? Leighton won't even entertain the idea of turning his human lover, simply because *she* would rather not. Well, I ask you. When did we as a species start putting the wants of humans above ourselves?" Parr raised a hand against the murmurings.

"It is one thing for this human girl to be kept in her natural state while her blood is of use. On that point, I do not argue. What I find objectionable is our Alpha's unwillingness to agree to an acceptable timeframe for her to be turned. She has seen too much. Knows too much. I tell you this. If we allow a few threads of law to unravel, so then follows the entire fabric of our supernatural society."

Oh, he was good...the son of a bitch.

Sean shook his head. Despite of his calm exterior, his exhaustion was clear, and Lily's heart broke for him. He'd been fighting windmills and getting nowhere.

"She has a name, Edward. It's LILY. And your disrespect sets my teeth on edge every time you refer to her as *the human*. Everyone here knows her biological status, and it's immaterial considering what she but has done for us. We have undeniable proof our survival depends on Lily's blood. There is no alternative cure. You want to talk timeframes? The doctor's at Leighton Research have already given us one, and they were *very* specific. One year. That is the time required for the vaccine results to be conclusive."

"Rubbish."

Sean's jaw tightened. "So you're a doctor, now? You're an excellent orator, Edward, but it's obvious your listening skills need work. Not more than eight hours ago, Dr. Ernst Volkmann himself said we need a year to be sure. Or is the word of our head geneticist not enough?"

With a smug look, Parr spread his hands. He was in his element, with all eyes, including Lily's, focused on him. His self-righteous expression said it all.

"What our Alpha doesn't know is I've since spoken with the good doctor. While it's true he would *prefer* to have the girl's blood intact for a year, Dr. Volkmann admitted by the next full moon, enough time will have elapsed that a forced transformation would most likely be without incident." He nodded. "That said, I've more than proven my argument. You, Leighton, have proven nothing except your desire to keep your human pet."

Pet?

Hell, no.

Throwing back her covers, Lily got out of bed, ignoring the shiver jolting through her exposed flesh from the chilled air.

"Well, fuck you very much!" Fists clenched, she needed to calm her anger, or she'd lose her hijacked mind link.

Sean stood slowly. His face grim. Even blocking her from their shared mind path, Lily felt every muscle in his body tense, including the one in his jaw as he bit back on his anger.

"Edward, everyone here knows what you're capable of, even if they won't admit it. I don't have to venture much of a guess as to what you said, or more likely did, to get Dr. Volkmann to give you what you wanted."

Even without the benefit of her psychic sense, Lily knew exactly how Parr had coerced, if not out and out threatened, Dr. Volkmann. The little geneticist may have been a heavy weight in their medical world, but against Parr and his henchmen, he didn't stand a chance.

Parr opened his mouth to argue, but Sean held up his hand. In the dual timbre of the Alpha, his voice layered power on power, never faltering as he stared down Edward's glare. "Enough! This discussion is over." The edict was clear. Lily was not to be touched.

Parr's entire diatribe on tradition and law had just backfired. The alpha had ruled, and according to their laws and the precedent Parr spent days preaching, the matter was now closed. Or was it? Lily could see the backpedaling scheme hatching behind Parr's narrowed eyes.

"This human has our Alpha wrapped around her finger, even as her legs are wrapped around his back. Our laws vary for no one. I have stated plainly she must be changed or cast out, but under these extenuating circumstances, and considering the Alpha's unwillingness to rescind his verdict, there is only one choice left. The human must be imprisoned until she is no longer of use."

Chaos exploded in the council room, with the majority demanding Lily stay, in essence, under house arrest, but also demanding Sean distance himself from her in exchange for a temporary truce. The Alpha's ruling may have been absolute, but the decision had come at a price. In their eyes, shunning her was the only way Sean could prove he had the Compound's best interests at heart, and not his own.

Lily hurled a delicate porcelain egg against the wall like a personal grenade. Severing her hijacked mind link, she picked up a pair of sweatpants from the end of the bed but threw them down in disgust. Did they honestly think she was the type of woman who'd sit complacent?

When pigs fly.

Stalking across the room, she picked up her leather jeans from one of the chairs facing the fireplace and pulled them on with a grimace. She threw on a plunging, black V-neck sweater and her leather jacket, stuffing her feet into her biker boots, mumbling to herself. From the side table, she grabbed her black wool scarf and her gloves and was out like a shot, slamming the door behind her.

Hell hath no fury? Bullshit! Forget scorned and try threatened and pissed off. They hadn't seen anything yet.

Lily looked like something out of Hell's Angels as she stalked across the frozen snow toward the great hall. Without stopping, she kicked open the double doors. Her gaze quickly swept the room. In one fluid motion, she grabbed a ritual lance from the sidewall and sent the lethal steel racing toward Edward Parr's head.

Fear flashed across the man's face, and he jerked sideways, barely avoiding the razor sharp edge.

The lance tore his sleeve, pinning the shredded material to the center of the chairback behind him. The spear pierced the wood to its core, impaling the chair's painted crest. Parr's crest.

Visibly paled, the man grabbed the hilt, but the lance wouldn't budge. Throwing his hands off in disgust, he narrowed his eyes and took a step toward Lily. Sean growled, moving from the Alpha's chair closer to where she stood, but Lily raised a staying hand. This was her fight.

Parr stopped, his eyes darting around. She saw his Machiavellian mind weighing the pros and cons of harming her in plain sight. Rearranging his robes, he shot her a slow, arrogant smile. "Hot-blooded. I'll have to remember that." His eyes swept her body.

"In your dreams, old man. The only thing you need to remember is watch your back." Lily's gaze swept the room next. "I have to thank you for including me in your deliberations. It's such a comfort knowing my well-being is so high on your list of priorities."

"How dare you spy on these proceedings!" Robert Stanton, delegate from the Avian collective, yelled as he moved to stand beside Edward.

"Gimme a break," Lily shot back, cutting the man off midsentence. "Spare me the self-righteous outrage, Robert. While you and the rest of your cronies were busy deciding my fate, you forgot I have my own specialized set of skills. Did you honestly expect me to accept my fate and come quietly?" Lily's tone was matter of fact, but her gaze was deadly.

Parr's face was a mask of indifference. "Don't look so put out, my dear. We mean you no harm. Evolution is a painful business," he replied with a silken voice.

Staring him down, Lily crossed her arms at her chest. "We both know that's bullshit, you pompous gasbag. You're not looking for these people to advance. You're looking to revert them centuries. That doesn't qualify as evolution. Or are you really as deluded as you sound?"

Parr's face hardened. "Our kind need a sharp reminder of the rich and powerful culture we once had. We are different from humans. Superior in every way. Eventually, you'll understand, but don't be dismayed. shifters have always had a weakness for humans. Titillating creatures that you are." His eyes drifted over Lily's lush curves.

Lily kept her face impassive.

"The council has taken our Alpha from you for the time being, but I'm sure another, more *satisfying* arrangement can be made." He hissed out the *'s'* in satisfying, his lewd tone making Lily's skin crawl. His tongue darted snake-like, wetting his thin lips, and he sent a mental image of her, naked and submissive, kneeling before him along the shifters common mind path.

Across the room, a menacing growl pierced the air as a heavy oak chair hurtled past, splintering inches from where Parr stood. Sean's gaze seethed. His eyes shifted from blue to yellow, as his body crouched, seconds from phasing.

Deadlocked, Lily looked from one man to the other. "He's baiting you, Sean." This was exactly the reaction Parr wanted, and Sean was playing right into his hand. "Don't give him what he wants. He's no threat to me. You know it, and he knows it."

Sean's muscles rippled and constricted beneath his skin. If he phased and attacked, everything they hoped to accomplish would be lost. Lily reached out to him with her mind. In his anger, he let his mental wall blocking her crumble, and Lily saw the effort it took for him not to kill Parr right then and there. His protective fury raged red and black, and her heart squeezed.

Don't do this, Sean. Can't you see it's a trap? Her voice was featherlight as it floated across his churning mind.

His eyes flashed to hers, and his mind calmed. She sent all her love along their shared mind link, leaving the channel open for every telepath in the room to see and feel the depth of their commitment.

Sean straightened. His eyes were still narrowed and furious, but at least they were his normal blue.

Mitch tossed Lily another lance. She caught it with one hand, sliding her legs shoulder width apart. Council members grumbled nervously where they stood, uneasy at having her armed and close. Especially after the show of solidarity from the Alpha's hunters.

Lily swung the lance with skill, the sound of the blade a sharp whoosh as it cut the air. Her gaze swept the room. Sean's lips curved upward. The words, *that's my girl*, feathering across her mind. She blew him a mental kiss.

A few of Parr's men took a step forward, but Lily stood her ground, sliding into a defensive stance with the lance held at an angle across her body.

Sean and Mitch moved to flank her on either side. "Not everyone's drinking the Kool-Aid, Lily. Problem is, they're too chicken-shit to stand up to Parr," Mitch offered. "But the rest of us have got your back."

Lily pushed the spear outward, its blade pointed right at Parr. "I know that Mitch, and I won't forget it."

Taking a step forward, Lily paused, smiling coldly before sweeping the blade within inches of Parr's men in a deft downward strike. They jumped back as she caught the shaft with a practiced hand, banging its blunt end to the floor. "I'm out gentlemen, and if you're smart, you won't try to stop me."

Fixing Parr with a hard stare, she continued. "And just in case your pack blowhard decides to twist my words, I want to set the record straight. I intend to do whatever I can to help your doctors fight this virus. I will make myself available to them should they need me, but I will do so from a distance. By turning your back on a leader whose loyalty is plain in everything he does, you've done nothing but prove to me how faithless you are."

"Lily—"

She ignored Sean. Not because she didn't care what he thought or felt, but because if she looked at him, she'd never have the strength to do what needed to be done.

Clearing her mind of all doubt, she turned a hard gaze to all. "If one man can sow division and fear enough to make you to turn on Sean, and then on each other, then you don't deserve as good as you've got. I have no intention of allowing myself to be turned. Ever. And in case anyone doubts my resolve—" Lily tilted the blade toward her hand. Without flinching, she ran her thumb over its sharp edge, her eyes never leaving theirs as blood trickled down her wrist. "I think you get the point."

Lily stormed off feeling dirty. Sean had his hands full with only a select few to help. She was truly on her own. Was her decision reckless? No. She had made her point. Now all she could do was hope common sense would prevail, and things would get back to normal—well, as normal as they could be in a community of supernaturals.

Yesterday, she had been certain it would work out. Now, not so much. Nevertheless, it no longer mattered. Suddenly Rissa's words hit her hard. *Once way or the other, you'll figure it out. Even if the answer takes a different path than the one you expect.*

She had drawn her line in the sand. She loved Sean, and he loved her, but she didn't have a choice. She refused to stay under house arrest or stay and split Sean's focus. There was something underlying this political ploy, and he needed his full concentration on the matter. The council may have separated them, but now it was on *her* terms. Sean understood that. Or at least she hoped he did. Either way, she was headed home to New York. Problem was, it no longer felt like home. Not without Sean.

CHAPTER EIGHTEEN

Lily sat up. Bleary eyed, she peered around the darkened room. Outside, the sun crept over the horizon cutting a pink and gold ribbon across the dark landscape. Her mind was silent, except for a dull ache behind her eyes from lack of sleep, and a throbbing hand where she sliced her thumb.

Running her fingers over the white gauze, she thought of how bruised and bandaged she was when Sean had first brought her here after Jerard's attack. Twelve short weeks ago.

Her bags were packed and stowed in the corner near the door. Not that she had much, but whatever she had, it was coming with her, except for the red velvet gown she wore the night of the Wolf Moon Ball. Had it only been weeks since Sean twirled her around the dance floor?

She exhaled. Her new world had seemed so full of hope and magic. That is until Edward Parr ruined it for them. She had reason to hate him before, but after tonight, the gloves were off.

The council dispersed after her announcement. To be honest, she was surprised no one tried to keep her from leaving the room. Still,

Sean hadn't returned yet, and she was grateful. If he asked her to change her mind about leaving, she didn't stand a chance.

Stretching, she tensed and released every muscle in her body. Opening her senses to their shared mind link, she felt for Sean, but only sensed the wind. He was in animal form. A soft whoosh always replaced the usual onslaught of thought whenever Sean phased, and he always took to the woods whenever he needed focus.

A slight tapping against the window broke the silence, and Lily turned toward the darkened glass. An owl perched on the sill. Its large eyes peering at her from the purple gloom.

Sean.

She shivered getting out of bed and padded across the cold floor to open the window. A blast of icy air gusted in, and she crossed her arms in front of her chest in a feeble attempt to ward off the chill.

"Sean, what are you doing? Are you crazy?"

The owl hooted low, spreading its wings. The majestic bird launched itself from the sill and did a single, lazy pass around the ceiling before setting on the bed. In a snap of electricity, the bird was gone, replaced by a very naked shifter with a teasing grin on his face.

"I thought you'd be happy to see me, especially now that you've calmed down," Sean replied, stretching his full six foot, three inch frame out on the bed.

Still standing with her arms folded, Lily smirked. "Aren't we a little old to be playing cat and mouse? Sneaking into my room like a horny teenager isn't exactly your style."

Turning, she closed the window, and then grabbed a throw blanket from the chair in the corner. "Trying to seduce me won't do any good. I'm still leaving in the morning," she added, wrapping the blanket around her shoulders, but the battle was lost before it even begun.

"You know—" He cocked his head with a suggestive smile spreading on his lips. "I can do a better job of warming you up than that blanket ever will. And in case you didn't notice, it's already morning."

"Well then, you can morph into a sparrow or some other harmless day bird and fly out the way you came, wolf boy. I guarantee the council had no clue what they got themselves into when they gave you the power to shift into any form."

"They knew exactly what they were doing."

Hmmph. "Like they know what they're doing now?"

"Different times, different circumstances. Besides, I'm still in charge, remember?"

"Sean—"

"Ssh. I am the Alpha Council, Lily. No one is going to question me about you. Trust me."

"But—"

"Lily," he said, pushing himself up and off the bed. "I'm not going to let you walk out of my life. You're my mate." He stood in all his naked glory, purposefully not manifesting clothes when he phased back to human form.

Lily couldn't help it. She licked her lips. He walked toward her, lean muscled, and as predatory and graceful as ever. Her heart skipped a beat.

"I did a lot of thinking out in the woods tonight. I'm done with trying to bend just to be politically correct. If Parr wants things the way they used to be, then so be it. Whether he likes it or not, I'm the Alpha. My will must be obeyed, or otherwise challenged. So if it's a challenge he wants, then bring it. Now, the only bending I plan on doing is bending you over until that gorgeous ass of yours is in the air."

With one long stride, he was toe-to-toe with her. Taking Lily's chin in his hand, he raised her face to his and kissed her. Running his tongue along the edge of her bottom lip, he whispered. "Besides, why should I resist what's mine for the taking?" He smirked. "That's right. Old school shifter. MINE."

"But—" Lily shivered, but not from the cold. Sean's hands dropped to her waist. In one swift motion, he separated her from her blanket and nightgown, and left her standing in front of him covered in nothing but gooseflesh. Pulling her to him, he pressed his body against hers, and his heat and desire flooded her, chasing away the cold along with any lingering reluctance.

His hands skimmed her waist, cupping each breast, grazing his thumbs across her nipples. They hardened under his touch. Stepping back, he lifted her, and Lily's legs wrapped themselves around his back. With a growl, he had her back against the cold glass, his cock hard enough to cut diamonds as he entered her with one thrust.

The window rattled in its pane, threatening to splinter as he impaled her over and over. Rough and untamed, Sean ravaged her body, his mouth sucking and biting, reveling in the taste of her like a man starved. His fingers bit into the soft flesh of her hips. The glass cracked in a long, thin sliver running the length of the pane, jerking his attention away from her for a moment. Without missing a beat, he spun them around toward the bed.

Lily's feet knocked over the lamp on the nightstand, sending books and an empty teacup crashing to the floor, but neither of them cared. Throwing the rest of the covers back, he lowered her to the edge of the bed. Holding her ankles locked together, he drove into her grinding her down, his hips relentless. Lily screamed as she climaxed, but Sean just grunted, flipping her onto her stomach. Pulling her back by her hips, he drove into her from behind, his inner wolf snarling for him to mark her.

Baring his teeth, his lips pulled back over his canines as they elongated both top and bottom. With a possessive howl, he bit down on her shoulder. Lily's back arched in pain and pleasure at the feel of his teeth on her flesh. Her inner walls convulsed, squeezing against Sean's cock as she came over and over, her fingers between her own legs, working herself even further into a frenzy. Sean's hips reared back, thrusting hard and fast, his balls high and hard. Throwing his head back, he yelled. He was primal, burying his cock deep within her as he came, his hands locking her hips to his.

He held her against him as the last spasms rocked his body. Then together they slumped forward on the bed. Four tiny rivulets of blood trickled from the four puncture marks on her shoulder. Pushing himself up on his forearms, he leaned his head down and licked them clean, healing them with his saliva.

At the raspy feel of his tongue, Lily stiffened. "Sean? What did you do? Please tell me you didn't just turn me! You know how I feel about the whole against my will thing."

Sean chuckled, giving her shoulder another lick. "It didn't seem as if things were against your will a minute ago— but no, I didn't turn you. I marked you. There's a difference."

Still buried deep inside her, he slowly rasped his tongue across the wounds once more. Her breath hitched as heat flooded her body making her lower belly clench in another aftershock of her climax.

"*Jeez,* will you stop with the tongue? I need to think!" She jammed her elbow into the middle of his chest, but all she got was quick jolt to her funny bone, and his lips curving into a smile against the nape of her neck. "What do you mean you marked me?"

Rolling her over so she could face him, he answered, running his hand over the curve of her hip. "You're leaving in a matter of hours, Lily. Did you honestly think I would let you go without marking you as mine? I said it before, and I meant it. You're MINE. To your mind it sounds archaic, making me something of a Neanderthal, but it's necessary." Leaning down, he nipped her bottom lip. "Especially since you're so stubborn and single-minded."

She pulled back, shaking her head. "Necessary? For whom?" she asked a little defensive, and to be honest, shocked he was actually letting her leave for New York.

"Necessary for *you*, that's who," he replied. "I have my hands full with uncovering Parr's true intentions. What he forced tonight is tantamount to house arrest, and I won't have it. I love you, Lily. You were right. Leaving here is the only way."

"Sean—"

He shook his head. "You're leaving here. You're not leaving *me*, right?"

"Of course not!"

"Well? It's the perfect strategy to let Parr think he has the upper hand while we both work to expose the truth."

"Team Wolf Bait." She smirked. "I like it."

"Cool your jets, killer."

Lily angled her head. "Is this why you marked me? For some weird shifter team-colors thing?"

"Interesting idea, but no. You're going back to Manhattan with a hell of a lot more knowledge about the supernatural than you had before you left. You're my mate. Whether you're here with me, or anywhere else. I couldn't let you go without giving you even the slightest protection. Marking you lets any shifter that comes within five feet of you know you're under my guard. Trace amount or not, you have shifter blood in your veins. When the moon is at its fullest, your blood will call to any male in your vicinity. Your scent will draw them. They won't be able to help themselves—" He hesitated, meeting Lily's eyes. "And regrettably, neither will you."

Pushing herself up, Lily sat on the bed with one knee tucked under. "Yeah right, nice tap dance. Now tell me the real reason why you bit me." When Sean didn't say a word, her brows knotted. "Wait. Are you saying I've become a lunar-driven nymphomaniac who sniffs around at the full moon after anything with a pulse and a penis? A monthly wolf-magnet, bitch in heat?"

Grinning, Sean propped himself up on one elbow. “Hey, some women would give their eyeteeth to be that irresistible.”

“Eyeteeth? Yeah, well, I prefer mine blunt. Or is that part of the package, too?” She exhaled, eyeing him. “Don't tell me I grow incisors the length of my pinky as soon as the moon crests.”

He laughed out loud at that. “Of course not! When we're together, my mark will make things very interesting for us. Apart, not so much. Without my mark, males would absolutely come sniffing around, or worse, but you won't have to worry about that. My mark mutes your scent, and says I've claimed you. You'll be as safe as kittens.”

“And when were you going to tell me about this character enhancement? Is there anything else I've inherited from Jerard's bite, or are you planning to surprise me again? What about a sudden urge to bay at the moon or an uncontrollable craving for dog chow?”

He rolled his eyes. “No self-respecting wolf shifter would be caught dead eating dog chow or anything else Purina makes, but I need to tell you, Cochran will be going with you to New York. My orders.”

“You're sending Jack with me.” Her brows knotted again. “What's the deal, Sean? And don't you dare lie to me. Is Jack going with me as a pack liaison for when I need to see Dr. Volkmann, or is he my new shadow?”

“Both.”

Lily stiffened, pulling away. Getting up, she took the top sheet with her, wrapping it around her body like a protective cover. “Like I said to your idiot council, don't you know me at all?”

“Lily—”

“Are you out of your mind, Sean? A babysitter? Haven't we been through this before? Because I'm getting a dizzying sense of déjà vu.”

Sean sat up, running a hand through his hair in frustration. “Why do you always have to go to extremes? Jack is not a babysitter. This thing with Parr is not going away. You know that. It goes way deeper than what we've seen on the surface, and my hands are tied until I find out what's behind his machinations. Why else would I agree to your leaving?"

He exhaled hard. "For Christ's sake, Lily, there are shifters out there who want to harm you! Edward's political maneuvering would be easier if you were out of the equation. Though, for the life of me, I can't fathom why." He nodded, as though convincing himself. "I'll get to the bottom of it soon enough. Like I said, you leaving is the perfect strategy. If Parr thinks you've thumbed your nose at *me*, then he'll leave you alone and hopefully drop his guard. Jack Cochran is going with you in case I'm wrong. In the meantime, cooperate for once in your life. I wouldn't put it past Parr to arrange a little accident for you."

Lily threw a hand up. "So what else is new? I think I've more than proven I can take care of myself. Christ, Sean, with all the supernaturals I've killed, and that includes a few vampires, half the Compound still thinks I'm a vigilante." She turned to eye him. "Did Jack volunteer for this mission, or is this another one of your mandates? The guy has no idea what he's getting himself into. I work cold case files, constantly. Do you know how hard it is for a psychic to gain credibility with the police? They trust me, and I've built a business on that trust."

She frowned. "That's if I still have a business left. I've been gone so long. Besides, my apartment has a strict no-pets-rule," she replied petulantly, plopping down on the bed next to Sean. "This is completely unnecessary, and utterly unfair."

Tilting his head to one side, Sean looked at her with serious eyes. "Which part? My marking you, or sending Jack to watch out for you?"

Lily pursed her lips, a sarcastic retort primed and ready, but seeing his expression, she realized the truth behind his question. She met his eyes before running her fingers along his cheek. "I wish it was you coming with me, instead of Jack."

"Me too. But it's not forever. Only until I figure out what's underneath Parr's bluster. Then it's you and me. Together."

She cocked her head. "Is that a promise, or do I have to bit you back?"

Sean chuckled, pulling her into his arms. "Difficult, dangerous, and utterly unreasonable. And people wonder why I love you."

Neither said a word as Sean carried Lily's bags downstairs to the front door. With the current council climate, Sean had no choice but to stay in Maine. There was no way around it, and nothing left to discuss. Problem was that issues at the Compound weren't just limited to Maine. shifters across the country were riveted, waiting to see if the united shifter experiment would self-destruct.

Rissa was at the bottom of the stairs, waiting for them by the door. "Good news travels fast, I see," Lily said, as she stepped onto the front foyer's polished tile.

Sean put the bags down and opened the door to call for Jack. A cold gust of wind followed, and Lily rubbed her arms against the chill as she leaned into Rissa's one-armed hug.

"Care package?" she asked with a chin pop toward the foil wrapped dish in her friend's hand.

"Toll house cookies for the ride."

Lily's mouth crooked upward, but she cringed inwardly. Rissa's eyes brimmed with worry, but there was a hint of steely indictment in their depths, as well.

"Seriously, Ris, you're the only person I know who would get up at dawn to make homemade cookies for a trip you're not even taking."

Deliberately avoiding eye contact, Lily turned to drape her jacket over the gleaming cherry banister, before placing her backpack against the curved rails at the bottom of the stairs.

As Sean stepped outside, it was just her and Rissa. The metronomic ticking of the grandfather clock on the landing almost deafening in the tense quiet. Lily pressed both hands to her stomach. Closing her eyes, she slid her palms to her hips and turned back around.

"All right. Enough with the sonic boom silent treatment," she said, meeting Rissa's pointed gaze. "I guess Mitch told you what happened at the council meeting."

Rissa didn't blink. "Yes, he did."

"And?"

"For Chrissake, Lily!" Exasperation exploded in her tone, even as her face flushed in uncharacteristic annoyance. Shaking her head, she floundered, at a loss. "You're not stupid, but I don't understand what goes through your mind, sometimes. Didn't it occur to you that confronting the council in that way played right into Parr's hand? And did you honestly think any of us would allow them to hold you against your will?"

Lily opened her mouth, but then swallowed her sarcastic reply. Rissa wasn't the guilty party in this, and her friend shouldn't bear the brunt of her annoyance. "I don't think that, but if Mitch told you everything, then you know the situation has moved beyond that point.

Rissa threw her hands up. "But why leave? Don't you think it's a bit extreme? Even for you?" She was at a loss. "Since when are you the type to cut and run?"

Lily flinched, watching the conflicting emotions play across her friend's face. Rissa wasn't the only one second-guessing her decision. Was the choice to leave truly best for Sean? For herself? Or had she simply convinced herself it was?

If leaving was for the best, then why was Terry's voice loud and clear at the back of her head, repeating the same two words over and over again? Selfish. Cowardly. She tried to ignore them but couldn't.

They mirrored her own doubt, and the fear she let her anger cloud her judgment. If Rissa thought she was taking the easy way out, then others would as well, and Parr would capitalize on it regardless of her speech in the war room last.

"Lily..." Rissa began, but Lily held up her hand.

"Don't, Ris. I understand. I know on the surface it seems as if I'm running, but trust me, that is not the case. Sean and I already went ten rounds about this and though he's not happy about my leaving, he agrees it's necessary. This is how it has to be. For now. You know he'd never let me go, otherwise. We've looked at every angle, and it's better this way. He needs to focus, and on top of everything else going on with the council, he doesn't need the added worry about me, our relationship and how I fit in, or don't for that matter. He can't do his job properly with me here, and I can't just sit around and wait. This way, it'll take some of the pressure off, at least politically." She shrugged, mentally crossing her fingers they were right.

Rissa put the foil wrapped dish on the small, corner table to the right of the door, and then linked her fingers over her belly. "I hope so, Lily."

Lily pulled her burgeoning friend into a hug. "It'll be fine, you'll see." She closed her eyes, sending a silent plea to Terry and whatever cosmic strings she could pull.

Sean came through the door with a small pink bundle in a snowsuit riding on his hip. "Look what I found outside," he said, picking frozen white lumps from the faux fur surrounding the puffy pink hood.

Strawberry blonde curls peeked out from beneath the brim, and a pair of big blue eyes stared at the two women from above the scarf encircling a tiny face. "She ambushed us with snowballs the minute Jack and I opened the trunk."

"Stephanie! What are you doing out of bed for one, and outside the house for another, young lady?" Rissa took her daughter from

Sean and put her down in front of them. "And where is nanny?" She squatted down to unwind the little girl's scarf, unzipping the top of her coat so the pink hood fell backwards.

"I had a nightmare," Stephanie said, her eyes moving between her mother and her uncle.

Rissa raised an eyebrow. "A nightmare, huh. So, you decided throwing snowballs at Jack and Uncle Sean would make it all better?"

A flash of tiny little white teeth in an impish grin showed for an instant. "Just Jack, but Uncle Sean kept getting in the way."

Lily bit the inside of her cheek, watching as Rissa pressed her lips together for the same reason. Sean laughed aloud, even as Rissa shot him a look.

"But why did you sneak out? You know you're too little to be walking around the Compound by yourself. Nanny was right there. You could have woken her up."

"I didn't want Nanny. I wanted you." The little girl's face dropped. Her small body tensed, and her eyes widened with fear. Trembling, her dread was so palpable Lily's senses went into high alert.

"What's the matter, honey?" Sean asked, glancing down at her.

Stephanie looked up at her uncle again, this time her eyes like saucers. "The lady. She's coming."

Rissa and Lily exchanged looks. "What lady?"

"The lady in my dream. She hurts people, and she smells bad, too. Like in the hospital where Lily helps Dr. Volkmann."

Sean leaned over and scooped Stephanie into his arms. "It was just a bad dream, munchkin. There's nothing to worry about." He kept a smile on his face, but over the child's shoulder, Lily's gaze caught his and locked. Stephanie was psychic, even more so than she. Could there be more to this than just a simple nightmare?

Stephanie leaned back in Sean's arms, her little cheeks pale. "The lady won't go outside in the snow. I think she's afraid of it, so that's why I went outside."

"*Ssh,* it's okay, honey. No one is angry with you for going out in the snow," Rissa cooed. "As long as you're safe, that's all that matters."

"No, mommy, you're not listening! Lily was in my dream too, and the lady hurt her." Stephanie turned back to Sean, her eyes pleading and much too intense for one so young. "Lily has to stay with us, Uncle Sean! Don't let her go away!" The words spilled from her lips, and she started to cry. Her knowing look melting with each tear.

Rissa took her from Sean and sat her down on the stairs, keeping one hand on her daughter's trembling shoulders. "Lily's fine, Stephie... See? She's right here with us. It was just a nightmare."

Stephanie cried even harder. "No! The lady wants to hurt people, and she wants to hurt us! She's coming here. I know it." Her wet gaze moved from her mother to her uncle and back again. "You don't believe me," she said her eyes wet and puffy, and her nose running.

"I do believe you, sweetheart." Sean squatted down, resting his hand on Stephanie's arm. "You don't have to worry because Jack will take good care of Lily while she's visiting her friends in New York, and I'll be here to take good care of you."

Stephanie hiccupped. "You promise?" Her eyes searched his, as if trying to decide if she believed him or not.

"Pinky promise," Sean said, and held up his little finger, waiting for her to do the same. Slowly she raised her hand and linked her tiny finger with his.

He gave her a brilliant smile. "That's my girl," he said with a wink. Pulling her into a hug, he looked at both women over her pink thermal-clad shoulder, one glance telling Lily she was no longer the only one concerned.

Lily didn't say a word through the whole exchange, instead gently probing the little girl's mind for any nuance showing it was no more than a dream. Problem was Stephanie's dream didn't feel like a dream. It felt like a vision—but there was no way she was sharing that tidbit with Sean at this point. They had enough problems without adding tilting at windmills to the list. In the meantime, she made a mental note to keep her guard up and her senses open.

Outside, Jack beeped the horn, and Sean picked up Stephanie, tossing her into the air and catching her before helping Rissa to her feet. With them both safely on their feet, he turned toward Lily.

A thousand unsaid words passed between them, and he slid his arm around her shoulders. "I hope you're sure about this because I'm not. No matter what we agreed."

Indecision reigned, and she opened her mouth, but no words came, so she just nodded.

His face was neither certain nor happy, and Lily's heart skipped a beat. Sean was everything she wanted and more. Now wasn't the time to let hormones and heartstrings sway what they both knew was the right thing. In the past, she was reckless in her decisions. Either flying by the seat of her pants or flying off the handle. After losing Terry, her selfishness had changed to an all-consuming anger and a need for revenge. She wanted to shred whatever made her feel vulnerable. Now she had opened herself to something bigger. Sean was her reason for fighting. Her only reason.

"We agreed. You need to probe what's going on in the Compound's soft underbelly. Besides, this is temporary."

"Temporary." He shook his head. "Still doesn't help."

Lily went up on tiptoe and kissed him. "We still have shifterlicious telephone sex to look forward to, right?"

"Just make sure you accept the charges when I call collect." The attempt at humor faltered for a moment as their eyes held. "I must be nuts letting you leave. Not because I'm a caveman or because I don't trust you. My head agrees there's method to this madness, but my inner wolf is pacing with anxiety. You're my mate."

Lily lifted a hand to his cheek. "You think this is easy for me? I'm a badass when it comes to Edward Parr and his cronies, but right now if you asked me to stay—"

"I know." He took her hand from his cheek and kissed her palm. "We're a team, and you're right. There's more going on here that meets the eye." Sean inhaled, nodding to himself. "Just promise me you'll call if you need me." At the smirk on her mouth, he put a finger over her lips. "Not the kind of *need* I meant, but that, too. I meant if your intuition homes in on anything off...any red flag. I'll be there in a heartbeat."

The two walked arm and arm to the car with Rissa on the porch with Stephanie, waving. Sean stayed at the edge of the drive as they pulled away, and as Lily watched his face, her heart squeezed in her chest. She glanced across the gravel and snow to her friend, and the little girl wrapped in her arms, and prayed Sean would find a way to end this mess. Soon.

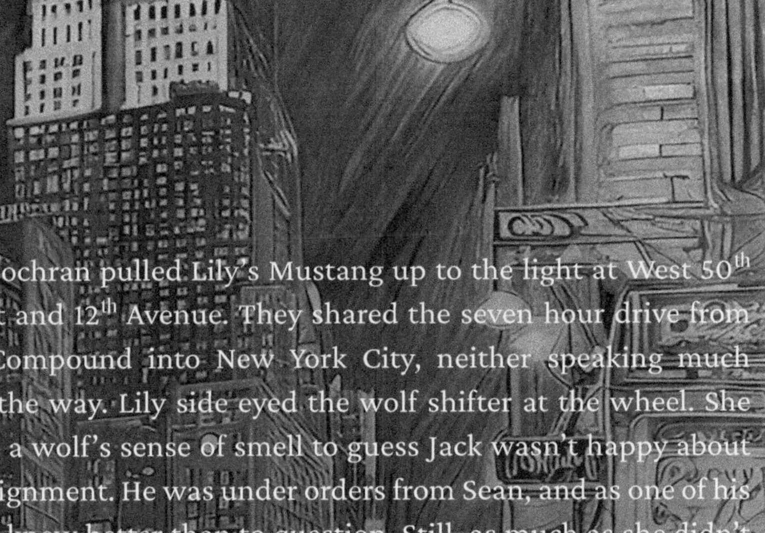

CHAPTER NINETEEN

Jack Cochran pulled Lily's Mustang up to the light at West 50th Street and 12th Avenue. They shared the seven hour drive from the Compound into New York City, neither speaking much along the way. Lily side eyed the wolf shifter at the wheel. She didn't need a wolf's sense of smell to guess Jack wasn't happy about his new assignment. He was under orders from Sean, and as one of his hunter's he knew better than to question. Still, as much as she didn't like the idea of Jack accompanying her to the city, she liked it even less that he was simply doing his duty. Last she heard Jack had been working at the Compound hospital. He was more orderly than security detail, and from what Rissa said, he was less than happy about it. Was sending him to New York a reward or did he view it as babysitting? Time would tell, but in the meantime the last thing she needed was a petulant pup.

The car idled while they sat in traffic next to the Manhattan Cruise Ship Terminal. "Looks like New York's winter cruise season is in full swing," Lily commented, looking at the crowds heading toward the departure terminal at Pier 90.

Leaning back in his seat, Jack stretched. "Why anyone would want to take to the sea in the middle of February is beyond me." Rolling his shoulders, he flexed his fingers, letting the blood flow back through his joints before dropping his hands back onto the steering wheel.

"You, okay?" Lily asked, taking a sip from her coffee. Traffic hadn't cooperated since they'd hit the interstate outside of York, Maine, making the strenuous drive even worse than usual. Grimacing, she turned from side to side looking for a place to spit. She rolled down the window and leaned her head over the edge of the glass, but with a traffic cop standing not ten feet from the car, she thought better of the idea. With no other choice, she scrunched her eyes and swallowed, putting the cup down in the holder between the seats.

"Okay... what was that about?"

"Nothing. The coffee tastes like it was made with vinegar," she answered with a wince, wiping her mouth on the cuff of her jacket.

Jack shook his head. "I told you the coffee didn't smell right back at the rest stop." Giving her a sideways glance, he smirked. "But that's what you get for trusting the bulb in the middle of your face, instead of my finely tuned instrument."

Shooting him a look, she huffed. "Bulb? Really?" Rummaging in her small leather backpack for a mint or a piece of gum she mumbled, "and Rissa wonders why you're still single."

"I heard that, and for the record, I do just fine with the ladies, thank you very much."

"Yeah, you're a real charmer. Why don't you work that magnetism and slide us on over to the curb at the next light? I should take it from here. After all, this *is* my neck of the woods, right?"

His lips curled into a smile, even as his hands curled tighter around the wheel. "I don't think so. I've seen the way you drive, and Sean made me swear I'd get you there in one piece."

The light changed, and Jack eased the car forward, but hit the brakes as a gypsy cab cut across two lanes of traffic aiming for the exit. With an aggravated sigh, he added, "He didn't, however, say anything about *me* arriving in one piece."

The cop standing on the brick median next to the crosswalk blew his whistle. "Move it, buddy! Whaddaya waiting for, an invitation from the mayor?" He waved at Jack to get going.

Leaning on his horn, Jack maneuvered around the cab that half blocked his lane. "Jesus Christ! Who designed this city? Gridlock my ass!" He rolled down the window. "It's called a signal, you asshole!" he yelled at the cabby, slamming his hands down on the steering wheel. "This is crazy! I can't believe you choose to live here and own a car! I mean, what the fuck?"

If Jack didn't relax, he'd steer them straight into Battery Tunnel, merrily on his way to the Brooklyn-Queens Expressway instead of Lily's apartment on Jane Street in the West Village. She smiled to herself at the thought of the wolf shifter trying to navigate his way back from there.

Chuckling, Lily glanced over as he flipped another driver the bird. She froze. Holy shit! His knuckles were hairy. Like, furry hairy! "Um, Jack?" she choked. "I think we need to pull over somewhere."

He shot her a look. "Why? In this traffic, are you nuts? Are you all right?"

Lily bit the inside of her cheek. "Um... yeah, I'm fine, but it's not me I'm worried about." Lily's eyes flicked from his face to his hands, and then back again.

Annoyed, Jack's eyebrows knit in a confused frown. His eyes tracked her curious gaze to his hands, and his mouth spread into a huge grin. "Lily, your face! Ha, ha, ha... Holy crap do you have a lot to learn about shifters! Did you think I was going to phase while behind the wheel? I can just see the tabloid headlines. NYC Traffic Gone to the Dogs!"

"Well, what did you expect me to think when your hands look like they're growing a pelt?"

"The unflappable Lily Saburi, freaked out by a set of hairy knuckles. Makes me wonder what we're in for the next few days when the moon is completely full. It'll be fine, family fun, don't you think?"

Lily crossed her arms in front of her chest. "Not funny, Jack. If this is a preview of the way things are going to be while we're thrown together, then you'd better get used to driving with one eye open, because I'm going to blacken the other one shut."

Jack smiled, his eyes crinkling at the corners. "Come on, Lily. You cut your teeth on things way hairier than my knuckles. Trust me it's nowhere near a sign of things to come. You have to understand between the stress of the drive, where the moon is in its cycle, and your scent, my nature was bound to manifest in some way. After all, I may be in control, but I'm not immune."

"My scent?" She slumped back against the seat, leaning her head back. "Oh no. Not you, too."

"I thought Sean talked to you about this?"

Lily shot him a look, but he laughed even louder. "Don't worry I'm not going to start humping your leg or anything. It's just the moon is waxing, and the closer it gets to being full, the more I sense things. However, you're fine. Trust me."

Even less sure about this than before they left the Compound, Lily didn't say a word. She exhaled quietly and turned her eyes back toward the traffic. A half hour later, they pulled onto Lily's Street, only circling the block once before finding a parking space.

"I've got to check in with Sean first, and then I'll bring up the bags. He made me promise to call the minute we arrived." He walked around toward the trunk. "I'm sure he wants to fill me in on what's going on at home, as well. Parr has to be having a field day now that you left. I don't trust the bastard. It sucks how fine a line Sean has to walk these days. It's not right. Not for an Alpha."

Lily followed him to the back of the car. "No problem. Just tell him I'm being a good girl and following your instructions to the letter."

Jack snorted, putting the key in the lock, and popping the trunk. "Yeah, right. You forget he knows you better than you know yourself. He'll trust matters more if I tell him how much of a pain in the ass you've been. All's right with the world when you're the bitch we all know and love."

"Oh, come on! I'm not that bad."

Jack raised one eyebrow.

At his skeptical look, she couldn't help but smile. "Okay, maybe I do have my moments, but that's what makes me so special."

"Ha! Why don't you make yourself useful and go grab some groceries? I'm sure there's nothing but a box of baking soda in that fridge of yours. I'll be right behind you. I'm not sure how long he's going to keep me talking."

Jack handed her a wad of cash, and Lily shoved it in the front pocket of her jeans. "Anything in particular you want? Dog biscuits. Maybe a rawhide bone?"

"Funny. I guess you want to carry your own suitcases upstairs, huh." He reached in for the biggest bag, lifting it out of the trunk with ease.

With a wry grin, she hiked her pack onto one shoulder. "Nope. That's what Sean sent *you* for."

"Yes, ma'am. I live to serve," he mumbled, flourishing a mock bow.

Chuckling, she headed across the street to the Korean market on the corner, stopping at the curb to look up at the red brick apartment house she had called home for the past five years.

Lily hadn't been here since she drove off a week after Terry's funeral, hell-bent on killing the creature that killed her best friend.

She sucked in a deep breath and headed into the market.

"Don't forget coffee!" Jack shouted from across the street, and Lily looked back over her shoulder to wave, but he was already on his cell phone.

With two bags of groceries in tow, she crossed the street, passing Jack as he unloaded the last of the bags onto the sidewalk. Sean had obviously kept him talking the whole time she had been in the store, and she cringed, wondering what the hell else was happening at the Compound.

She unlocked the vestibule door and then stepped onto the black and white subway tiles of the main lobby. She glanced up the stairs and then back over her shoulder at the small but heavy pile of luggage out on the sidewalk. The building was a five-floor walkup, so regardless of how hairy they were, she was grateful for Jack's supernaturally strong arms.

The hallway smelled of street dirt and Pine-Sol, with an underlying scent of sesame oil from the Chinese takeout next door. She was home.

The lobby door opened. "Where do you want these?" Jack asked, carrying all the bags at once.

"Fifth floor," Lily said shoving her leather keychain into his mouth. "I've got the penthouse."

"Great," he mumbled and started up the stairs, her keys jingling from his teeth.

"Wait! I need the mailbox key."

Jack put two of the bags on the step and tossed her the set of keys.

She wiped the wet teeth marks on her pants, unhooked the brass colored key and then tossed the rest back. "The square key with the black rubber grip is the key to my apartment. I've got the whole fifth floor."

Jack growled, keys jingling from his mouth again.

With a chuckle, she put the grocery bags on the floor and then unlocked the mailbox. A rush of envelopes and magazines fell in a cascade at her feet, with the rest crammed all the way to the back of the narrow box. She sighed. "Two months' worth of junk and overdue bills."

She pulled the key from the lock and reached for the rest, finding a note from their mailman stuck to the inside cubby.

Lily—

I was so sorry to hear about Terry. With the mail piling up, I figured you were away trying to sort things. Not to worry. I've been keeping the rest at the post office until you get back. My prayers are with you, sweetie.

Henry

Tears pricked the corner of Lily's eyes. Terry's death had left a fist-sized hole in her heart that none could fill. Not even Sean. She was better, but she'd never fully get over it.

With a deep breath, she stuck the note in her pocket and then bent to gather the letters from the floor. "It doesn't cost anything to be nice," she whispered, repeating the words Terry had said after taping a thank you gift for Henry to the inside of the mailbox before their fateful trip to Maine.

She picked up the grocery bags, adjusting her backpack before heading up the stairs.

Jack had left the door ajar. Guess the big bad wolf needed a lesson on life in the big, bad city. She nudged the door the rest of the way open with her foot. "Hey! How about a little help," she called, struggling in with the groceries and the mail now overflowing from the top of the paper bags.

"What's all that?" Jack asked, coming out of the bathroom.

"My mail."

"I guess you never got the chance to put it on hold, huh," he said, taking one of the bags from her.

"Uh, no," she said, putting the other bag and her backpack down on the kitchen table.

"Nice place, Lily. With the stories you hear about New York rent, I didn't expect it to be so big."

"Thanks." With her hands folded across her chest, Lily looked around the apartment. Wrinkling her nose, she rubbed the end of it with her knuckle. There had to be at least a half inch of dust on everything.

Stifling a sneeze, she pinched the end of her nose between her fingers, her eyes watering in the process.

"Oh, that's classy."

"Trust me, sneezing would only make it worse," she said, taking the box of tissues he'd rummaged from one of the shopping bags.

Lily blew her nose and walked into the living room. Except for the dead plants and the cobwebs, it was just as she and Terry had left it. Down to the empty ammo boxes on the coffee table.

The apartment might be huge by New York standards, but it was crammed with memories. Everywhere she looked there were poignant reminders of where her life had been, in contrast to where it was now.

On top of everything else, the answering machine blinked FULL across its digital LCD. The fact they still had a landline complete with answering machine was Terry's idea. It was for Terry's tech-challenged parent's more than anything else, and she cringed inwardly wondering how many messages were from them.

Jack sat on the arm of the sofa. "How about you take a shower, and I'll make us something to eat."

Lily exhaled, watching the tall, dark haired shifter watching her. Perhaps Sean was right. Whatever Jack's function, she was glad she didn't have to face the emptiness alone.

"Sounds good." Nodding, she gave him half a smile and then turned to grab one of her suitcases and head down the hall.

Terry's door was to the right, and she hesitated as she passed. The two had been roommates since college, but they had been friends forever.

A born pack rat, Terry saved mementos from almost

everywhere, cramming them into every nook and cranny. Now the small ten by twelve room was bare except for the plain oak furniture.

It was clear Terry's parents had been by to collect her belongings, and Lily ached at the thought. Jack had already dropped his bags on the floor next to the bed. He would have to sleep somewhere, and she knew she couldn't relegate him to the couch. Not with an empty bedroom available. Still, logic couldn't stop the idea from jabbing at her heart.

"Get a grip, Lil. It's not like the man hijacked the room or anything," she muttered, opening the hall closet for a clean set of sheets.

She placed them on the bare mattress and then took a comforter from the chest at the foot of the bed, smoothing the top of the soft fleece as she placed it beside the linens.

With nothing else to keep her, she turned for the door but then stopped. Terry's room faced the street, and in the sooty glow from the streetlight outside the window, she spotted a wooden box atop the tall chest of drawers in the corner of the room.

Squinting, she walked closer, and delight and sorrow dueled between her heart and mind as recognition dawned. Terry's parents must've found the box when they packed up the room, leaving the memento for Lily to find when she finally came home.

Twice the size of a cigar box, she lifted the wooden rectangle off the dresser, stopping to brush the dust from the faded pictures and magazine cutouts glued to the lid. Inside were things she and Terry had collected and cherished since the fifth grade. Some silly. Some tender. All priceless.

Drawing a breath, she tucked the box under her arm and crossed the room, leaving the door ajar as she headed into the hall.

In her own room, everything was in its place as well, including her cell phone still in its charger. She had purposely left it behind when she left for Maine, not wanting anyone to find her or hinder her plans for revenge. Not that it would have done any good.

She sat on the bed and slid the memory box onto her nightstand. The outside edges of the rectangle and the homemade latch were fashioned with braids made from old, multi-colored telephone wire the girls swiped from a shelf in Terry's garage.

As if it would lessen the pain, she lifted the lid slowly. Lily's hand went to her mouth, and a sad smile spread beneath her fingers. Tears gathered and she blinked, the droplets falling onto the back of her hand. Terry had left her a time capsule. With layer after layer of mementos and memories. A true testimony to their friendship.

On top were the pictures they took before prom. Terry looked young and beautiful in her blue satin, with her hair swept up in curls and baby's breath. Lily shook her head looking at herself in the photo, as well. She had felt like a Barbie, all powdered and pink in her organza gown. Organza. Her. Terry had insisted, telling Lily her penchant for black leather was the complete antithesis of prom. She argued that was the whole point, but in the end, didn't have the heart to disappoint Terry.

Underneath, hidden behind seashells and clandestine notes saved from study hall, were two rope friendship bracelets. Lily slipped them on her wrist, and it was as if time slipped away.

They had each turned twelve that summer, and Terry's parents, Beverly and Carl, had taken them to Mystic Seaport in Connecticut as a surprise. A Tall Ships Festival was in town for the weekend, adorning the harbor and the surrounding town with all kinds of events.

Shops and tents dotted the graveled path winding through the nineteenth century museum village. Giggling, the girls had gone from craft to craft until they'd found an old man sitting on a stack of barrels beside one of the whaling schooners. He was tying sailor's knots in scraps of rigging.

"Pretty girls should have pretty things," he said with a wheezy laugh. With a wink, he had held out pieces of rope, and then laughed even louder when Terry stepped back, scooting behind Lily. "Ach, lass, don't be shy. I mean you no harm. I'll teach you to make a Claddagh braid then. Something pretty for two such pretty sisters, eh?"

Sitting on the edge of her bed, Lily ran her fingers over the rough rope, tracing the intricate patterns in the braid. "Pretty sisters," she murmured.

It was true in every sense of the word except blood. Unlike Lily, Terry was forever the romantic, and when she discovered the Claddagh braid was an ancient symbol of love, friendship, and loyalty, she swore the old man must have been a fae messenger, and that something extraordinary was going to happen. She even stole Carl's penknife that night, determined they'd be blood sisters, binding them to whatever magic came their way.

Lily ran her fingers over the faded scar at the center of her left palm. It had hurt like hell and bled like a stuck pig, but Terry wouldn't take no for an answer. Silly as it was, she even tied their hands together with one of her mom's scarves like she saw in a movie once, and boy, did they catch hell for it. Not only for the bloodstains on her mom's favorite scarf, but because Beverly swore they would end up with tetanus.

Lily sniffed away another tear. "Something extraordinary. Right." Her world had gone way past extraordinary, rocketing straight through to surreal. Only problem, Terry had gotten caught in the crossfire.

She looked at the cordless phone in its base next to her cell phone. The messages blinked, almost disapprovingly, as she sat with her memories. With a sigh, she pushed herself up from the bed.

"Shower first. Messages later." She reached to unzip her bag for her toiletries.

Once showered, she toweled off, and feeling human again, she slipped into a pair of fleece pajamas. It was barely seven p.m., but it was pitch black outside, and the glow from the streetlights cast shadows around her room.

The aroma of fresh-made coffee and buttered toast filled the air, and her stomach rumbled. She hadn't eaten a thing since before they left the Compound.

Running a wide-toothed comb through her hair, she then wound it into a knot at the top of her head before jamming her feet into a pair of shearling slippers and padding out into the kitchen.

"That smells amazing." She peeked over Jack's shoulder at the eggs sizzling in the pan.

"Huevos Rancheros. One of my many specialties."

Lily inhaled, appreciatively. "If Sean told me you could cook, I wouldn't have complained as much as I did about you tagging along as my babysitter."

Jack shot her a look. "Babysitter?"

"Isn't that why Sean sent you? To keep an eye on me? Keep me out of trouble?"

Jack turned off the burner, pushing the frying pan to the back of the stove. "Lily, do you honestly think anyone at the compound thinks you need a keeper? Sean? Mitch? Me?"

Lily didn't answer. She grabbed a mug from the drain board and filled it with coffee. Taking a sip, she held the warm ceramic in her hands and stared at Jack over the rim.

"Answer me, as I'd honestly like to know. Especially since I'm the one who volunteered for this jaunt."

He volunteered. Hmmm. Guess she wasn't as clearheaded about things as she thought.

"Honestly, Jack. I don't know. I know Sean loves me, but sometimes I think he sees me as a fragile possession. He's never going to relax and let me be me, at least not until I become a full shifter."

She shrugged. "I meant what I said, though. I have no intention of that happening. At least not right now. So where does that leave me? I don't need a shadow. Like I told Sean, he needed to deal with his Alpha business without me getting in the way. In the meantime, I have a life to live. Work to do. And while I refuse to be a pawn, I also won't let Sean's anxiety over my fragile human state get in the way. I'm not fragile. Like you said, I don't need a keeper."

"Okay, I get it, but why don't you try thinking of it like this... in our world, Sean is tantamount to being the President or a Prime Minister."

"So, that make me what? First Lady?"

"Yes. Like it or not, it does."

"And I suppose that makes you my secret service detail?"

Jack flashed an entirely wolfish grin. "Exactly. With a few enhanced abilities."

Lily burst out laughing, spilling hot coffee over her hand. "Ow! Jeez! See what you made me do?"

"Hair of the dog, baby. Hair of the dog."

Lily snorted, drying her hand on a dishtowel.

"So, do we have a truce, then?" Jack asked, refilling her coffee cup.

Lily took a sip from her mug. Regardless of how much she complained, she didn't have much choice in the matter. Sean would never let her be here on her own. Not until he was certain she was safe.

Tapping the side of her mug, she pursed her lips. "I suppose. If we're going with this silly analogy, you gotta promise me no nicknames. No talking into your wristwatch saying stupid stuff like, the sparrow has flown, or anything like that."

"Sparrow?"

"I'm serious, Jack!" She flicked him with the damp dishtowel. "I want this to be as normal as possible."

"Okay, okay. I promise. Can we eat now?"

"Sure, but I'm keeping this locked and loaded just in case." She twisted the dishtowel again. Her cell phone rang in the bedroom, grabbing her attention. "Be right back," she called over her shoulder. "Dishes are in the middle cabinet."

Lily rushed down the hall, but the call had already gone to voicemail. She punched in her retrieval code, expecting Sean's voice on the other end. It wasn't.

Lily. It's Mark Phillips. We have a case that needs your particular talents. I'd rather not get into it over the phone. If you can meet downtown at ten a.m. tomorrow, it would really help me out. Give me a shout if that time doesn't work for you. Hope to see you then.

She pushed end on her touch screen. It looked like she still had a business after all. The feeling was bittersweet, but she'd take anything to help her from heading back Maine first chance she got. If only to kiss Sean and then punch Edward Parr in the face.

Sean needed time to root out the rot at the Compound, and she had to give him that time while convincing Edward Parr he succeeded in his plan to divide and conquer. Keeping that between them meant keeping Jack in the dark. As hard as it was, keeping her in New York and Sean in Maine gave them the perfect cover.

"In the end the truth will out." She murmured the quote from Shakespeare's *Merchant of Venice*. It was one of Terry's favorites, so the fact she thought if it now spoke volumes. So much pain and so much sacrifice. She had to believe Parr's scheming would be revealed, and that he'd get his comeuppance. All the better if delivered courtesy of her steel-toed boot.

Lily scrolled the missed calls on her phone again. One from Sean, one from Rissa, and the other from Mark Phillips. Closing her eyes, she dragged in a breath. All she needed was faith and patience. Faith in Sean, and in their commitment to each other. Faith that truth would prevail over bullshit. Faith that none of it was in vain.

Patience was another story. Still, what better way to cultivate both than to keep busy? She picked up the phone and hit redial on the last call received. It barely rang before answered on the other end.

"Mark. It's Lily Saburi. I'm returning your call..."

Thank you for reading! Did you enjoy? Please add your review because nothing helps an author more and encourages readers to take a chance on a book than a review.

And don't miss more in the *Cursed by Blood* series with the vampires in BLOOD LEGACY available now! Turn the page for a sneak peek.

Also be sure to sign up for the City Owl Press newsletter to receive notice of all book releases!

SNEAK PEEK OF BLOOD LEGACY

Avalon
Condemned Church-Turned Nightclub
New York City, midnight

Carlos pulled onto the street and slid his black Jaguar XLR to the curb across from the club. The music's pulsating beat vibrated blocks away, and his blood answered in anticipation.

He got out of the car, eyeing the ritual line-up of players and wannabes well under way behind the red velvet ropes. Most were teenagers out for an illicit night of fun, their excitement radiating like steam from a subway vent in winter. Gliding past, he inhaled their mingled scent, savoring their collective flavor.

With barely a nod, he breezed past the bouncers and up the stairs to the main doors. Avalon was a church turned nightclub, an anomaly not unlike himself. A blend of the contemporary and the old world, of the sacred and the profane.

His hand trailed the door's brass handles, lingering for a moment on the embossed cross still intact on the pull. He couldn't help but chuckle at the Hollywood irony.

The club's main level was awash with life. Surreal in a setting so dim he wondered how anyone was able to see—that is, anyone without the help of preternatural senses.

Winding his way past the main bar, he paused for a moment at the edge of the dance floor. The space had once housed the main body of the church, and apart from the bodies in motion, he could still feel the lingering shadow of the old pulpit.

Carlos scanned the upper galleries. The gothic arches of the old steeple, and the streamlined chrome and neon bar that now sat nestled in its arms, instead of the organ that originally occupied its place.

Climbing the stairs, he settled into a quiet corner in the back. Plush low couches and small tables lined the gallery. The lighting was like candlelight, dim enough to be intimate, but bright enough for conversation.

By New York standards the night was just getting started. A small crowd had already gathered in the gallery lounge, and it would certainly get more crowded as the night progressed. By then, too many would either be too drunk or too drugged for his liking.

No, he preferred the earlier crowd. The eager young ones who came looking for excitement, anticipating a taste of the forbidden. The youth of America went out every weekend looking for a thrill, and those who found Carlos usually got more than they bargained for.

So far, no one had sparked his interest, though from this vantage point he could survey the entire club. He smoothed the front of his black silk shirt. Dressed in a pair of dark grey jeans that molded his body, Carlos looked as though a he belonged on the cover of *GQ*. Dark and gorgeous with a hint of mystery and underlying danger.

He wielded his presence like a finely honed sword. With one look, he could leave women breathless and men questioning their own sexuality. It didn't take much to lure them in, but Carlos prided himself on being proper, always giving his chosen ones a choice.

His family, as he liked to call them, hadn't had any new blood in quite a while. Not since the plague that rampaged through undead ranks these past months.

He grimaced. The thought of wading through the throngs made his head throb. Still, regardless of recent events, he was exacting in his choices. There had to be a fire or spark of soul to the ones chosen, something that left him wired with anticipation.

Unfortunately, it appeared his efforts tonight were fruitless. He wasn't looking for another pretty face. He was bored of the jaded and superficial, and lately had been looking for more. Craved it almost as much as he craved blood. Except now, even blood didn't fill the void in his life. In him. He wanted something else, only he didn't know what.

"Can I get you anything?"

Carlos looked up from his musing. The waitress stood over him, her pad and pencil leaning on a little round serving tray.

"Rum," he replied. "A tumbler, no ice...and bring the bottle."

"Sorry, I can't—"

He lifted a hand, holding her mesmerized before sliding a wad of cash onto her tray. "I think we understand each other. *Comprendes*... Susan?"

The waitress mumbled something and walked away, shaking her head as if trying to clear a fog. Carlos smiled as he watched her head back toward the bar.

"Hi!" a pretty brunette chirped, walking up to where Carlos sat. "Mind if my friends and I share?"

"The more the merrier. *Por favor*." Carlos flashed a suggestive and slightly predatory grin.

The brunette shivered. "I, um, I...I'm Brandy," she stammered, obviously flustered. She cleared her throat. "Whoa, and I haven't even started drinking yet. Let's try this again. I'm Brandy, this is Sharla, and this is Gwen."

They slid in one after the other, Brandy now flashing Carlos a brilliant smile. "Thanks for letting us join you."

"*De nada*," he replied, inclining his head with a hint of amusement.

The three were all fresh and beautiful. They couldn't be much over eighteen, and their eagerness made the air taste faintly of electricity and perfume.

"Ladies, I'm going to have to see some I.D.," the waitress said as she walked over again.

As the girls fished through tiny purses, Carlos considered spelling the waitress into letting them pass. Still, none of them sparked his interest, so he let it go.

"I don't seem to have mine with me," the blonde said, giving the waitress a hopeful smile.

"Sorry, then I can't serve you," the server answered with an apologetic smile of her own. "I think maybe you girls should go back to the dance floor."

They got up with a collective huff, and Carlos couldn't help but chuckle. Jerking her head around, the brunette shot him a look that left him laughing even louder, his hands up in mock defense.

The waitress stood at the table waiting until they disappeared down the staircase. "I did you a favor, my friend. That was disaster zipped into a miniskirt. Underage girls can get guys like you into a heap of trouble." She nodded once before hooking her tray onto her hip. "I'll get you your drink." However well-intentioned, she was off by a mile.

He was the dangerous one.

She brought his order and winked as she set the tumbler and the bottle on the table. "Will there be anything else?" she asked, pouring his first glass.

"No...no, thank you, Susan."

"In that case, would you mind settling your tab? My shift's up and my tables need to be closed out before I can leave."

"No problem," he answered, handing her a credit card.

“Thanks. I’ll be right back with your receipt.” With a nod, she pivoted on her high heels toward the bar again, but then stopped. “Oh, and thanks for the added tip.” She patted her pocket. “I really appreciate it.”

Added tip? Shrewd. Very shrewd.

Amused, he lifted the glass she poured. The dark liquid hit his tongue, familiar and satisfying, and he nearly groaned. He closed his eyes and inhaled, savoring the underlying scent of molasses and sugar cane.

The Bacardi did nothing for him, neither the alcohol nor the taste. He loved the rum’s warm, sweet aroma. The scent rendered so many memories from his human life, memories he was glad weren’t lost to him. He had read somewhere that olfactory memories were the earliest and most poignant, the ones most likely to be preserved. That rule obviously applied to vampires as well.

He picked up the bottle and ran his thumb over the label. Funny, of the limited human fare he was able to consume, the one he liked best had a black bat for its logo. Classic Boris Karloff irony.

In the time since the girls left, the club grew crowded. The music pounded, and the dance floor gyrated with so many disconnected arms and legs moving to the frenetic rhythm.

Carlos took his glass and walked to the railing overlooking the throng. Leaning on the polished chrome, he watched the human drama unfold. Different scents tinged the air, each a glimpse into a host of human thought and emotion.

Anticipation. Disappointment. Money. Pleasure. Sex.

Closing his eyes, he lifted his head and inhaled. His eyes snapped open. “What the—?”

His eyes narrowed and he reached out with his senses. A variation flickered amid the human cacophony. He scanned the club for its origin, and he growled low in his throat.

“No way.” He exhaled an annoyed breath.

"Youngbloods."

Inhaling again, he caught the scent of fresh blood from a stairwell near the back downstairs bar. "No fucking way!"

Pushing himself from the railing, he was within five feet of the fledglings in seconds. The two youngbloods were in an alcove and had managed to lure a girl to the far end of the empty stairwell.

She was clearly underage. Even more so than the three girls he encountered earlier, and she was drunk. Their wards were clumsy and haphazard. A hasty attempt to obscure their activities from the humans. And from him.

Had someone invited them? If so, who? Admittance to his territory was by invitation only. Anger clenched his jaw, but experience told him to watch and wait.

Vampire politics was even more corrupt and fickle than anything the human world could imagine, and the consequences infinitely more brutal. He wanted to save the girl, and maybe even teach the youngbloods a lesson they'd never forget, but he also didn't want to incur reprisal against his entire family.

The girl was on her knees. One of the boys had his fangs buried deep in her throat while the other was buried deep between her legs.

As the first one drank, sloppy, sucking sounds coupled with the girl's pleasured moans drifted through the wards.

Blood dripped from the fledgling's chin, splattering the concrete floor with red.

"Dude don't be a pig. Leave some for me." The one nailing her from behind slapped a rhythm against her bare ass.

Jerking his head up, the other pulled his fangs from her throat with an audible pop. "What are you complaining about? No one hunts here and no one patrols, so it's all good." He scraped his finger across his chin, the way a child would lick cake batter from a mixing bowl. "*Mmmm*, sweet!"

Hey, man!" He picked up one of the girl's shoes and threw it at his friend. "Hurry up. And don't get any ideas. I call first dibs on the next one."

Carlos's lip curled in disgust. He had seen enough. For ages, he tried to distance himself from exactly this kind of behavior, and now it was in his own backyard.

Without warning, he walked through their wards and grabbed the closest one by the hair, yanking him backwards.

"Oi! What the fuck, man!"

The young vampire didn't stand a chance. He screeched, hissing as Carlos dragged him off the girl with his pants twisted around his ankles.

With a flick of his wrist, Carlos sent him crashing into the wall. The youngblood slumped to the ground in a cloud of concrete dust. The other one backed away, leaving the girl covered in blood and writhing in an ecstasy high.

The other's eyes darted back and forth while he crouched, baring his teeth like a character from a B-rated horror flick.

"That Hollywood vampire act isn't going to work on me, amigo. Tell me, didn't Sandro warn you about coming here? Or are you playing hooky from daddy tonight? This territory is mine. As Sandro well knows."

The one who hit the wall got to his feet. He turned, cracking his neck before smearing a trickle of his own blood from his mouth with the back of his hand.

"What makes you think we care what arrangements you have with Sandro?" he jeered, pulling up his pants.

Carlos looked at them. They were typical. Unbelievably beautiful but dumb as stumps. Sandro's type. Not surprising, though. Sandro liked to surround himself with pretty boys, and he couldn't care less if they had any intelligence. In fact, he preferred them that way.

"Yeah, right. We know all about you, *amigo*," the one covered in concrete dust sneered, mimicking Carlos's accent. Taking a step forward, he spit, raising a defiant chin.

Carlos growled in warning, but the youngblood ignored him. "Sandro says you're a pussy," he pressed. "He says you used to be a real badass, but you traded your fangs and your balls for a bunch of crybabies wishing you were still human."

"Is that so?"

"Yeah." The youngblood sniffed. "Why don't you do all of us a favor and toast yourself, huh? Leave things for the real vamps."

With a low, feral snarl, Carlos let his fangs descend and his face and jaw distort completely. He threw his arm up, solidifying their tattered wards with one word. Taking a step forward, he let his eyes flash from black to red. The full impact of his intentions hit, and when the two vampires' eyes went wide, he sprang.

"Holy crap! Run!"

Anger vibrated in his veins. His body taut. The two pivoted for the warded exit, but Carlos cut them off in a blur of speed.

He grabbed them each by the throat, raising them above his head. "I warned you." Their eyes bulged before he threw them full force against the back wall.

A deafening crack echoed behind the wards, shattering egress windows, and splintering glass all around. Sheet rock and base cinderblock crumbled as sparks flashed from snapped wires.

The two vampires crumpled in a heap. Carlos squatted in front of them, menace dripping from his voice. "If you ever trespass in my territory again, I will pull your fangs out with my bare hands, and they won't grow back. Do not disrespect me again."

He took each of their arms and in one swift move, snapped them over his knee like so much dried wood. "Unfortunately, you'll heal. Too quickly for my tastes, but not before you have to explain what happened to Sandro."

Carlos stood up, leaving the youngbloods in a broken pile on the floor. Looking around, he snuffed out any potential fires, but decided to leave the smashed wall as a message for any others lurking in shadow and looking for a challenge.

Turning, he spotted the now terrified girl cowering in the corner. The glamour they had spelled her with had worn off, and her eyes were wild with fear. She screamed as he approached, scrambling even farther back against the wall.

Gently, he held out his hand, spelling her so she would calm enough for him to help her to her feet. He cleaned her neck and shirt the best he could, healing her wounds completely. Straightening her skirt, he then wiped her memory. "Find your friends. Tell them you feel ill and need to go home immediately. Under no circumstances are you to linger."

As he picked up her purse from the floor, he awakened her, handing it to her as if she only just dropped it. With a subtle wave of his hand, he let her walk out ahead of him, confused but otherwise unharmed to disappear into the crowd.

"What a waste." Carlos sighed, looking at the mess before glancing toward the darkened club on the other side of the wards. The girl would be all right, he hoped, but wiping her memory was the best he could do.

The youngbloods stirred. Stupid and arrogant, yes, but the instinct for self-preservation was a vampire's greatest asset. They'd skulk off into the night licking their wounds, talking trash as soon as they were at a safe distance.

He exhaled, clenching his fists. They deserved final death. It would be so easy. A skim of dirty ash in a broken stairwell. That's all that would remain of their undead existence.

"Not your monkeys, not your circus," he muttered. Vampire law said they weren't his to end. They were Sandro's problem.

With a last look of disgust, he brushed debris from his clothes.

Minuscule shards cut his palms, healing instantly before they could even bleed. Music penetrated the wards. Behind the miasma it was just another Friday night regardless of Sandro's untrained fledglings.

Picking the last bits of concrete from his tie, he glanced up. A woman stood in the open doorway, staring at him. A round silver tray hung limply from her hand, and her pen and pad were on the floor by her stilettoed feet.

It was obvious she could see through his wards, and from the look on her face, she'd witnessed the entire spectacle.

"Fuck." He needed this added complication like a stake through his heart.

Carlos moved quickly, positioning himself to silence her if she screamed. The woman didn't move or blink. She stared at him with the greenest eyes he'd ever seen, and if it weren't for her heartbeat, he'd swear she wasn't breathing.

He could smell the fear on her skin, keeping her immobile. Yet there was something else about her. Something in her scent he couldn't place.

Raising his fingers to her face, he expected her to flinch, but she didn't. "The back stairwell is off limits. It's being renovated." He brushed the side of her cheek, glamour radiating from him in waves. "You know this. You. Didn't. See. Anything."

She tilted her head and exhaled. Her breath, sweet and full of life in his nostrils. Her eyes glaze over as expected, but then she blinked a few times, meeting his gaze dead on. "Like. Hell. I. Didn't."

Stunned, Carlos blinked, but before he could question her, she disappeared into the throng on the dance floor. He blurred after her, scanning the club as he ran, but the place was too crowded to decipher anything.

There was no sign of her. But how? How did she get away without warning? How could she see through his wards? Resist his glamour?

He opened and closed his fingers, squeezing them into his palm.

His cool flesh tingled with the lingering feel of her skin. What was it about her scent he couldn't place?

Anticipation coursed through his veins as he picked his way toward the bar. He searched the faces on the dance floor and the surrounding tables.

"Can I get you anything?" the bartender asked, putting two bottles of Heineken on the bar.

"What?" Carlos barely acknowledged the question.

"Drink, dude. What can I get you?"

"Yes, sorry," he replied, still distracted. "Bacardi 151. Neat." Carlos's mind raced with possibilities while the bartender filled his glass.

Throwing a twenty on the bar, he picked up his drink, but stopped halfway to his mouth. The girl had a tray in her hand.

An order pad and pen dropped at her feet.

He frowned. Talk about being slow on the uptake tonight. Catching the bartender's eye, he raised his hand, calling him over. "There's a cocktail waitress...long, auburn hair, really green eyes. You know her?"

Putting a couple of glasses under the tap, he gave Carlos a quick once-over while working the levers. "Sure, I know her. What's it to you?"

"She's a very pretty girl. Just wondering what her name was, that's all."

Putting the two drafts on the bar to settle, the bartender picked up a towel and wiped his hands. "Look, you're wasting your time. You'd do better with any one of the honeys trolling the dance floor. They're the ones on the prowl, not Trina. She's not the type."

Nodding, Carlos raised his glass to his lips. "Thanks for the tip." Turning around, he leaned his back against the bar facing the dance floor. He inhaled, taking in all the heightened scents.

"Trina," he whispered.

The taste of her name lingered on his tongue, and for the first time in centuries, the dark alcohol burned as it slid down his throat.

Don't stop now. Keep reading with your copy of BLOOD LEGACY

And sign up for Marianne Morea's newsletter to get all the news, fun tidbits, and special email-subscriber-only specials at www.mariannemorea.com/contact

CHARACTER INTERVIEW

A special Anniversary Edition interview with Sean Leighton, Alpha of the Brethren, from Marianne Morea's *Cursed by Blood Shifters* Fantasy!

Interviewer: *Tell about yourself, Sean.*

[Chuckling, Sean raised an eyebrow] "What's there to tell, really?" [He runs a hand through his hair, a sexy half smile teasing the corner of his mouth] "I'm a wolf shifter. I've been blessed with dual natures, both human and wolf forms. Other than that, I grew up not much differently than you. I had a mother and a father and a younger brother. Unfortunately, I'm all that's left of my family."

Interviewer: *I think there's a lot more to you than you're letting on. Your position hold tremendous weight in your world. As to you being the last of your family, didn't your brother have children? And let's not forget about Lily.*

[Sean snorted] "I couldn't forget Lily even if I wanted to! But, you're right, of course... Jerard is survived by his wife, Rissa, and their daughter Stephie, and that little one is something special, and not just because she's my niece. She's responsible in a huge way for saving more than one life, but you'll have to read the saga to find out about that. So, I suppose you're right. One day Lily and I might have children of our own as well. It might take some convincing, though. [He winks at Lily sitting off camera] Especially since I haven't been able to convince her to go wolf."

Interviewer: *"Trouble in paradise, big guy?" [The interviewer winked at Sean]*

"Lily's middle name is trouble, so I would tread very carefully if I were you. She'll deny it, but she's as possessive and jealous as any wolf I've met. As to my relationship with her, she's headstrong and hard to handle, yet compassionate, super smart and fierce. Not to mention beautiful. She's everything I never knew I wanted, and I wouldn't change a thing. So, trouble in paradise? With Lily, it wouldn't be paradise unless there was trouble."

Interviewer: *"What did you want to be when you grew up? Did you imagine you'd hold such a powerful position?"*

"As a child, I never really gave it much thought. In my world you are born into your dual nature and are automatically part of a pack or pride or whatever grouping is specific to your animal nature. I knew I was destined to be the Alpha of my pack because of my blood line. Blood challenges are far and few these days, but never in my wildest dreams did I think I'd be the Alpha of something as unusual as the Brethren. Or that we'd have anything like our experimental Compound. Shifters, like any other group, need to evolve and adapt to the times. Inclusivity is key. When you shun members because they want to grow and flourish, you risk alienation. You need to adjust to the world around you, or risk losing the younger generations."

Interviewer: *"Out of all the dual natures with which you were gifted when you became Alpha, which is the most fun?"*

[A sheepish grin spreads across Sean's face] "My hunter's will never let me live this down, but it has to be the gift of flight I received from the Avians. Flying is an unbelievable rush. The only thing that comes close is racing the full moon. Our Compound may be multi-specied, but each group still thinks their particular set of skills is king. Me, I love being a wolf, but flying is amazing."

Interviewer: *"What are you passionate about these days?"*

[Smiling broadly now, he glances over his shoulder at the pretty honey blonde sitting off to the side of the interview set] "Lily. She's my whole existence now. Her and the survival of our Compound. Though I do wish she'd change her hair color back to her natural dark chestnut. Don't get me wrong, she'd still be beautiful even if she was bald, but I miss her thick, rich dark hair. Don't tell her I said so, but I think she changed her hair color because my ex, Delia, was dark haired. Like it mattered at all. No one hold a candle to Lily. Not in my world. Not ever."

[Lily blew a razzberry at him off set.]

Interviewer: *[chuckling] "Well, you know what they say about blondes having more fun..."*

[Raising an eyebrow, Sean cocked his head to the side] "With Lily, you never go right to fun, but it's definitely a roller coaster worth riding."

Interviewer: *"What is your favorite meal?"*

"You're kidding, right?" [With a sly grin, Sean leans forward in his chair, letting a bit of a growl rumble in his throat for effect] "I crave what any four fanged carnivore craves, something succulent with the promise of dripping wet, juices... [the interviewer scooted back in her chair, making Sean laugh out loud] "Sorry, I just couldn't resist. I guess my favorite meal is a big, juicy steak. Rare, of course."

Interviewer: *[clearing her throat]: "What do you do to unwind and relax?"*

"I run in wolf form through the forest. It calms me and helps put things into perspective. It clears my mind." [Looking over his shoulder again, he smiles, shaking his head] "Lily hasn't joined me yet. Like I said, she's still debating whether or not she wants that particular part of our lunar driven world."

Interviewer: *"If you could apologize to someone in your past, who would it be?"*

[Sean takes a deep breath, letting it out slowly] "I'm not really sure how to answer that question. I guess I would have to say, my brother, Jerard. With the Compound, and the coming together of all shifter species, I was preoccupied and didn't see that his marriage was crumbling, or that he had lost his way. If I had paid more attention, perhaps he'd still be alive. I miss him. He wasn't a good husband to Rissa, or a good father to Stephanie, but he was still my brother.

When you love someone, you don't give up hope they can do better. Be better. Unfortunately, our father wasn't the best example, and Jerard took after him. I'm more like my mother. We understood the good of the pack had to come before our own wants and needs. People like Edward Parr used my love for Lily to paint me as the opposite. Unfortunately, we dual natured are as bad as humankind when it comes to believing spin instead of facts. Parr bet on that, but his scheming will be his undoing. Mark my words."

Interviewer: *"What is something people would be surprised about you?"*

"That unlike Hollywood stereotypes, shifters are not bloodthirsty, mindless beasts ruled by the full moon. We can shift any time, any day. We are as comfortable and as cognizant in our animal form as we are when we're in our human form. We're really not that different from anyone else. Just like humans, we have our good days and our bad days. We get angry and vent, we laugh, we cry, we bleed when hurt, we have prejudices that we need to rise above. We're just trying to find our way in this world. Just like you."

Interviewer: *"Lily, would you like to take the microphone and spill the tea on Sean or anyone else in the saga?"*

[Sean grimaced, but with a twinkle in his eye.] "Buckle up, buttercup. This is not going to be pretty."

"What makes you say that, wolf boy?" [She fluttered her lashes with a smile] "And for the record, I did not change my hair color because of Delia. I did it because I was bored. Let's put it this way. If Jack doesn't want to be one of your hunter's anymore, he's got a career ahead of him as a colorist.

[Sean's mouth dropped] Jack. He did your hair?

"Yup. He sure did. While we shared a bottle of pinot gris and watched the Real Housewives of New York."

"Ha. I knew you were lying. Jack hates reality TV"

[She angled her head.] "You sure about that? Jack has many layers, and some of them might surprise you."

"Lil, please tell me you didn't..."

[Lily laughed] "No, Sean. I did not take a walk through Jack's head, though I know he's hiding something, but I don't know what."

Interviewer: *"Guys, do I need to be here for this?"*

[Sean and Lily look at the interviewer before bursting out in laughter.] "Sorry about that. We're like an old married couple already."

Interviewer: *"Sean…was that a hint? Are you two planning to get hitched?"*

[Lily crooked her finger, and then leaned in close.] "You'll have to read the books to find out.

Interviewer: *"If that's not a tease, then I don't know what it! You heard it here first, folks. Lots of promise and maybe even a for better or for worse! Sean… Lily… thank you both for taking the time to give us a small glimpse into you world behind the scenes.*

About the Author

Marianne Morea has always been a scribbler. From the time she could write her name, she has been making up stories, writing characters and dialogue in the corners of notebooks.

She has been married for 28 years, has three beautiful kids, three dogs, and a cat. She is a 2nd degree black belt in traditional Japanese karate and loves to travel. Her romantic and spontaneous husband shares that passion with her, so her stories get plenty of inspiration!

She is also a founding member and previous President of The Paranormal Romance Guild, a not-for-profit organization for readers and authors of the genre. She resides in New Milford, CT.

mariannemorea.com

 facebook.com/mariannemoreaauthor

 instagram.com/marianne_morea

ABOUT THE PUBLISHER

City Owl Press is a cutting edge indie publishing company, bringing the world of romance and speculative fiction to discerning readers.

Escape Your World. Get Lost in Ours!

www.cityowlpress.com

facebook.com/CityOwlPress
x.com/cityowlpress
instagram.com/cityowlbooks
pinterest.com/cityowlpress
tiktok.com/@cityowlpress

ADDITIONAL BOOKS

MARIANNE DAMBRY

(PARANORMAL WOMEN'S FICTION)

There Goes My Midlife Crisis Series

Jeepers Reapers

Where'd You Get That Keeper

One Scythe Fits All

M.A. MOREA

(YOUNG ADULT FICTION)

The Legend Series

Hollow's End

Time Turner

Spook Rock

www.ingramcontent.com/pod-product-compliance
Lightning Source LLC
Chambersburg PA
CBHW071255290726
48958CB00018B/190

* 9 7 8 1 9 6 4 9 5 1 1 2 6 *